PROLOGUE

The last place Augustus Keats, the Marquess of Talisker, wanted to be this evening was a ball. He'd just arrived from his home in Scotland and had much business to attend to but let his long-time friend Lord Edward Findley convince him he needed to attend, if for no other reason, it would let people know he'd returned.

His life had been in tatters for over a year. Flippant ways led to him owing to friends, now former friends, a ridiculously vast sum of money from his gambling. His brother-in-law, the Duke of Hightower, loaned him the money to pay off his debts, but that had come at a cost. Hightower, at least for the immediate future, held an interest in the family whiskey distillery. The agreement made with his father left Augustus with a slim share of the profits.

Unwilling to live off the meager amount and finding him forced out of the day-to-day operations, he started his own distillery with a generous loan from his aunt. His first two batches were aging and wouldn't be ready for at least two years. He readied for a third bottling, and in the meantime, he found himself forced to live off his estate's meager earnings, and the pittance from his father's whiskey business.

Findley suggested he find a bride. One with a generous dowry. Not that he hadn't thought of that before. That would take care of a lot of his immediate problems, a marriage of convenience. After she bore him a couple of sons, he could set her up elsewhere and he wouldn't have to set eyes on her.

As the heir to a dukedom, life had never been an easy road for Augustus. He and his father shared little in common, which, until recent years, hadn't caused a problem. They worked around it. Now a rift had grown between them, and he blamed his sister and her husband for making things worse.

Glancing across the ballroom, he saw her. Lady Beatrice Steele, older sister of his brother-in-law. Beatrice was even more attractive than the last time he'd seen her. She was tall, willowy and her figure curved like an hourglass in all the right places and stunning, just as he remembered.

The pair became friends while she and her sisters visited for their brother's wedding in Scotland, and he found himself attracted to her. She was bold and opinionated, much like his sister Cora, but unlike his sister, Lady Beatrice knew where boundaries lay.

Though he tried to further their friendship, Lady Beatrice made it known she wasn't interested. Seeing her two younger sisters settled was important to her.

Their eyes locked and she flashed him a seductive grin before turning and making her way to the French doors leading out to the gardens. What was she up to, going outside alone and unescorted? There were always one or two rakes who bided their time waiting for someone like Lady Beatrice they could easily take advantage of.

She looked seductively over her shoulder at him one last time before disappearing.

Intrigued and worried for her safety, Augustus hurried across the room and out the French doors. She was nowhere to be seen.

He ventured out into the gardens, the pathways lit by torches, until he found her. She was sitting on a wooden bench in front of a pond the Countess of Mulberry was famous for. The countess had seen one similar on a journey she and her husband made to the Far East, and immediately upon their return had one installed in both their London home and their country estate. Or so the story went.

Upon seeing him approach, she rose from the wooden bench. Her golden hair sparkled in the moonlight. She looked like a goddess in a dark blue silk confection that hugged her luscious curves in all the right places.

Augustus approached without saying a word. He had kissed her once before when she came to Scotland for her brother Sebastian's wedding to his sister Cora. He had not made the impression on her he'd intended. This time, she would remember exactly who he was. Taking her arm with one hand, he cupped her face with the other and boldly kissed her. Lost in his lust and need for her, he parted her lips with his tongue. She seemed to enjoy his advances, opening to him. Perhaps a little too easily.

The next thing he remembered was Lady Beatrice pulling back, ending the kiss, slapping him as hard as she could across his face before pushing him into the countess's pond.

"What was that for?" he sputtered. He landed on his backside, not an inch of him left dry. Looking through wet hair now plastered to his face, he saw her backside as she hurried off without a glance.

Suddenly she stopped and turned back around, her eyes bore through him. "What's that for? You really have to ask? That's for assuming I wanted you to kiss me. You're no different than any other man. You're a rake and a scoundrel and I don't associate with either." She turned and was gone.

Augustus threw his head back and began laughing, his rumbling baritone echoing throughout the gardens. Wiping his face with his hands, he pushed wet hair out of his eyes. The minx. What had he done to deserve such a greeting? His interest was now piqued. Lady Beatrice wanted him to kiss her, she just wasn't ready to give in to her feelings. He could play her game of cat and mouse for as long as she wanted. Sooner or later, she would tire, and he'd capture her.

After a lifetime of chasing women, he never actually allowed his heart to become engaged, to never fall in love with any of them. And there'd been plenty of them. He chased them all, played all the games until he came out victorious, kissing, caressing and making love to them. Being the rake he was, he would simply walk away, because they wanted more than he was willing to give.

Things changed the moment he met Lady Beatrice. His entire world shifted as he fell so hard and so helplessly in love with her.

Once again his heart was unable to maintain the façade of the merry rake he portrayed when he was around her. Was this what love felt like? He'd never been in love before and had no idea how he should act. He had broken his own code of conduct by allowing a woman too far into his heart. He was going to burn in hell.

1

Four years later

Lady Beatrice Steele looked up from the letter she was writing. Her assistant, Mrs. Hughes stood in the doorway of her private office. She was a middle-aged woman, a bit plump with steel gray eyes obscured by round spectacles. She was as efficient at her job as her husband was as butler at Steele House.

Her offices were on the third floor, separate from the rest of the people who worked for her. When she took possession of the building her aunt left her, she made sure to make this her main offices. It was a three-story brick building, and her business interests were housed throughout the two top floors. Tenants occupied the ground floor. Some of them had been there for years. The second floor housed employees. Some oversaw specific properties, others kept paperwork in order while still others went out and inspected her properties on a regular basis. There was an architect on staff for the time being to oversee the department store she envisioned.

"What is it Mrs. Hughes?"

"There is gentleman here to see you."

"Does he have an appointment?" Beatrice asked putting her pen down.

"No, but he was quite insistent you would see him without one."

"He'd better be the bloody Prince of Wales."

Mrs. Hughes shook her shock of gray hair. "I'm afraid not. The gentleman is the Marquess of Talisker, my lady."

Augustus Keats, the brother of her sister-in-law, the Duchess of Hightower. She smiled to herself. The last time she'd seen the marquess she had slapped his face and pushed him into the Countess of Mulberry's Koi Pond.

What was he up to? Better yet why was he here after all this time? He certainly had nerve to just show up unannounced.

"Show him in," she sighed. She put aside her pen and correspondence.

A moment later Mrs. Hughes returned, a tall, towering, familiar figure behind her. He entered her office, glass green eyes following her. Beatrice moved across the room to greet him.

"My lord. It's been far too long. What brings you all the way to London?" She asked. She turned her sight to her assistant. "That'll be all Mrs. Hughes. Please see tea is brought. Other than that I do not wish to be disturbed."

She didn't want to be disturbed until she found out what he was up to. For four years he avoided her, but she had been too busy to keep up with whatever escapade he was up to, and she was sure the rake would not disappoint if she dug deeper into his activities.

He bowed. "Lady Beatrice. I'm here on business."

"Really? How interesting," she said. She sat down

behind her walnut desk and motioned him to sit in one of the burgundy upholstered wing-back chairs on the other side. "If I remember correctly, you opened your own distillery with a loan from your aunt."

"I did. The first batch is ready for release and I'm looking for a place to store it once it's arrived from Scotland. I understand you own several warehouses and might be able to accommodate me."

"I might be able to help you out. For a price, of course."

"Of course."

She had never forgotten him, not really. They were like oil and water until they got to know each other better. Still, she never forgot the kindness he showed her while she came to terms about her brother marrying his sister. But that was over four years ago and much had changed.

"How is your aunt?"

"I'm afraid she died about two years ago of a heart ailment."

Suddenly Beatrice felt sympathy and sadness. His aunt had tried her best to help raise both Augustus and Cora, though as she remembered she was far fonder of Augustus. After all, she loaned him the money for him to break free of his family whiskey business and her brother's monetary involvement.

"My deepest condolences, my lord. I had no idea."

"Thank you. I find it curious you hadn't heard the news from either my sister or your brother."

She tapped the top of her desk with her finger. "I rarely see them. Sebastian hardly approves of what I'm doing. He believes I should have let things continue on as my aunt had done."

"It's not so unusual for women to have their own businesses these days. Look at my sister."

"Not to this extent. At least not the hands on managing I do." There was no point in going through the list of what she owned. He would see it as bragging.

"I was surprised when they told me you owned several warehouses. Not a business one would think a woman would own."

She arched a brow. "You've seen them? Sebastian and Cora?"

"Yes. They visited a few months ago."

"I see." Theodora and Matilda had never made mention of this, but then her sisters had no qualms about telling her how odd it was for a woman to wield so much power. They constantly reminded her nothing good would come from it.

Sebastian was at his estate in Berkshire, where his wife trained horses. He rarely came to town except on estate business. She hadn't seen him in a fortnight when they had dinner together at the family home. Their businesses kept them both busy and sometimes the only time they saw each other was at dinner.

At that precise moment, Mrs. Hughes, entered the room with a brass cart, filled with a tea service and plates loaded with sweets and small sandwiches. She made a note to herself to talk to her assistant later. High tea was not how she wished to entertain her guests. Especially someone like Augustus Keats.

They sat in silence until Mrs. Hughes left then Beatrice rose and began to pour for them. Once they settled in with refreshments, she chose her words very carefully. There would no misunderstandings in what transpired.

"How are you intending to move your whiskey from Scotland?"

"Rail would be quicker."

"It would. If you had it brought by rail, it could be unloaded and taken to one of my warehouses."

"It is secure?"

"Of course it is," she said. "You think because I'm a woman I don't know even the most minute details of running such a business?"

"I'm sure you are more than capable. Hightower mentioned you and your sisters were beneficiaries from your own aunt."

"Yes, my aunt left us with all her business interests. As my sisters have no interest in such matters, they left it to me to oversee things."

"Something happened?"

"Yes. The moment word got out about their inheritance in addition to their dowries, men appeared out of nowhere. They wanted to marry my sisters and take over the running of everything."

"Yet, you're sitting here so I take it you were more persuasive than any of these men?"

"No. I bought my sisters out."

The edges of his mouth twitched upward. "Cora said you're a ruthless businesswoman."

"Which makes me wonder why you've really come, Augustus."

He took a sip of tea. There was a hesitation in his answer. "The inheritance my aunt left Cora and I is tied up. A nephew from her late husband's family has challenged her will."

"I see, but what does that have to do with shipping your whiskey?"

She did know. Augustus's distillery had no income yet. No one wished to purchase futures for whiskey that had never gone to market, and what little he got off the family-owned distillery was a pittance since her brother Sebastian had stepped in to help.

"I'm short on funds to pay the shipping charges, taxes, and warehouse space."

"Do you have any buyers?"

"A couple. Others have told me to revisit them once I had product to sell. I plan to call on them with samples."

She set down her cup and once again chose her words carefully. "I need to think on this, Augustus. I'm not a charity. I'm in business to make money."

"I realize that. I've come to see if we couldn't work something out until I sell the whiskey I plan to ship to London."

"In other words, you want me to pay the shipping and taxes."

"A loan. If you could help me out this once, I would be forever in your debt. All I need is a loan to pay the shipping fees and taxes."

"What about use of my warehouse?"

"I will pay whatever you charge once I've sold the whiskey."

Beatrice stood and paced the floor, walking up and down the thick, light blue colored carpets. "I'm not saying no. Your proposition is unique, and I must think this through."

"I see," he said. He put his cup down on the table.

"I will have an answer for you by tomorrow morning."

She knew she'd loan him the money. It was too good an opportunity to pass up. If his whiskey was as good as what his family produced, Augustus's single malt would quickly be in demand. It was a chance to secure another profitable customer. And Augustus's whiskey would be profitable.

"Thank you, Beatrice."

"Don't thank me yet. You may not like my terms," she said.

"I'm sure we can reach an agreement."

Beatrice pointed to the plates of sweets and sandwiches. "Please, help yourself. We wouldn't want to offend my assistant nor my cook now, would we?"

He smiled and took an empty plate from the tray. In a moment his plate was piled high. Beatrice wondered how dire his finances truly were. He acted as though he hadn't eaten all day.

"Where are you staying?"

"I've taken rooms in St. James. Right now, it's best that my father and I keep some distance between us, and it's not feasible to open my house for just myself. At least until I show some profit."

"I understand."

"Besides warehouses, what other businesses did your aunt leave you?"

Beatrice leaned forward and took a piece of shortbread and contemplated her answer. "I never knew what she owned until after she died. I was in awe of her when I found out she'd left me with some residential buildings, farmland, and factories, as well as the means to do more. After my late uncle died, my aunt hired someone to oversee everything. But, she was still well involved in the operations. She was just keenly aware of men's attitudes about women in business so she chose to ignore their comments and sideway glances and concentrate on what her husband had left her."

"That is indeed amazing," he replied. "May I ask what these factories produce?"

"One produces the rail needed for railroads. The other makes locomotives and rail cars."

"Passenger cars?"

She took a bite of shortbread. "We manufacture whatever a client desires: cars for livestock, enclosed freight cars. The possibilities are endless."

"I imagine you're in great demand."

"Yes, we are."

She felt slightly uncomfortable discussing her newfound wealth and the successes of her companies when he was struggling to get his fledgling whiskey to market. She had been handed her success where Augustus had done it from nothing.

"Are any of your warehouses at the docks?" he asked as he gobbled down his third ham sandwich.

"Yes. Why?"

"Merely curious, that's all."

"That is where my aunt's husband had started his fortune. The docks are still quite important but having warehouses near railroad stops is even more lucrative. I plan to expand these to include more stops. Make it convenient."

For now she wasn't going to share the detail since she'd shared the idea. Too many things to be studied before final decisions were made.

"I wish you nothing but success, Beatrice."

"Thank you. I know your whiskey is going to be a smashing success. All it will take is getting in the right doors."

"Yes. That's the purpose of my visit to London."

"What about Edinburgh?" she asked. "Have you thought of hiring someone there to do what you're doing this trip?"

The corners of his mouth curled up into a smile. "I've started distributing there myself. I intend on expanding my work there upon my return, though I would rather work London myself and hire someone for Edinburgh."

"Once you get this first year out to market, you'll be in high demand."

"Yes. I set some of the first batch aside to age ten years, and I'll do that with the next two as well. Maybe even age some longer."

"Yes, you should. If this first batch is as good as you claim, holding a few barrels aside to age longer would be phenomenal."

She knew Augustus had to have already thought of all this. He knew whiskey well and just needed a push. At five years old, it was young, but mature enough to release part.

"So smart. You amaze me, Beatrice."

"How's that?"

"You don't know much about whiskey, but you certainly know marketing and how to make money, but you forgot one thing."

"What's that?"

"Bottling. I plan to bottle and sell along with selling casks."

"I will be sure to place an order," she said, smiling at him.

"It's been wonderful to see you, Beatrice. I should go. I've taken up enough of your time."

She stood. "It has been too long. I promise to have an answer for you in the morning. My assistant will set aside some time in the morning."

He nodded and rose to his full height. "Perhaps we can meet again socially while I'm in London. Dinner perhaps?"

"I would like that."

What in hell was she doing going against all her rules? She had boundaries regarding Augustus. He was a danger for her to be around. She had let her guard down years ago, and it would not happen again.

She had too much at stake and she would be damned if she'd marry and let a man, even Augustus, get too close.

Taking her hand in his, he bowed slightly. "Enjoy the rest of your day, and again, thank you for considering my proposal."

"You do the same," she said.

Augustus turned and walked out of her office without looking back. His proposal appeared to be sound. She would make some inquiries. Unless something out of the ordinary was found, she would agree to his venture. He needed a boost, just something to help get him started, and since he was floundering on his own, she would rescue him this once. It was the least she could do. He had been through so much. Leaving the family distillery, opening his own with little to no funding, yet striving to ensure his whiskey among the best. He was making strides, but it would take time.

~

AUGUSTUS WALKED BACK to his rooms, the biting March wind cutting through him like a knife. Having been in the same room as Beatrice rattled him, and he found the need to go for a walk. Although he wasn't sure of the reason, walking had always helped in the past whenever he had decisions to make or was worried about something. But London was a poor substitute for the open spaces and fresh air of Scotland.

Beatrice had always been a confident, outspoken young woman, but now, now she was wielding her self-confidence like a weapon, running her own corporation. Never in a hundred years would he have thought Beatrice would have taken on something as intricate as business in a predominately man's world. What he saw today impressed him. Rather than let men run the businesses their aunt left them, Beatrice bought them out and personally took over the day-to-day operations.

Appointments awaited him this afternoon at two of London's more upscale gentleman's clubs. These weren't on the scale of grandeur as White's, Brooks's, or Boodles but they were both sought after by up-and-coming gentlemen who had yet or could not gain entrance to any of the others.

He had made his contacts months ago and the management, though interested, wanted to wait until they could sample the product. Not an uncommon practice and Augustus couldn't blame them. He was considered the disgraced son of a duke who had walked away from a lucrative family-owned distillery to form his own. He was a fool to some, to others a brilliant strategist. All he wanted was to produce the finest whiskey in Scotland. He'd been on the way to achieving that with the family brand, which had been around for hundreds of years. Now he wanted it for his own fledgling distillery. He wanted to be the best.

He hurried along the crowded street. Ordinarily he would think nothing about hiring a hack but needed to use his funds wisely. Extravagances were now something he closely monitored. It would all begin to turn around once he had more orders. The response thus far had been sterling, and no one hesitated in placing orders once they'd tried his whiskey. Beatrice was right--he needed to hire a man who knew Scotch whiskey to take care of procuring buyers. He certainly couldn't be everywhere, nor could he afford to make trips to London on a regular basis. At least not now, but soon.

He couldn't get Beatrice off his mind. He knew it was time for him to take a wife, a woman who would become his marchioness and later his duchess. His financial troubles made him an unwelcome suitor for most young ladies. His decision to walk away from the family business was thought of by some as a bold move. Others though he was a fool. Beatrice didn't seem to mind and even seemed to encourage his new business.

He crossed the street. The rooms he let were housed in an old mansion and quite comfortable. The proprietress, a Mrs. Maple was particular about who she rented to. Rhys Littleton, Viscount Leeds, a friend from university had told him about the lodging and helped him secure his rooms.

He would have enough time to grab the case he kept his samples in and hail a hackney to take him to his first appointment. When that one concluded, he had one more. He felt both would be successful meetings, and afterwards he'd return to his rooms. Later he would go out for a quiet dinner.

The rooms were warm as he came through the door. Divesting his greatcoat, he sat in front of the fire in a dark green upholstered chair to take the chill off.

With any luck, Beatrice would help him out of his predicament and things would begin to turn themselves around. His father would be proud and perhaps then the two of them could make up for lost time and harsh feelings.

He smiled thinking about what sort of terms would come from dealing with Beatrice. He needed use of her warehouse and her funds too much to negotiate with her. She wouldn't let the past come between them--or would she?

He had treated her disrespectfully a few years ago

but stupidly pushed her away even though he cared deeply for her. His world had been falling apart and he'd been angry at everyone. His father, sister, anyone who got in his way. At the time he'd been unwilling to let anyone know how dire things were. He pushed everyone away, including Beatrice. She tried to befriend him then and he had been anything but nice to her.

A knock on the door drew him out of his thoughts. He rose and opened the door. Mrs. Maple, a petite, round middle-aged woman stood there holding an envelope.

"This came for you while you were out, milord. The viscount's boy told him to make sure you personally got this."

"Thank you, Mrs. Maple."

She nodded and without another word turned and walked away. He was glad she wasn't one of those nosey ladies who felt the need to know everyone's business.

He shut the door and tore open the envelope. Rhys had written him, wanting to know if he was available this evening. They could enjoy a nice dinner at Brooks's, the club the viscount frequented. It wasn't what he'd planned but perhaps what he needed. An evening out with an old friend. Placing the paper into the fire, he found his case and made sure there was enough whiskey for sampling. He shrugged on his greatcoat again and headed out the door. The biting cold wind hadn't let up as he opened the door and hailed himself a hack.

2

"Lady Beatrice will see you now. Right this way, milord," Mrs. Hughes said before turning and leading him to Beatrice's office. She knocked gently on the oak door before opening. The older woman nodded, and he proceeded.

He took two strides and entered Beatrice's inner sanctum. The space was large and comfortable, though utilitarian. He hadn't noticed the day before, but there were few pictures or personal effects that indicated a woman occupied the office. Augustus quickly concluded Beatrice did this intentionally. Doing business with a man would be better suited in a room void of feminine trinkets.

She was reading through a stack of papers, but quickly put them aside when she saw him.

"Good morning."

He nodded. "Good morning."

He was anxious for her decision and Beatrice was aware of this. He could feel his hands shake, his palms were sweaty and his stomach was churning. His future rode in her hands. She indicated one of the two chairs in front of her desk. He sat and observed her demeanor, her confidence and how unreadable her face was.

She folded her hands on the desk. "I won't waste your time, Augustus. I'll get straight to the point. I've decided to go ahead and help you out."

Suddenly he felt as though a huge weight had been lifted from his chest. All his sleepless nights would now be behind him. This was an answer to his prayers.

"Thank you," he murmured. What else could he say?

"May I ask how much whiskey you brought with you?"

"My sample case and about a dozen bottles. It will do until I can get the first shipment moved here to London."

She nodded. "I've requested my solicitor ready a contract immediately. It should be ready by tomorrow. Until then, I've informed my man to make sure space is made available for you at one of my warehouses for when you're ready to ship your whiskey."

"Thank you again, Beatrice."

"Don't thank me too fast. You may not like my terms."

"What are the terms?"

She steepled her fingers. "I will pay the shipping charges and taxes as we discussed. I'll rent you space in my warehouse for a fraction of the cost, and I believe the interest rate is far better than anything else you might be able to negotiate. I'm even willing to extend repayment until you've sold your first shipment."

"That's reasonable."

"I'm not finished."

And there it was. The ruthless businesswoman had emerged.

"What is it?"

"I want a small portion of your distillery. Ten percent should do. If you agree to all my terms, I'll pay for any and all shipments until the whiskey begins to make a profit."

He sat back and studied her for a moment pondering his answer. He really had no other options. He would accept. Perhaps at some point in time, when things were better, he could buy her portion. "You and your brother are fierce negotiators. I accept your terms. I only ask that we revisit this every year."

"That's excellent, and yes, I think revisiting this yearly is a good idea. I'll have my lawyers draw up the necessary paperwork."

He nodded, still watching her with fascination, and with admiration for her determination in such a male dominated world.

She opened a desk drawer and pulled out an envelope. She slid it across the desk. "I don't know how your credit is, but this should help should you run into any problems."

He picked up the envelope, not daring to open it in front of her. "I can't accept this."

"This isn't a gift. It'll be written into the contract."

"Thank you. I would expect nothing less from you," he said.

She gifted him a smile before rising from her desk. "I took the liberty of ordering tea. I thought we could discuss your plans in more detail. That is if you have time."

"Of course. I cleared my morning." That wasn't a lie. He made sure to free up his morning once Beatrice showed an interest and asked him to return today.

She walked to a corner and pulled a black cord. As she directed him to where they sat the day before,

Mrs. Hughes brought a tea cart. Neither said a word until she left. Beatrice handed him a steaming cup which he accepted and sat back in the leather chair.

"I do have one favor I would hope you would grant me."

"Name it," he said.

"I wish two casks of this first batch of whiskey."

She wasn't asking the impossible. Beatrice had figured it out. Such an offer could easily be taken for the allowance he made for breakage. It wouldn't play into his profits. She was far savvier than he first gave her credit for. But why would she want that quantity?

"Done," he said. "Though I must ask why."

"It's simple. It's a smart business move. Should your whiskey be as good as you claim, I will hold a cask back from the initial batch. It might be worth quite a lot to some men," she said. "Consider it partial payment."

He laughed. "I should have known."

"In fact if you like, come for dinner this evening, and bring a bottle. You can introduce me to your skills."

There was a twinkle in those lapis blue eyes and for a moment he wasn't sure what skills to which she was referring. He quickly regained his composure.

"I would be delighted to dine with you, and I'll be sure to bring a bottle with me."

"Excellent," she said. She put down her teacup and looked at him. Her face was unreadable. "I really have faith in your abilities, Augustus. I wouldn't be doing this if I didn't. I think you're going to be a huge success."

"Thank you. You have no idea what that means coming from you."

"You went through a phase. All young men do it. You were reckless and made some bad choices. I don't think you should be judged by your past. If you weren't serious about this, you would simply be living off whatever your father provided or finding schemes to make money quickly. Regardless of its legality." She smiled again.

He took a sip of tea, not sure how to respond. She knew his story far better than most, having heard a lot of the details from family.

He gazed at her as she sipped her tea. Perhaps they might renew their friendship and the fledging romance which had developed a few years ago. From his own research, he found out no one was courting her. She was only interested in her businesses. Was she using them to hide away from any pain? He had offended her a few years past, but he was a different man back then.

She certainly had grown into a beautiful, desirable young woman. Back when they met, Beatrice was already a beautiful young woman. None the less, she was one without the experience and wisdom of the woman who now sat next to him. She might be two years older than he and Sebastian, but it had never been important to any of them. Some men would think she was about to be on the shelf, too old. Rather than be bored by the idle chit-chat of other young ladies, he found her wisdom refreshing in a woman.

"Augustus?"

He turned his attention back to her. "I'm sorry. I just try not to think of that period of my life. I was a disappointment to everyone."

"But you're making strides to change that."

"I am," he nodded.

"Excellent. Dinner at seven?"

"Yes," he said. He rose to his full height, taking her hand. "I know you're busy. I won't keep you. I'll see you this evening."

"Until this evening." She looked down at the case he brought with him. "Off to another appointment?"

"Yes. Wish me luck."

"You'll do fine, Augustus."

He turned and walked out of her office, case in hand.

LEAVING her office Augustus felt as though a huge weight had been lifted from his shoulders. Beatrice had agreed to his proposal, her terms not to his dislike. If she hadn't have agreed to help him, he might have been forced to go to his brother-in-law Sebastian or his father which might have ended in failure. He'd had little to do with either man since Sebastian seized control of the family whiskey business by paying off his debts and putting the distillery to rights. It had been the answer to a lot of problems, but Sebastian's terms had not been to Augustus's liking. He'd formed his own company. Now it was time for all his hard work of the last years to come to fruition. He would make this work.

There was much for him to do, details to be sorted out. Then he would contact Duncan Lindsay, the man who oversaw his distillery about arranging for the whiskey to be shipped to London.

Perhaps for the first time in a very long time he had something to celebrate.

He hailed a hack and instructed the coachman to take him to a local fried fish shop. It was a business appointment with his friend Thomas Thigpen, Viscount Montgomery, and it was a place they frequented while at university. He and Thomas had been friends during that time and like Augustus had somehow managed to survive this formative time in their lives.

Augustus had kept in contact with his friend throughout the years. Thomas's family owned vineyards in Italy and France, so his friend was not unfamiliar with the shipping and distribution on the continent. In a couple of years, once his whiskey had a firm footing in the market, he would look to expand his horizons to the continent. He and Thomas had spent many an hour discussing how they could become rich and powerful men on their own if they just put their heads together.

Thomas also had connections to Brooks's and White's since his own family's wines were sold to the clubs and had promised to introduce Augustus to the manager and man who purchased spirits for Brooks's. This was a break he needed. Knowing Thomas and how charming and charismatic he could be, Augustus had no doubt he would walk out of the club with an order.

The hack pulled up in front of the small shop which was now booming with the lunchtime crowd. Shops like these were found all over London. Workmen and aristocracy alike frequented these establishments as an alternative to a heavy meal in the middle of the day. Besides the popular fried fish, one could buy a lobster salad, dressed crabs or a nice plate of beef or ham. A man could be in and out of such a place in thirty minutes.

He spotted his friend immediately and after placing their order the pair took their mugs of ale and sat down at a corner table. His friend was extremely tall and rail thin with dark hair and fair skin. His features were sharp-cut, and he had the ability to make people around him uncomfortable with his hard gaze.

"I have to thank you for arranging this meeting," Augustus said.

"Think nothing of it. I remember how hard it was for my father to get his wines into more exclusive establishments. If I can help you avoid some of that, the better for both of us."

"How's that?"

"Let's wait on that discussion for another time."

"No, go ahead. Give me something, even if your idea is not ready for me."

"I can help you get your whiskey to market on both the continent and America. I was thinking perhaps we could discuss it again, say, in a year?"

Augustus nodded. "I'm intrigued, and a year is plenty of time to have my whiskey firmly planted in London."

Thigpen smiled and lifted his mug of ale and downed half the contents in two swallows. The man sitting across from him was intelligent, articulate, and confident. He knew a good business deal the moment he saw it, rarely delving any deeper. His instinct was always correct.

"So tell me, are you truly reformed?"

"Not by choice," Augustus replied. "I'm afraid I've had to give up my roguish ways as they wouldn't be good for business."

"Yes, of course."

"That doesn't mean I'm not against going out now and then and having a good time. My business must come first that's all."

"I understand completely, but how are you going to find a wife if you don't socialize?"

"I'll manage when the time comes." He smiled. "I'm having dinner tonight with Lady Beatrice Steele."

"Something I should know about? I thought the two of you were not fond of each other."

"I think we've matured past that. She's quite successful in business."

"Which a lot of gentlemen don't like."

Trying to drown a sudden grin, Augustus took a long swallow of ale. "So she's told me. She also doesn't give two figs about what gentlemen think of her."

"Is that so? She sounds like one to be wary of. I've heard rumors she quite ruthless."

"She doesn't scare me. Besides, we're sort of related. Her brother is married to my sister, Cora."

His friend put his now empty mug down on the table. "I understand she plans to open a department store on the outskirts of Mayfair. The building is nearly finished."

He hadn't heard that but it didn't surprise him. Not after negotiating with the young woman. "Nothing would surprise me." He would find out more this evening at dinner, like why she hadn't thought to mention such a large undertaking.

"Something like that might do exceptionally well if it were just for women, but from what I've heard the store is going to have everything under one roof."

"Like Fortnum and Mason?"

"Yes. I don't know all the details, but I'm sure you can find out the next time you see her."

Augustus shook his head. "The only business dealings I want to have with Lady Beatrice is warehousing my whiskey when I ship it south."

"She's going to lease you warehouse space?"

"Of course. What is family for?"

Thigpen threw his head back and began to laugh

deeply. "You sly dog. Here I thought you were barely able to tolerate your family."

"That's only a temporary situation." He had no intention of letting his friend know the exact reasons he'd gone to Beatrice in the first place. That was between him and the lady.

Thigpen reached across the table and clapped him on the shoulder. "Come, we best get going. We have whiskey to sell."

The pair left the fish shop and headed down the street towards Brooks's. It wasn't a long walk, but the time would give Augustus a chance to go over everything in his head.

Thigpen led him to a corner of the salon where they made themselves comfortable in leather wingback chairs. The viscount ordered a whiskey for both.

"Who is it we are going to talk to?" Augustus asked.

The very efficient footman approached, tray in hand with two glasses. They each accepted one and waited for the young man to leave.

"Mr. Armstrong," Thigpen replied. He lifted the crystal glass to his lips and took a drink of the amber liquid. "All liquor and wine sales must be approved by him."

"I've met him a few times on my father's behalf."

"Excellent. He knows you and is familiar with your family's product. It shouldn't be hard to sell him on yours."

Augustus drank his whiskey and put the half full glass on a table beside him. "I hope you're right. I'm not here selling my family whiskey. This is my own."

"Here he comes," the viscount murmured.

Mr. Armstrong had been at Brooks's since he'd first come. He was a man in his fifties. His dark blond hair had given way to silver and the lines on his face were becoming more pronounced. The man had started as a footman and rose through the ranks. A knowledge of spirits and wine made him an asset. Augustus wondered who would replace him when it came time for Armstrong to retire.

He immediately recognized Augustus as he made a slight bow in front of both men. "Milord, it's an honor. I understand you've branched out onto your own."

"It's been far too long, Mr. Armstrong, and yes, I began making my own brand of whiskey. The very first batch is ready for consumption."

He nodded. "If you gentlemen will come with me, we can finish our discussion in my office."

Augustus and Thigpen rose from their chairs and followed Armstrong from the public rooms to the inner workings of the club. Augustus noted it hadn't changed much since he had been here. The office was small, but efficient. Bottles of various spirits lined a shelf behind the man's desk.

"I've tasted your whiskey, milord. It is quite good. Almost as good as your family's brand."

"Almost?" Augustus sputtered. He'd hoped for better from the chief spirit purchaser at Brooks's.

"It's your first, am I right?"

Augustus nodded. "Yes."

"It is good and with a couple more years of aging it will mature into something even finer."

"Thank you."

Armstrong leaned back in his chair. "I'll place a small order to see what the members think of it. If it does well, I'll increase the order. If it doesn't, I'll wait until it's had a chance to age more."

"I appreciate your confidence."

"Your family produces one of the finest single malts. I have confidence yours will be as fine. In fact, I would like to purchase one extra barrel to keep aside for a couple of years. If that meets with your approval, milord."

"I have a better idea. I'll sell you a cask but keep it at my distillery where it can mature under proper conditions. If that works for you."

"It does and you're right. Being in a different environment might change the way it ages."

Armstrong slid a piece of paper across his desk. Augustus picked it up and found an order for a single cask plus the one he would keep for another couple years. He'd hoped for more but was grateful to get this. A cask would go a long way for a new whiskey.

"Thank you, Mr. Armstrong. I'm honored to have my whiskey served at Brooks's."

"I have no doubt you'll go far, milord. You have the knowledge and know good whiskey."

Armstrong was in demand, and he knew there were probably people lining up to see him. "You're a busy man and we've taken up enough of your time. I'll be in touch."

They said their goodbyes and Thigpen and Augustus walked back into the public rooms and out the front door.

"That went well," Thigpen said when they reached the street. "I didn't realize you knew the man."

"I've met him through my father, but I hadn't been able to procure an appointment with him. So having you put this meeting together was a boon."

"Glad to help."

They walked down the street to where a couple of hackneys were waiting for customers. "Can I give you a ride?"

"Thank you, no. I think I'd like to walk."

"I'll be in touch."

He stood and watched Thigpen climb into the hack. The vehicle pulled away into the London traffic, leaving Augustus on his own, but happy. Happy he had made significant progress today.

3

Augustus arrived at Steele House promptly at seven. He was shown into the blue and gold drawing room he remembered from the time he'd been a guest of his sister and her new husband. As he waited on Lady Beatrice, he glanced about the room. It was furnished elegantly, but not overdone. Richly upholstered blue and gold furniture caught his eye as being quite comfortable. A hearth was ablaze at one end of the room. He walked toward the crackling fire as he waited on his hostess to appear.

A moment later the door opened, and Beatrice stepped into the room. Her golden hair sparkled in the light and complemented the cornflower silk gown she wore. The gown was simple by the days' fashion. Rather than jewels, she wore two rows of pearls and matching earrings that added a subtle addition.

"I hope you haven't been waiting too long," she said as she closed the distance from doorway to the fireplace.

He caught a whiff of the perfume she wore. The same orange and vanilla he remembered her wearing four years ago. He tried to hide a smile as she neared. "No, I haven't been waiting but a few minutes."

"I thought it would be nice to catch up."

"Catch up? Before yesterday, I hadn't seen you in what? Four years? After the incident with the countess's pond, we've avoided each other like the plague."

She arched a brow. "I'm sorry. I haven't been avoiding you. I've been much too busy to do something so childlike."

Childlike? "Forgive me. Perhaps this isn't a good idea. It might be better if we kept our relationship purely professional," he bit out.

"I would, but it seems my brother and your sister both have other ideas. Sebastian made it abundantly clear I was to entertain you while you were in town."

He barked out a laugh. "And did Sebastian know I called on you professionally?"

"Why would he?"

"Oh, I don't know. He's your brother and a very powerful man."

"He may still think I'm not capable at what I do, but be assured, I am, and I do not report to him."

"Still, he's your brother."

"Our business arrangements, whatever they end up being, are between you and me. Nothing we discuss goes any further."

He wasn't surprised at her ferociousness. Beatrice was always protective of what was hers--whether they were people in her life or now her businesses. She was loyal to a fault.

"Then let us call a truce."

"I can live with that," she replied. "Whiskey? Or brandy?"

"I think a good brandy sounds in order."

She glided across the room with grace to a table of crystal liquor decanters and began to pour two healthy snifters of brandy.

"I thought this might be better than whiskey. I'm sure even you get tired of it."

"Not at all, unless of course it's some of the swill they pass off as whiskey," he replied, smiling.

"Spoken like a true master."

Beatrice passed him the snifter and sat down on a gold upholstered couch. Augustus followed suit sitting in a nearby dark blue damask chair. He took a sip but said nothing for a moment.

"I'm surprised you haven't bought your own house."

"Sebastian and Cora are in the country where they prefer a quieter life so for now, I don't have to worry about family underfoot. But I have bought a townhome and am currently redoing the interior."

"Good for you."

"I thought the marquess had his own home in London."

He nodded, taking another drink of brandy. "I do, but it is more cost effective to keep a skeleton staff and not run up all the expense of such an upkeep. At least for now."

"Things will get better once you get your product out in front of the masses."

"That's what I'm counting on. In the meantime, my father and your brother are watching me quite closely."

"That doesn't sound like Sebastian or your father."

"No, they are waiting for me to fail," he replied lowly.

She placed her glass on the table beside her. "That's only because of your past actions. I have the utmost faith in you, or I wouldn't have agreed to your proposition."

At that very moment the butler opened the door

and announced dinner. He waited for her to stand and followed her to a small dining room. He deduced this would normally be used as the breakfast room, and Beatrice quickly confirmed that.

"I hope you don't mind dining here. I always prefer it when there are only a few guests. Much easier to talk and enjoy our meal, don't you think?"

"Yes, I would have to agree with you," he said.

He stood while a footman assisted her before sitting across from her.

"I had the cook prepare something much simpler than what might usually be served. I hope that agrees with you."

Augustus nodded as a footman set a fish plate in front of him. Scottish salmon with a dill cream sauce. It amazed him how she could go from a fiery business-woman one moment to a thoughtful hostess the next. Perhaps he should take lessons from her.

"This looks wonderful," he said.

"I thought you might like it," she replied as she raised her fork.

The salmon was mouthwatering, and he quietly wondered how she knew this was one of his favorites. There hadn't been time for her to go to Cora for recommendations, and he had a hard time believing she would remember something so trifling.

Clearly the Beatrice he'd come to know a few years ago had matured in a great many ways. She intrigued him and sometimes that wasn't necessarily a good thing for him. He needed to keep their relationship completely professional for now. He needed her connections, her money and her warehouses to launch his whiskey. Perhaps later, she might stop looking down her nose at him and welcome him as an equal.

He was most curious to learn more about her and how she did business. He needed to take things slow and let her think she was in charge. Well, she was, but who knew what might transpire?

"What other businesses are you interested in obtaining?" Augustus asked after the roast chicken was served.

She arched her brow and then responded. "A weaving mill in Scotland and I've got a few other things which I would like to do."

"How can you find the time to keep track of it all?"

"It's really not that hard if you plan out your time carefully," she replied.

"Plus, you have a good assistant."

"Yes. I don't know what I'd do without her. Mrs. Hughes keeps me looking good."

Any other things you're looking at?"

She chose her words carefully. "I'm flattered you're interested in my businesses, Augustus, but why?"

He shook his head. "No reason. Merely curious."

"A department store."

"Like Fortnum & Masons?"

"Yes, but I want everyone to feel like they can shop there affordably. I'll have high end departments, of course, but I want there to be those where a working man or woman can come without feeling out of place."

He nodded. "That makes sense, and I must say, I'm quite impressed."

"Thank you."

They moved to the drawing room for a brandy. Augustus was quite amazed at how the more time he spent around her, the more at ease he was. There was none of the old Beatrice that showed, at least not publicly. He was sure she had her moments. Otherwise, she wouldn't be able to survive in what was predominantly a man's world. She could hold her ground better than a lot of men he knew, and for that it would take some of the spunk and sass of the Beatrice he once knew. But he liked this new version of her.

"Would you care to see the warehouse I have in mind to store your product?" she asked swirling her brandy.

It caught him off guard. He figured she'd send one of her lackeys instead. "Yes, of course, but do you have the time?"

"Yes. I'd like to go so we can discuss it with my warehouse manager in person. That way there's no misunderstanding about how much space you'll need or anything else."

He swirled his brandy before taking a swallow. "I think that's a good idea."

"Good, I'm glad you agree. My warehouse near the Camden Town station will be perfect to house your whiskey."

"I look forward to seeing it."

"Come to my office around ten and we'll leave from there. That will work for you, won't it?" she asked before swallowing the remaining brandy. The fingers of her other hand pushed an errant strand of blonde hair behind her ear.

He set his glass down. "Yes, that'll work."

"Excellent."

He rose to his full height. "It's getting late. I should go."

"I've enjoyed this, Augustus."

"As have I. I'll see you in the morning."

He took her hand and made a small bow before

turning and heading out of the drawing room. He needed to get away from her so he could think straight. For some reason being around Beatrice did strange things to him.

BEATRICE SMILED as she heard the front door close behind Augustus. The evening had been productive and an excellent way for the two to reunite. So much had happened to each of them over the past years, and she wasn't sure it was fair of her to hold things against him. Still, the thought of his face when she pushed him into that pond that evening still gave her great pleasure.

From what she'd been able to find out about Augustus, he wasn't involved with anyone. He wasn't courting any young lady and certainly wasn't betrothed. Unfortunately for Augustus, his fall from grace would put him on an entirely different list of eligible bachelors. Lucky for her, he wouldn't be thought of as a very good catch for any peer's daughter.

She groaned silently as she poured herself another brandy. Brandy before bed always helped her sleep better. Her mother would have reminded her that young ladies did not partake in any spirit stronger than wine. But Beatrice enjoyed finer liquors such as good French brandy. She had even cultivated a taste for whiskey over the years which would prove helpful with her endeavor with Augustus.

Augustus. What did she really think about him?

Setting aside the past incident, she found him to be quite pleasant to be around. The damage to the relationship with his father and Sebastian had humbled him, but he realized what he was capable of and was ready to move on in his life. The old Augustus would be arrogant, a man who thought about no one but himself. He had grown a lot since their incident in the garden at the koi pond. She would be interested to see how it all worked out for him. If she could be a small part of his success, it would please her.

She would accompany him tomorrow and hopefully once he met with Mr. Little, the two of them could work out the details and she wouldn't have to be involved any further. She had other projects that needed her personal attention, and besides she wasn't sure if she dared spend so much time around Augustus.

Sitting in front of the fire, she finished her brandy before heading to the study. She had some invitations she needed to respond to, and tomorrow she wouldn't have much time. This was something she should let Mrs. Hughes handle but couldn't let go of. She wanted to be the one to accept or decline. So she'd made the decision that Mrs. Hughes would handle the correspondence sent to the office, running everything past her when it came to personal invitations. For now, what came to her home was something she would address herself.

Sitting down behind the massive oak desk, she picked up the invitations which had arrived. There weren't a lot since most of the peerage were enjoying their homes in the country. It didn't take long for her to put them all into two neat stacks One for rejections, and the other for acceptances. Fortunately, or unfortunately, this pile was a great deal smaller than the first one. She simply had too much to do and the last thing on her mind was spending an evening at some musicale or small gathering to listen to all the latest gossip.

Hearing the clock over the mantle chime midnight, Beatrice pushed away from the desk and made her way upstairs to her bed. Her day would start all over again before she knew it and she looked forward to a good night's sleep.

4

Augustus peered out the window as the carriage weaved its way through the London traffic heading north. The day was starting out as one of those dreary London mornings. Mist from the Thames gave an eerie effect as the horses clopped along the cobblestones. Out of the corner of his eye he saw Beatrice looking straight ahead. If he didn't know better, he'd say she was looking at him, but decided she was lost in thought and nothing more.

She blinked and turned her attention toward him. "Have you given any thought about expanding to other English cities?"

He turned his head and nodded. "I have. Once I get a foothold in London, I'll look to expand."

"Might as well conquer England before moving on to the continent," she said smartly.

"I don't look at trying to expand to the continent for at least another year, perhaps two. My focus is here."

He watched as she pulled at her bottom lip with her teeth as she considered her answer. "Have you used any of your old contacts from your family's whiskey business?"

"Yes, of course I have. But, I've tried to be discreet for fear my father or your brother might put an end to that."

"That's a wise move on your part, but you can't live in fear of them. Your father is established, you're just starting out. I would think there's enough room in the market for you both. Besides, I have the feeling once people figure out your ties, they won't hesitate to buy your new brand."

"How do you figure that?"

He watched her roll her eyes and arched a brow. "Do I have to spell it out for you, Augustus? You are already known to produce fine whiskey. People will want to take a chance with this new brand."

"I want to do it on my own."

"And you are. You've spent a lot of time marketing to these men. Use your contacts. The worst that could happen is that your father or Sebastian will ask you to stop."

He grunted. "You're probably right."

She smoothed her skirts with her gloves. "Of course I am," she said and flashed him a saucy grin.

He turned his attention back to the slow London traffic. She did something to him, and he was unsure how much longer he could keep his feelings at bay. Right now, he couldn't afford to mix business with pleasure. He needed her help too much.

She was a complicated woman, more so than he remembered from the younger woman of a few years ago. He wondered what Sebastian's true feelings were about his sister's many businesses. She had indicated the pair didn't see a lot of each other and he had the feeling she didn't share everything with him. Today he would see firsthand how she interacted with men she employed. He was sure she was a fair employer but had certain expectations of them.

"We're getting close," she said.

More and more large buildings–warehouses began coming into view. These huge brick structures dominated the scene. Augustus imagined most had been in service for years as he craned his neck to look across the carriage and out the window at the large building Beatrice pointed at.

"Is that it?"

"No, but when I see Smythe's warehouse I know I'm close. My warehouse is only a block away."

"Quite a difference from the docks," he murmured.

"It is. I feel safer coming here than I do the docks."

He cocked his head. "I certainly hope you don't come here alone. Even here is not safe for a woman."

"I always bring an extra man if I need to come here. Little stays in contact and even comes to my office if needed."

Augustus felt a cold chill run through his body. He knew Beatrice was headstrong, but surely, she wasn't foolish enough as to go places that weren't safe for women. Yet she came here. He knew there was no point in arguing with her. He couldn't afford to have her back out of their arrangement. Not now. Perhaps he could have the discussion with her once they became reacquainted.

"Augustus!"

He jerked his head around. "Yes?"

"You're wool-gathering."

"I'm sorry."

The coach slowly came to a stop in front of yet another brick building. They all looked the same. The door opened and one of the coachmen extended his hand to help Beatrice descend. Augustus followed. He looked about at his surroundings. He needed to familiarize himself with the area since the next trip he made here might be without Beatrice. She had been generous with her time, but he was beginning to feel a bit guilty for taking her away from her other work.

"Come," she said, her dark blue skirts swooshing as she passed him.

He nodded and followed her to a non-descript door that opened just as they approached. A man with curly brown hair and a moustache stood at the doorway. He was stocky and strong. Augustus mused the man had probably always done this sort of work by the looks of him and wouldn't want to cross the man if he met him on the streets.

"Lady Beatrice. It's good to see you as always." He gazed in Augustus's direction. "Is this the man you wrote me about?"

"Yes. Mr. Little, this is Lord Talisker. I wanted to show him the warehouse where his product will be stored."

"Milord. It's nice to meet one of her ladyship's customers. I have space set aside for your casks. If you'll follow me, I'll show you around."

Augustus turned in Beatrice's direction expecting her to remain behind in the office while he went out on the warehouse floor. Instead he was surprised to find her brush past him. The corners of her pouty pink mouth turned up as she walked on behind Mr. Little.

The warehouse was busy as they walked across to a corner which had been cleared for his whiskey. A dozen or so men were working moving crates to the few empty areas. In one case men were busy moving a shipment onto the back of a delivery wagon to its new owner. "Is it always this busy?" he asked Little.

"Yes, milord. And don't worry, your whiskey will be quite safe here, which is why I decided to put it back here out of the way. Less chance of casks getting broken."

Or stolen.

"You keep watchmen I presume."

Little nodded as he stopped at the cleared area. "I keep two most nights. Not because it's unsafe or that we've been broken into. Because one man can't be everywhere in the building."

"I told you it would be quite safe here."

"Yes, you did. That makes me feel better."

"Will this be sufficient, milord?" Little asked.

"Yes. I plan to personally oversee the shipment this once. If you don't mind."

Little shook his head. "Not at all milord."

"Shall we go to the office and discuss the particulars?" Beatrice asked, as she lifted her skirts and began to walk back across the floor without waiting on either one of them to answer.

The office was just as Augustus figured it would be. Quite plain, small, and well used. Judging by the stacks of paper cluttering up his desk, he doubted Little spent much time in here aside from tending to the paperwork that came with each delivery or departure. They spent the next half hour going over every detail, and by the time they left, Augustus felt more at ease that his whiskey would be in good hands.

"We won't keep you as I'm sure you have plenty to do. His lordship will be in touch," Beatrice finally said, ending the conversation.

Little nodded. "Just let me know when to expect the shipment so I can have men at the station to unload it and bring it here."

"I will. As soon as it is scheduled to leave Edinburgh I'll be in touch."

Beatrice rose, and the two men followed. They bid their goodbyes to Little and made their way to her waiting carriage. He assisted her back into the coach and followed her. He sat down across from her, leaning back against the back of the seat.

"What did you think?" she asked as the carriage moved forward.

"I'm impressed. Very well run. Little certainly knows what he's doing."

"He wouldn't be in his position if he wasn't the best."

He arched a brow. "He seems to be just that and will be easy to work with."

"I'm glad you think so."

"A lot of men would just sit in the office and leave the actual work to others. Little seems to be very much involved."

"When will you send for your first shipment?" she asked.

"I intend to return to oversee the first shipment as soon as I finish with my appointments, which should be done at week's end."

"Would you mind if I went along?"

He stared at her in disbelief at such an offer, but quickly reminded himself whom he was dealing with. "We can certainly discuss it."

"Good because I'd like to see where your whiskey is made. It would be exciting to accompany you while you ship the product to London."

Augustus was at a loss for words. "I suppose it would be a good way for you to see the process in person. From the time it leaves the distillery until it arrives at your warehouse."

"That's what I was thinking. Now, would you like lunch? Mrs. Hughes is expecting us. I took the liberty of having her arrange lunch sent to my office."

"Yes, I would love to. If you have the time. I don't want to keep you from your work."

He was thrown by her boldness. Not that Beatrice hadn't always been one to speak her mind, not caring what others thought. It was one of the things he had always admired about her. Still there was a limit. Arranging his schedule was one of them. In one swift conversation she had gone from inviting herself along to Scotland to telling him he'd be dining with her for lunch.

BEATRICE WAS CERTAINLY glad to be walking in front of Augustus as they made their way to her private office. She was trying hard not to laugh at his annoyance. No matter how much he tried to hide it, Augustus was failing miserably. If he couldn't mask his face with her, it was understandable why he was so bad at gaming.

If she was going to help him out with this first delivery of whiskey she wanted to see where his distillery was, how it was made and where it was stored, she needed to accompany him back to Scotland. She could observe this new Augustus on his own ground and see what sort of business owner he might be. She had her own ideas running through her mind, but before she could act, she needed to see the distillery firsthand. For now, she would be content with what they had agreed upon.

She led him to the private dining room just off her office. A mahogany table stood set for two. Beatrice walked toward the table and a footman pulled out her chair. She beckoned Augustus to sit. This was often where she ate. If she didn't have an appointment away from the office, this was convenient. In fact she probably spent too much time in her office, but then how could she succeed if she didn't work? Her brother had told her to find someone she could trust to help her out. Sebastian didn't think it was good for a young woman of her breeding to be away from social events. Which, with her brother, meant finding a husband.

But she wasn't interested in marriage. Not right now. She was too intrigued by a world few women had dared to penetrate. She had half-heartedly looked for someone to work alongside her but hadn't found anyone she felt she could trust. Most men wanted to tell her how she should run her business when she preferred that they observe, do their work, and if they found a problem, inform her of it. Then, and only then, could they offer their opinion.

She turned her attention to Augustus as a footman placed a plate in front of her. She had requested something more elaborate than her normal lunch fare. Mrs. Hughes had done well. Succulent roast chicken with fruit, cheese and bread was quite filling, and she watched as Augustus began to eat. She spied seed cake to one side. Remembering it was a favorite of Augustus's, she'd asked Mrs. Hughes to have it served for dessert.

Why was she trying to impress him? She was doing a friend a favor, nothing more. True he was easy to talk to. Far more than most men. He didn't make disparaging remarks about what she did for a living, tell her she needed to be at home bearing children for her husband. Oh yes, and her favorite: no man is going to want to marry you if you insist on inserting yourself in a man's world.

When she had visited Scotland with her sisters for their brother's wedding to Augustus's sister, Cora, she found he was the only one who seemed to understand her hesitancy in the marriage. It had been the four of them, and at the time she had been unwilling to let go of her brother. But Augustus showed her everything would be fine if she just let nature take its course.

"This is delicious, Beatrice, and far better than some noisy restaurant."

"I thought so."

"How long before you move into your new home?" he asked as he picked up a piece of robust Stilton cheese from his plate.

"Soon, I hope. I want it completed before Sebastian and Cora return to town, and I'm sure the workmen will meet their deadline."

"I'm sure it's going to be beautiful."

"Yes. It was rather dark and out of date. Everything worked out to allow the workmen plenty of time to complete the project without feeling forced by a short deadline."

"When do you plan on opening this department store of yours?" he asked.

"We're on schedule for an early autumn opening. The kinks can be worked out before the holiday season."

"I'm sure you'll attract lots of customers."

"Thank you," she replied. "Not to change the subject, but what are you doing while you're here in London, when you're not selling whiskey that is?"

"Not a whole lot. I think with all that's gone on I need to keep a low profile right now."

"But Augustus, that was years ago. You're back and trying to make things right. Just choose your friends more wisely this time around," she said with a smile.

"That's what I'm doing. I must make this work. I must prove not only to myself, but to my father, that I am more than capable of running a business. I want him to know when the time comes, I'll be more than capable of taking over the dukedom."

This new Augustus piqued her curiosity. He spoke for the first time about the title he would one day inherit. He wanted to make his father proud. So many men in his position and rank never cared about such things. They lived off their allowances, some dabbled in business, but they waited for the day when their fathers would die, and they would inherit their titles and everything that entailed. It was refreshing to see Augustus was unhappy he'd hurt his father by his bad decisions. He would be fine, and he would do well if he kept going down this path.

"Would you like to accompany me to the theater some evening? I have use of Sebastian's box and I understand there's a fabulous rendition of Hamlet being presented."

What was she doing? He was going to find her far too bold, asking him out as though she were desperate. No, she was helping a friend and as such they could certainly accompany each other one evening. It would do him good to be seen socially, and she certainly could use a night out of her house.

"I would like that. When did you want to go?"

She found herself fascinated by the shadow of his beard on his jaw, but quickly admonished herself for such thoughts and brought herself back to his question.

"Tomorrow evening?"

He nodded, the corners of his mouth pulled up to smile. Had he caught her daydreaming?

"I look forward to it."

"Wonderful, I'll send a note to you later with details."

Augustus set his napkin aside. "I should go. I know you're busy and I do have an appointment this afternoon."

"Yes. I should get back to work as well. I've enjoyed this, Augustus."

"As have I," he replied. He rose to his full height after she stood. He was taller than she remembered.

She watched as he left the room before turning to walk to the windows. There she stood and watched him as he walked off rather than take a hack and for the first time found herself feeling sorry for him. He was a proud man and it had been difficult for him to come to her. She turned around. He would be fine. With the orders he had so far, word would surely get out about how good his whiskey was. Yes, he would be just fine.

5

They arrived at the theater the following night in Beatrice's black carriage. There was a large crowd present, more than most nights. Not because it was a fine production of the Shakespeare play, but because it had been rumored the Prince of Wales would be in attendance. Everyone in the ton came in hopes of catching a glimpse of him in the royal box with his wife, Princess Alexandria.

Beatrice couldn't care less about such frivolous things. She wasn't one to socialize much. Not since she inherited from her aunt. Most men she met now were only interested in her wealth. She just smiled when introduced to men and prayed that's as far as it would go.

She and Augustus had arrived together, and she was sure eyes were on their box as they settled in. The gossips would be abuzz with the fact she had been in the company of the impoverished and banished marquess. Glancing at Augustus, she found him to be relaxed, making her wonder if he had any idea as to what their appearance might mean to some.

Augustus brought her a glass of champagne and was just about to ask her something when the door opened and the Earl of Heplin strode in. He was an ordinary man of average height with unremarkable features. She was aware the man was looking for a rich wife and knew he had her in mind.

"Lady Beatrice. I saw you from afar and had to come say hello," he gushed, taking her hand.

"My lord. Good evening. May I present the Marquess of Talisker."

The two men acknowledged each other. Heplin immediately saw Augustus as a threat to any chance he might have of gaining her attention. The earl's reputation preceded him in Beatrice's eyes. The man was too arrogant and cocky for her. He lived off the earldom and was going through money at an alarming rate. He refused to modernize his estate and knew the bulk of his money still came from agriculture and his tenants. As far as she knew he had no gambling problem, but loved to spend money on lavish clothes and trips. He might think he could fool her, but Beatrice had done her research on just about every man of the ton looking for a wife and it would take a lot to get something past her.

"Heplin," Augustus said.

"Talisker."

Beatrice tried to not show her amusement at this age-old male ritual as they both, mainly Heplin, sized the other up. She thought she'd let it play out and see what happened.

Unfortunately for Augustus, Heplin had heard about the rumors swirling about state of the Marquess of Talisker's finances.

"Bad luck with the inheritance your aunt left you. It could be caught in the courts for years," he said shaking his head of dark brown hair. "What a pity to be left without an income."

"I don't know where you're getting your information, milord, but I can assure you things aren't as dire as you paint them to be."

Heplin knew he'd hit a chord with Augustus. He had an arrogant smirk on his face as he considered his answer. "It's a well-known fact you're broke." He turned to Beatrice and in a concerned voice said, "I thought you should know, my dear. I meant only to protect you from men after your fortune."

"I appreciate that, milord, but it is you who is seeking a wealthy woman's fortune. If you're trying to make the marquess look bad, you will find you'll not succeed. He's a family friend and my brother-in-law," she shot back.

"An unmarried family friend," Heplin replied.

"And that is none of your concern, sir." Augustus said staring the earl straight in the eye.

"Gentlemen. I appreciate both of your concern but be assured I can take care of myself. I can spot a man interested in only my money from a mile away."

She took a sip of champagne waiting to see if the earl would back down or if he was going to be as persistent as he was known to be. She glanced in Augustus's direction. He stood there, his face masked. She knew he hated this. People doing exactly what Heplin was. Putting his finances out for all to hear.

Heplin wasn't about to be run off. "May I call on you tomorrow, Lady Beatrice?"

He blatantly used her given name without her permission and that was an instant warning sign to her. The man had other things in mind and had no regard for women.

"I'm afraid I won't have time."

"Another time. I forgot how busy you are with your businesses," he drawled with a smirk.

"Yes, they keep me quite busy, but I like that."

"You really need to find a man to run them for you. If you'd like I could recommend a couple of gentlemen," he said.

"I have no plans to relinquish control of my businesses, and I take offense that you would even think I would."

She turned and walked away from both men to the edge of the box. Beatrice made a quick assessment of the other boxes and who occupied them before sitting down with her glass of champagne. She'd dismissed Heplin and hoped he had the good sense to leave. She had certainly made it clear she had no patience for men like him and his catty little comments. At least Augustus understood her, and if he didn't agree with what she did, he had the good sense to keep it to himself.

Beatrice heard the door close behind Heplin and she held her breath as she waited for Augustus to join her. What was it about him that made her do silly things? Why did he take her breath away? She had no time in her life for dalliances with him or any other man. Besides they would never suit. They were complete opposites--oil and water. She would help him with his first shipment of whiskey and be done with him.

Why did she keep telling herself this?

"He's gone," Augustus whispered in her ear. He was behind her, bent over. He was close, too close, but she didn't seem to mind his nearness. He walked around and sat down beside her, handing her a fresh glass of champagne.

"Arrogant prig. Who does he think he is coming in here trying to tell me how to run my life?"

"As you said–arrogant prig. Let's not let him ruin the evening."

"Oh, I don't intend to. I've forgotten about him already."

FOCUSING her attention on the play as it began, Beatrice immersed herself into what was unfolding below her. Shakespeare had always been a favorite and this rendition was the best she could recall ever seeing. The actors and production brought Shakespeare's words to life. It was easy to see why royalty made time to attend. This was the first time in a long time she had been able to let go of her responsibilities and relax. It was something she needed to make the time to do more often.

Instead of the play, Augustus found himself watching Beatrice. For the first time in a long time she seemed to be able to relax and enjoy the play. Women wouldn't bear such a heavy burden, but Beatrice seemed to thrive and if they were to ever become betrothed or married, he would never ask her to give any of it up. Not that she would. Betrothed, married? Did he dare dream of a life with her?

She seemed to be content with their relationship as it stood. If he was patient, and she saw he wasn't out to control her, hopefully she would soften.

Beatrice had proven her distrust of men this evening when a certain gentleman tried to talk down to her. It backfired on him. She saw right through him for what he was. A man like all the others; after Beatrice not for herself but her vast array of businesses and money. Marrying a man like that would cripple her, strip her of her spirit.

He reached over and took her gloved hand in his.

She didn't object and continued watching the stage. Finally she did glance away and smiled in his direction. Not a word between them. None were needed.

He leaned over towards her. "Would you like to leave at the end of this act, or do you wish to see the entire play?"

She smiled. "Are you bored, milord?"

"No, not at all. I thought perhaps after Heplin's remarks you might want to leave," he replied.

"No. I refuse to bow to Heplin or the gossips. We'll stay until the end."

"I thought you might." He squeezed her hand.

"I should tell Sebastian about this encounter, so he'll be aware the man is searching for a wealthy woman he can make his bride and control."

"Yes, you should. He needs to be told. Your sisters don't need to be around him. He'd ruin one of them to get her money."

She wasn't listening. The crowd had turned its attention from the stage to the royal box which it seemed was occupied after all.

"You would think he would know he can't sneak in unnoticed," Beatrice said shaking her head of blonde curls.

"I'm sure he does, though I'd be willing to bet he likes making a grand entrance."

She leaned forward, her attention on the stage below. It was a far better diversion than what the latest interest society had. One of the reasons she loved the theater was she could lose herself in what the actors were doing on stage. Immerse herself in the characters. An escape from reality, if only for a while.

6

Two days later, on a rainy London morning, Beatrice walked into her warehouse. She had come, spur of the moment, curious to see if everything was ready for the first shipment of whiskey. It was his first release, and she knew he had to be excited and proud of such an accomplishment. Especially under the circumstances. He'd overcome a lot. He started his own distillery after a parting of the ways with his father and her brother. He'd poured every bit of money he had into this day. She thought he could use some good in his life.

They would leave for Scotland as soon as Augustus had all his orders together. She had told him if she were going to invest in his endeavor, she wanted to see the process all the way through. Though the whiskey wouldn't be made while there, she would get to see his distillery and learn how the whiskey ended up at in the customers' hands.

She looked down at the warehouse floor from the large window in the office overlooking the hustle and bustle. She spotted Augustus, suit coat long abandoned, his shirt sleeves rolled up helping the men move unneeded wood out of the corner where his whiskey would be stored. His mahogany red hair was tousled, and an errant lock kept falling over one eye. She turned away seeing the sinewy muscles of his forearms flex as he pushed a cart filled with wood and other items. She had no business thinking the thoughts that were going through her mind. Yes, she and Augustus had shared kisses at one time, but that was a long time ago and a lot had happened since then.

He turned, finished with that cart, saw her standing at the window and waved. He looked happy and satisfied with the progress being made. She waved back before turning away. Walking to a chair in front of the desk, she sat and waited. She knew Augustus well enough to know he would be coming through the door any moment. Not that he was predictable, but he appeared to be a different man now that she had agreed to help him with this first shipment.

Moments later she heard the door open. Instantly she was aware Augustus had entered the room.

"Everything is going smoothly?" she asked without turning around. She wasn't sure her face wouldn't give her away if he were attired, without a jacket, as he had been when she saw him minutes ago.

"Aye. Little certainly runs a tight ship. Everything has gone very smoothly. I look forward to a continued relationship."

"Oh, you plan on renting space here in the future?" she asked coyly.

"I can think of nowhere else I'd rather trust my whiskey."

"Thank you. I'm sure Mr. Little would love to hear that as well."

"I have some appointments left the day after tomorrow, but then I'll be finished."

"I thought we were going to Scotland then?"

"Aye, we are. My appointments are in the morning, we can leave afterwards."

"You really need to hire a man here, Augustus. You can't do it all."

"I know, I know."

"Augustus if money is the issue, I'd be happy to help."

"I will hire someone once we return from Scotland."

He was too proud to ask for more help. That was one of the things she was coming to admire about him. No matter how much he went through, Augustus managed to pick himself up and carry on. He might have a bump or two along the way, but he determined to win.

She rose from her chair. "If you need anything else, please let me know. If not, I'll be at your door to pick you up for our train ride."

"Thank you for everything, Beatrice." He hesitated, then the corners of his mouth curved up. "There is something you can do for me."

"What's that?"

"Have lunch with me. I'll take you somewhere you won't soon forget."

She really didn't have time, but what would be the harm?

"I doubt even you can surprise me, but I'd like that."

"Wonderful. Give me a moment to speak with Little and grab my jacket."

She shook her head. "I'll be right here. I know how long-winded Little can get."

"But he's very knowledgeable."

"He is that, and he knows people, which is always good."

Beatrice gave a sigh of relief. She really couldn't afford to take any more time away from her office. There was too much going on, but maybe it wouldn't hurt to have a little fun now and then. Augustus made it easy. When she was around him, she could relax and be herself, something she found refreshing. She could never let her guard down around other men; she never knew when they might be out to try and take advantage of her.

Perhaps she needed a reliable assistant as well as Augustus. They could sit down and talk about her finding a man. If Augustus had time, he would be a perfect buffer and he would know who is a rake and just after her money, and who was financially stable. One who was settled. A man who would accept her as their equal.

~

DESPITE BEING ELBOWED AND SHOVED, Augustus led her to the counter of the fish shop so they could place their order. He'd brought her here for two reasons: the food was good and to remind her that there was a whole other world outside the world she controlled. He glanced at her and was surprised to see that if she was unnerved by the crowd she wasn't giving anything away.

"What do you recommend?" she shouted in his ear when they finally got to the counter to place their order.

"Everything is good. I've never had a bad meal here."

She frowned at his non-commitment. "What are you planning to have?"

"Me? The fish. It's fried to perfection and served with chips."

"I'll have that."

"With an ale?" he inquired with a grin.

"Yes."

Augustus placed their order, and they were quickly served. Handing her both ales, he led her to a counter at the side of the shop. It was too cold to stand or sit outside and he always enjoyed watching the people.

They stood in silence and ate the crispy fish. They ate in silence as the crowd was loud and didn't allow any meaningful conversations although the crowd has lessened quite a bit since they arrived. He decided to find out what she was thinking, because knowing Beatrice, there was no way her pretty little head wasn't spinning with thoughts and ideas.

"What do you think?" he asked. He lifted his ale and took a swallow, his eyes studying her closely.

"Very noisy and crowded, but I like it. Thank you for thinking of this."

"My pleasure."

"Do you come here often?" she asked.

He nodded. "I find it's a nice change from my club. I've come to learn I don't need to spend hours over a leisurely lunch, when I can come to one of these shops, eat and get back to my day."

"Yes. I detest wasting time with a long, drawn-out lunch. I feel the same way about tea. I can have that served in my office with no fuss every afternoon."

"Don't you feel like you're missing out on life?"

She shook her head. "Heavens no. I have everything I need."

"Hmm," he replied.

"What? Don't you think I do?"

"Yes. You have a vast empire. But do you have anyone to share it with?"

She stared at her plate as though trying to figure how best to answer him. "Do you?"

He finished off his ale. "Dodging the subject, Bea?"

"If you're done, I need to get back to my offices. I've been away far too long."

"Beatrice..."

"We can talk tomorrow on the train to Scotland."

"Promise? None of this avoiding the subject like you're doing right now?"

She gifted him a smile. "Of course. We can talk about anything you want...within reason of course."

"Of course," he said as he guided her out of the busy shop. The sidewalk was still brimming with people coming to eat. He kept his hand on the small of her back as he continued to guide her away from the crowd.

Finally, about a block away from the food shops, Beatrice stopped and faced him. "There's no need for you to continue with me. I can find my way back."

"I'll see you back to your offices myself, and you'll give me no argument."

"Really, Augustus. I'm not some young innocent girl."

"I never said you were," he growled. "But you are a successful businesswoman, and I won't see you walking unescorted back to your offices."

She sighed and shook her head, knowing she wasn't going to win this round. Augustus had made up his mind and there was no changing it. "Very well. Have it your way."

"It's for your own good."

"I know, and I appreciate your thoughtfulness. I'm just not used to anyone, let alone having a man be concerned about my safety and well-being."

"What about your family? Friends?" He asked as he guided her towards her offices.

"You know the situation with my family. Sebastian's married now. And friends?" She laughed. "That's another story. My lady friends are all married or betrothed. If they aren't, they're looking to make a match. None of them understand, some are even horrified."

"I completely understand. It seems most of my friends weren't really friends after all."

"I know and you're better off without them."

"Seems like we live similar lives, though I will admit yours is much more successful and exciting."

"Don't sell yourself short, Augustus. You have something you've made from nothing. Your whiskey didn't exist until you put it together and aged it. That alone is successful."

"I thank you for that," he said lowly.

"Don't thank me. It's the truth."

They continued walking until, a few blocks later, they stopped in front of the dark red brick building which housed Beatrice's offices. He started up the steps behind her. Beatrice stopped and turned around. "I can make it from here."

"I insist. What sort of gentleman would I be if I didn't escort you all the way?"

"Augustus..."

"Really Bea, you don't need to be so serious."

"I'm not," she snapped. She instantly regretted her response and tried to soften it. "You've seen what I'm dealing with. One day, I promise I'll return to the old, carefree Beatrice. Until then, please bear with me."

She started towards the door now being held open by a waiting doorman.

"Very well. I guess I'll see you in the morning on the train."

"Thank you for being so understanding. I'll see you in the morning."

He stood and watched as she disappeared before turning and continuing on his way.

7

Augustus slid open the door to the compartment and stepped in. Surprisingly, he found it empty and void of Beatrice. Most likely she had gotten caught up in the line of carriages dropping off passengers headed north to Scotland. After storing the one case he carried, he made himself comfortable, sitting next to the windows of the oak paneled compartment and waited.

Outside people were bustling to their designated trains even though the skies were cloudy, and threatening rain. As usual, the weather was unpredictable, and he was thankful to have arrived before the rain set in.

Remembering he brought a book, he found his case and pulled it out. He had little time to read and was grateful to have time to do so. Knowing Beatrice, she would probably be absorbed in reports most of the journey. She needed to relax and give herself the luxury of some free time but knew she would find an excuse not to.

Setting the volume on the seat next to him, he once again sat back and observed the crowd of people outside before closing his eyes and listening to the sounds of the train.

Moments later he heard the door opening and the rustle of skirts. He cracked an eye open and watched as Beatrice, dressed in a deep blue traveling ensemble, stepped into the compartment. Her lady's maid followed, carrying what appeared to be a picnic basket. A few minutes later he heard the door shut and Beatrice sat down on the seat across from him.

"I know you're awake, Augustus. I saw you watching."

He turned toward the sound of her voice and opened his eyes. "You're very observant."

"I hope you haven't been waiting long. The line of carriages is long and it's starting to rain."

He shook his head. "No, I haven't been here long. Just long enough to settle in."

"I took the liberty of bringing a meal. I didn't know if you'd want to go to the dining car or not so I had my cook prepare a variety of things we can enjoy."

"That was very thoughtful of you," he said.

At that moment the train began to slowly lurch forward. As it pulled away from the station the rain became more evident. The skies were dark and ominous.

"I'm certainly glad we don't have to make the journey by carriage," she said.

"Yes, it would be cold and miserable. Not to mention all the stops," he agreed.

"I certainly don't miss any of that. I can remember traveling to Scotland for the wedding with my sisters. It was one of the worst experiences I've ever had to endure with them."

"Why is that?"

"Being confined with two chatty girls and all their

questions," she said. She folded her hands on her lap and turned her attention to the landscape that was rapidly changing from the town to farmland. "Thank goodness they're Sebastian's problem."

Augustus smiled and shook his head. "You don't really mean that. Don't you want to see them both make good matches?"

"Yes, of course I do."

"Like you said, not your problem."

"No, it's not," she sighed.

"Perhaps one day you'll find the perfect husband."

"I'm not counting on that. The only thing men seem to want out of me is my money."

"He's out there. Of that, I'm sure."

"You have more faith than I do," she said. "What about you? Any prospects?"

"No, but as you well know I'm the one women avoid because of my situation."

"Former situation," she corrected.

"Yes."

"Like I've told you, this is only temporary. Things are already turning around for you."

"Yes, you're correct. They are turning around."

He watched her closely as she diverted her attention to the changing landscape outside the window. The rain was evident by the way it pelted the window.

"It'll be dark when we arrive."

"Yes, I know," she said, her eyes never leaving the window.

"Is there anything you'd like to do while we're in Scotland besides visit the distillery?"

She turned her head to face him and nodded. "I would like to see the weaving mill I've purchased. It is right outside of Inverness, and I understand we can take a train to get there."

"We can."

"Good. I want to arrive unannounced."

"Why is that?" He was curious, but in the back of his mind he knew the real answer.

"Though the mill was purchased using the company name, I'm sure that word of a woman being behind the sale might not be as well received as one might expect."

"This way they'll have no way for them to prepare for your visit."

She nodded, smiling. "Exactly."

"That's actually a very good idea," he said.

Beatrice moved to the corner of her seat, near the window, sat back and closed her eyes.

"You look tired, Bea. Have you thought of hiring a clerk? Someone to help you with the day-to-day tasks?"

"No, I'm perfectly able of handling things," she snapped.

"I'm not saying you aren't. I think it would take some of the weight off your shoulders. Allow you to focus on more important matters."

She sighed and opened her eyes. "Perhaps you're right."

"When was the last time you took a day off for Beatrice?" he asked.

"I can't remember."

"Then you're going to do it while we're in Scotland."

"But..."

"No excuses. You're taking some time away from your responsibilities and when you return to London you're going to hire someone to assist you."

8

———

The sound of screeching metal was the first thing to wake Beatrice. Why? Was something on the track? She glanced across the compartment where Augustus was awake and staring out the window into the darkness.

Whatever was blocking the track, the train could not stop in time. The sound of the engine's brakes screeching into the night was all she could hear.

They were falling through the air as the car they were riding in derailed, as others followed and the sound of inhabitants shrieking out in terror as glass shattered and the coach groaned. Finally the car slid to a stop on its side.

Silence. Nothing but silence filled the dark. Then slowly the sound of people was heard. Talking lowly amongst themselves. Crying and shrieks of horror followed as the reality of what had just happened was setting in.

"Beatrice? Are you okay?" Augustus shouted from somewhere in the dark of the compartment.

"I think I'm fine. You?"

"Fine."

She called out to Harriett, her maid, who by now

was sobbing. The sound of a pistol nearby had the young woman panicked. "We're being robbed!" she wailed.

A thud from above as shots rang out. Without warning, the window imploded, shattered glass raining down on the trio.

They looked up and, came face to face with a pistol and a man wearing a mask. A light rain was still coming down.

"You'd be correct."

He tossed a cloth bag to Augustus. "Your jewels and money. Now!"

"I can assure you we have no jewels and little money," Beatrice challenged.

A beefy hand reached down and grabbed Beatrice's arm, all the while his pistol fixed on Augustus. "Don't make a move."

He pulled her through the opening and into the darkness before throwing her to the wet, muddy ground. She remained still and silent as she lay assessing the situation. Where were they? By her calculations they had to be near the border with Scotland. The robber was English, uneducated, and judging by his accent was probably from London.

Robberies like this were not uncommon. The trains were slow enough to make them an easy mark for highwaymen. She'd heard stories of robbers commandeering a train without even having to stop it. These men were brazen and bold and let no one get in their way, leading her to believe they had done this sort of thing many times before.

The bandit came back to Beatrice, hauled her to her feet and dragged her across the mud to where a small group of passengers stood huddled together in the darkness. Shots rang out in the night. Were they simply intimidating passengers? How many had been hurt in this horrific accident? She had to keep her head and not let her emotions get in the way.

"Give me your jewels and money. Now!"

Saying nothing she hesitated, but not before the robber ripped the gold chain from her neck and dropping it into his bag. The chain had belonged to her late mother and for some reason she had not added the piece of jade that went along with it.

"What else have you got?"

"Nothing." It was the truth. She had been smart enough not to bring along valuables, and the ones she did have in her possession were high quality paste.

He grabbed her hand and held it up to see the fake ruby bracelet she wore.

"Lyin' bitch!" He swore before backhanding her across the face as he ripped the bracelet from her wrist. She fell to the mud, her hair now filthy, unpinned and stuck to her face. She brushed aside a strand from her eyes thinking perhaps if she lay perfectly still the man would leave her alone. His attention was now diverted to others lined up against the overturned car. He would be too busy taking valuables from them, giving her time to assess the situation.

Where was Augustus?

The sound of a man whistling nearby told her the robbers were finished. The longer they stayed, the more time they risked being discovered. Surely another train would come before long. Unless that was their plan--to rob another train while they sat here on the tracks.

What if his orders were to kill everyone and leave no witnesses? No, that was too big a risk. They'd done what they set out to do and were ready to make their escape.

The robber quickly finished and taking his leather bag disappeared into the darkness leaving her and the others alone and frightened.

It was eerily quiet with only the sound of a few people whispering among themselves. She had to find Augustus and Harriet and make sure they were both all right. But where were they? She was disoriented by all the carnage of overturned train cars.

Hauling herself to her feet she glanced around before calling out, hoping one of them would hear her cries.

"Augustus! Harriet! Where are you?"

In the nearby distance came a familiar voice. "Beatrice! Over here. Follow the sound of my voice."

"Are you unharmed?" she asked as she stumbled through the mud and briars.

"Yes. I just climbed out. I'm trying to get Harriet out."

"I'm on my way," she said shakily. Moans and people crying out came from the darkness and beyond.

Torches began to appear out of the wreckage. Employees had begun to light them to find and guide passengers. More importantly, a fire had been lit on the side of the track in front of the wreckage to light the track for approaching trains. Looking to her left, where she'd heard his voice, Beatrice found him leaping off the side of the overturned carriage, carefully helping her maid down from the side of the gnarled metal. Thank God they both appeared unharmed.

Upon seeing her, Augustus neared, his hands grabbing her by the shoulders. "You're sure you're unharmed?"

"Yes, I'm fine." She turned her attention to Harriet. "I'm happy you're okay."

"We need to see if there's a carriage that's not over-turned," Augustus said.

"Why?"

"For people to shelter from the rain."

She nodded. "If we're lucky there might be one or two at the end that are left on the tracks. People could gather in there."

"Good idea."

"Harriet, wait for us here. We'll be back as soon as we can."

Her maid nodded and joined a small group of passengers huddled near the wreckage.

They walked away in silence along the tracks and overturned cars. The rain was cold making Beatrice shiver. She couldn't think about herself as there were people who needed help right now.

"You're sure you weren't harmed?" Augustus asked as they trudged through the wet ground.

"He struck me in the face with the back of his hand and was forceful in the way he grabbed me. I'll probably have some bruises, but I'm fine."

"I'm afraid there might be some deaths. These men seemed ruthless in getting what they were after."

"Yes, they were. I think they were after something else and robbing the passengers was simply a way to keep us occupied." She had heard the gunshots and prayed none had been used to kill innocent people.

"But what could they have been after?" he muttered.

"Maybe the driver or one of the crew can tell us."

"Someone has to know."

They trudged backwards in the darkness and rain

alongside the track. No cars were standing. The robbers had set a large pile of stones and lumber on the track. The force of the sudden stop had caused every single one to derail. Bea could make out they had come across the enclosed cars used to transport passengers' luggage and commerce. One lay on its side, the other had somehow managed to stay upright. As they drew closer it was obvious to her that the robbers had gone through the two directly in front of them. Bags and crates were thrown out on the ground. It made a large disorganized mess outside the freight car.

"Whatever they were after must have been valuable or important," Beatrice said as she struggled to survey what lay around her. Her eyes had adjusted to the dark but despite that, it was a struggle not to trip over debris.

"What do you think?" he asked, taking her hand.

"This would get people out of the rain and somewhere dry until another train comes along."

"Yes, it would work considering the circumstances and we need somewhere to put the injured."

A pair of men that were lighting a fire at the end of the train caught Augustus's attention. "Stay here. I'm going to go see what I can find out."

She shook her head. "I'm coming with you. I want to hear just how dire things are. Besides they surely might know when and from what direction the next train might be coming from."

"Very well. Just be careful."

The walked closer through the wet grass, weeds, and nettles to where the men were working.

The men had lit a fire and were adding whatever they could find to feed it as they approached. Pieces of crates seemed to be the best fuel. Both men were hard at work and didn't hear them approach.

"Anything we can do to help?" Augustus inquired.

"You can fetch some wood from the broken crates," one man said. He was a tall, older gentleman and from the sounds of his accent, Beatrice deduced he was from Scotland.

Augustus walked over to a shattered crate and took a handful of wood. "Any idea how many people are seriously hurt?"

"No," the man replied. "Not sure how many were injured from the derailing. It's too dark to tell."

Augustus wiped his dripping wet hair from his face. "We found two freight cars that are in decent enough shape we could put passengers in to get them out of the rain."

"And who's going to do that? There are only a few of us who are alive or uninjured enough to help," the other man said.

"We'll take care of that," Beatrice said. "Do you know if there's a doctor aboard?"

"I have no idea."

"Very well. We'll start gathering people up and moving them to the two cars. Are there any at the front of the train that might be useable?"

"No. The front took the worst of it all."

Augustus turned to her. "Let's work with what we've got. We can figure the rest out as we go."

"Any idea when and from where the next train might come through?" Beatrice asked.

"There'll be one bound for London, but it won't get here until early morning. Dawn."

She nodded and joined Augustus. They began walking back toward where they had left passengers sitting. She knew they needed to evaluate the situation and determine how many more passengers there were. The more severely injured needed to be among the first to be moved, and if there were a lot of souls another car would need to be found.

She shivered from the chill and rain and moved closer to Augustus. She had no concept of what time it was. Time seemed to drag on since all of this started. What she wouldn't give for a dry dress and warm fire. But there were others to think of and they took precedence to her own personal comfort. Once everyone was taken care of, she and Augustus could find shelter, and if the rain let up, they could find a fire to stand near and warm themselves.

She said nothing as they walked side by side for a few minutes. "I think we should start at the front of the train. That's what took the brunt of the crash and where the more seriously injured may be."

"Agreed."

They continued walking, the outline of the chaos of the derailed and crushed cars which had landed on their sides, snapping connection with other cars and skidded to their final destinations seemed to be larger and ominous in the faint light. The closer they got to the front of the train, the more dire the landscape. Looking around she finally found the engine laying a good distance from the rest of the train, a couple of cars still connected.

The first thing that caught her attention was the quiet. The utter silence. Beatrice wondered how anyone might have survived. Regardless they would search each and every car and the surrounding area. They already decided to put them in the baggage/freight cars. Hopefully, they had enough room for all the injured. The rain had yet to let up and it was cold. Biting cold. She was wet making matters more dire. She glanced at Augustus who wasn't faring much better than she was.

"We need to assess the situation and then find a dry place," she said.

"Yes, I agree."

Faint sounds of people groaning and crying caught their attention. They began walking closer and soon came upon a small group huddled together to trying to stay warm. Surprisingly no one was seriously injured and after assessing the situation, Augustus suggested everyone move underneath anything that would shelter them until help arrived.

"Still want to build train cars?" Augustus inquired as they headed back down the carnage.

"Yes. One incident will not change my mind. It doesn't matter how well built they are. No car could have survived this. I will build them better."

By the time they reached the end of the wreckage they found everyone inside of the baggage cars and out of the cold and rain. Beatrice herself was so cold and wet she was beyond shivering. She motioned to the fire that was roaring. Some were standing around it in an attempt to warm up.

The faint gray of dawn was beginning to light up the sky. Rain still came down, though she noted it was heavier than earlier. Surely the southbound train would be there before long. Even one headed to Edinburgh would be a welcome sight. Whichever arrived first, they still wouldn't be going anywhere soon. The track was littered with cars and debris making travel in either direction impossible.

She glanced over at Augustus. He appeared spent. Tired, wet and cold, just as she was. But something was off. He'd been working tirelessly all night and she needed to get them somewhere dry--at least for a while. They both needed to rest.

"Come, there's nothing more we can do. Let's get out of the weather, if only for a short time."

He nodded, never uttering a word. He walked alongside her as they approached one of the cars being used to shelter passengers.

"Are you all right?" she asked.

"Yes, I'm fine. Just cold and wet as everyone is."

Beatrice didn't know whether to believe him or not. Something was off in his actions, but she quickly dismissed it for what he told her. A train would arrive soon.

"You know they'll send someone out to look for our train since we didn't arrive."

"That's what I'm hoping. We're a good four hours late. Surely that's enough time to cause concern," he said.

"No southbound train then?"

"Probably, but not until they find out where we are," he said. "We'll see."

The car they approached was filled with passengers all attempting to stay out of the inclement weather. They found a spot near the opening and sat after others moved over to give them room. Everyone was subdued, quiet and miserable, yet thankful to be uninjured and out of the cold and rain.

ugustus slid down until he reached the bottom of the carriage. It felt good to sit. Neither of them had taken a break in hours and they were both exhausted. Another wicked pain shot through his shoulder, but he chose to ignore it. Once help arrived he would have it looked at, but he knew what had happened. One of the robbers had fired in his direction, missing a young woman, the bullet going clean through his shoulder. Thank goodness Beatrice hadn't been around when this occurred. There was no way to judge how she might have acted.

Glancing down at his coat he was surprised there wasn't more blood than what he saw. Good because he didn't want Beatrice to know and worry. He just had to hold on until help arrived.

The cold numbed him to the bone. He couldn't feel his toes or fingers.

He judged that Beatrice was miserable but wasn't going to let him know. Her hair was wet, and all the pins holding her hair up had long been lost. Her dress was saturated and her boots were a muddy mess. She'd be a trooper and forge on, putting everyone's comfort before hers. She was an amazing woman in so many ways. Recently, she'd been right alongside him offering him advice and cheering him on as he attempted to make his own way in the world. Bea had a mind few women had when it came to complex business matters. No one had schooled her, it was all Beatrice.

The best part was they seemed to have worked through whatever misunderstanding there had been four years back. He quietly wondered if it might be possible to take things to a new height. He would love a chance with her. She'd make a perfect duchess when the time came, and together they would find success at whatever they chose. She was smart, well-spoken even a little outspoken, and she had a mind like a steel trap.

Most of all he found his feelings had only deepened and wanted desperately to show her. Once they got out of this mess and to his estate there would be plenty of time for expressing his feelings.

Going to her that fateful day in London had opened the way to a whole new avenue he never allowed himself to imagine he could take. Though Beatrice was guarded, her feelings seemed to be thawing.

Right now he needed his wits about him. Hopefully help in some form was on its way.

"Are you all right, Augustus?"

"Yes, of course. Why do you ask?"

"You look awfully pale," she said.

"Small wonder. We're both soaking wet and have been for hours. I'll be surprised if we both don't get sick from this."

"We're not going to think that way."

She playfully patted his injured shoulder, causing him to flinch in pain. Pulling her hand away, Beatrice glanced at her hand, noticing a small amount of blood on her palm.

"It's nothing," he assured her. "I fell trying to get some passengers out of one of the cars, that's all."

"You're a terrible liar."

"Let's not worry about it right now. I promise to see a doctor as soon as we arrive in Edinburgh."

If he made it that far. The pain was increasing; probably because he was sitting, doing nothing. Before he had been helping passengers, keeping his mind off his shoulder.

"You need to keep it immobilized. I don't think moving it about is good."

"We have nothing to use," he said.

"Take off your cravat," she instructed. "I'll use it."

He grinned at her. "I think I'm going to need some help doing that."

She arched a brow and shook her head. "Of course you are."

Augustus enjoyed her closeness as he took in everything about her. She began to untie the neckcloth as carefully as possible, but even so he let out a moan of discomfort.

"I really need to look at this," she said.

He shook his head. "Not now."

"I need to see how bad it is," she insisted.

"No. I can wait. Just do whatever it is you want to do."

Beatrice fashioned a makeshift sling out of his cravat without saying another word. The look on her face told him she was concerned and trying hard to keep her thoughts to herself.

"There, that will have to do until I can get a better look at your injury."

"You mean a doctor, don't you?"

She pushed back her wet hair off her face. "No, I want to assess it before we get to a doctor."

"But why?"

"I can then give the physician more details. You on the other hand would downplay things."

"I would not."

"You're a man, of course you would. You're expected to put on a brave face."

He smiled knowing she was right. Not that he'd ever let her know. It was best to let her think she was in charge right now. He enjoyed the attention she lavished on him. He wanted to kiss her, hold her, and reassure her everything was going to be fine. But he was injured and now wasn't the time. Perhaps once he'd seen a physician...

No, she'd be bossy and make him follow whatever instructions were given to him. The traits that had gotten her where she was today. She didn't back down from anything, and ignored the looks, snickers and comments men made. She wasn't out to prove men wrong about what a woman could do, Beatrice just went about her business and did whatever her businesses required. Still she needed someone to assist her. A good, trustful clerk. Someone to help with the small things, letter writing, overseeing her schedule and making sure things ran smoothly. He would work on that while they were at his estate.

"There are others who need to be tended to more than me."

"It won't. Now I don't know about you, but I'm cold, tired, and wet. Hopefully someone will come for us soon."

"And you're very good at diverting the subject if you don't wish to talk about it," she said.

She was partially right. He went out of his way to

not talk about anything that made him uncomfortable. But he was trying to change. There were a lot of things he needed to change. Working on them all took time, and right now wasn't the time or place. They'd just been through a horrific train crash and robbery and he needed to direct all his attention to what was going on here. He felt himself becoming lightheaded from the bullet wound. He needed to keep his wits about him because once help arrived, he was going to have to help with whatever was needed.

"Yes, well that's something we have in common."

"I do not avoid the subject on anything. As you well know I speak my mind."

"Except in matters of the heart."

She bit out a laugh. "I think you've been in the rain far too long, or your injured shoulder is making you say things you wouldn't ordinarily mention."

"Am I? You're the one who keeps me and other men at arm's length."

"That's because the majority of men want to control me, my businesses, and my money."

"I'm not," he said. He studied her for a moment, watching as she sat there trying to mask her emotions. She was good, he had to give her credit for that. Beatrice would probably make an exceptional poker player. No one would know whether she was bluffing or not.

"I know you're not. Now you need to sit back and rest while you can. I'm sure someone will be here shortly."

Augustus closed his eyes, hoping he would remain conscious until the rescuers arrived. The pain was becoming excruciating if he moved or if Beatrice accidently jostled him. He didn't want to worry her and knew he'd get an earful when she saw what his wound might look like. Nothing to do but sit and wait.

The car was eerily quiet except for the occasional sound of the other passengers. Everyone was trying to do exactly what he and Beatrice were. Huddling together for warmth, though their wet clothes did little to make that possible. But it felt good having her close. He felt safe.

And then his world went dark.

~

"AUGUSTUS! AUGUSTUS! WAKE UP!" Beatrice pleaded to him.

He had slumped over into her lap as he lapsed into unconsciousness, scaring the wits out of Beatrice. She helped him out of his coat, and laid it to one side. Quickly she ripped the shoulder seam open on his shirt on his injured arm, revealing more dried blood... and a bullet hole. Upon examining the wound closer it appeared the bullet had gone through his shoulder.

"Silly fool! Why didn't you tell me you were so seriously injured?"

She pulled the sleeve back up, hoping not to expose the wound to the air any more than necessary. There was nothing she or anyone else could do for him until help arrived except keep him as comfortable as possible.

It was now daylight, the rain was still coming down, cooling the air. As she stared down at Augustus, tears filled her eyes. He had to be all right. They had just reconnected, and both seemed to like the course their renewed friendship was taking.

"When we get out of this, I promise I'll never let

you far from my sights. You've got to get better, Augustus. For us."

His body seemed to twitch, and he groaned from the pain. Then he stilled once again, seemingly content as Beatrice ran her fingers along his jaw line.

The sound of a train whistle nearby caused her and the others to look up. Cheering began as a couple of the men left to see who their rescuers were from the north or the south. At this point it didn't matter. If they had somewhere dry and warm, Beatrice didn't care. She bent down closer to Augustus after the men left.

"Hold on, help is here," she whispered.

Moments later a pair of men arrived looking into the car and inquiring about everyone. Another man appeared carrying a litter. They'd come to get Augustus. Slowly, one by one everyone walked out of the car so they could lift Augustus and take him to the waiting train.

"Where are you from?" she asked as she relented Augustus to them.

"Edinburgh, milady. When your train didn't arrive, they sent us out in search of yours. You were extremely lucky."

"How's that?"

"There has been an increase in robberies on the tracks, especially at night."

"Those men were ruthless," she said watching as they began walking, taking Augustus carefully with them. He hadn't made a sound during the transfer, and she was thankful. At least he wasn't feeling any pain for the moment.

"Yes, they don't think twice about killing anyone that gets in their way or who doesn't do what they say," the older man said. She wondered if perhaps he was

with the railroad security. He certainly was well informed in the matter.

She nodded. "Yes, that's exactly how they acted."

"If you'll follow us, milady we'll take you to the
waiting train. A doctor waits to assess your husband's
condition, and you'll be able to get dry and eat."

She was about to say something to the effect that
he'd made an error in assuming Augustus and she
were married but decided against it. If they knew she
most likely wouldn't be allowed to remain with him.
Instead she lifted her damp skirts and followed the
litter carrying Augustus in the mud down the tracks to
a waiting train. It was a most welcome sight.

"How far are we from Edinburgh?" she asked.

"About an hour, milady," came the answer.

She wondered if Augustus would be able to travel
to his home or if they would have to stay in Edinburgh
for a few days. She was unaware if he or his family
had a home there. Once Augustus regained consciousness, she would ask him and when they arrived in
town, she would make the necessary arrangements for
them.

A young red-headed man helped her onto the
train car, and she followed the men transporting Augustus to a dining car which was now being used for
the doctor to assess the wounded passengers.

"If you'd like to wait in the next car, milady, I'll
send for you once I've assessed your husband's condition," a graying man said as he indicated where he
wanted Augustus placed. It was obvious by his famil-
iarity with the injured, this was the doctor.

"I'd rather wait here with him," she replied.

The man looked exasperated, but said nothing,
simply nodding his head. "As you wish, but I will warn
you, this may be more than you can bear."

"I've already seen his wound, doctor. It went clean through as far as I can tell."

"I'll have a look." He gestured to a chair, dismissing her. She walked over and eased down in it.

Never had anything felt as good as this dining chair. It was far better than sitting in an overturned railroad car exposed to the elements. What she would love was a hot bath and dry clothes.

It bothered her that he still hadn't regained consciousness. She was going to ask the doctor about it but decided the fewer questions she asked until he made his evaluation, the better.

Someone brought a blanket and placed it around her shoulders while another brought her a hot cup of tea. The cup felt heavenly in her hands, warming them up for the first time in hours. She gratefully took a sip and let out a contented sigh. Her stomach growled in protest. What she wouldn't give for something to eat. Hot would be better, but considering all, she would settle for anything.

The shades had been pulled on the windows, so she was unable to see what was happening outside. She could hear muted conversations both in the car and near the windows. They ought to start back before long but without being able to get a view of the area, and how bad things were, she couldn't judge. All she knew was that the situation was dire.

Beatrice sat and enjoyed her tea, making a list in her head of what needed to be done once they arrived in Edinburgh. She'd learned his family kept a townhome in town but she doubted the staff would be expecting them, and there was no other way than to simply show up. They would stay there for a few days until Augustus had the strength to travel further.

At that precise moment she heard the distinctive

voice of Augustus, cursing the doctor and anyone else around him. She smiled as she realized he was conscious as the doctor was tending to his wound. Filthy words spilled from his mouth as she glanced in his direction for a better look. Unfortunately she couldn't see a thing because Augustus was surrounded by a group of men holding him down.

"Augustus," she called out cheerfully, "stop being such a pain in the arse, and let the poor doctor work."

"Beatrice?"

"Yes, I'm here. Do you really think I'd let them dismiss me?"

"No, never," he groaned.

"Now rest. We'll be headed to Edinburgh before you know it."

"Not until I see you," he said hoarsely.

To her amazement, the doctor turned in her direction, nodding his head, bidding her to Augustus's side. She rose and setting her now empty teacup on the chair walked over to where he lay. The first thing she noticed was how pale he was. The next was his naked chest. She'd never seen a man half dressed. No, that wasn't true, she'd seen her brother plenty of times when he was outside working. This was different. It wouldn't be seen as proper, but then she'd lied about her relationship to Augustus.

The men seemed to disappear as quickly as they'd appeared, moving on to other passengers brought to the doctor. It left her alone with him.

"What did you do?" he asked.

"What do you mean, what did I do?"

"You're standing here alone with me, and I'm half dressed."

She smiled coyly. "I might have told a tiny fib."

"And pray tell what that might be?"

"I told them we were married." She shook her head. "Actually, I believe they assumed that, and I just played along with it."

"Married? Clever woman."

"If I hadn't, they would have sent me to another car, and I wouldn't have known what was going on with you."

"I'm surprised they didn't, considering this isn't a place for women."

"So you say. I'll have you know lots of women are in the medical profession these days."

"As a nurse perhaps," he replied.

"There are women physicians too."

"God help us," he muttered.

She placed her hands on her hips. "If you weren't hurt, I'd remind you you're injured."

"I'm sure you would."

"We'll stay in Edinburgh until you're able to travel."

"I'm able now."

"No."

"Concerned about me, Beatrice?"

"Of course I'm concerned about you, you thick-headed man. You hid the fact you were injured from me. It could have been so much worse."

"It wasn't, but if you want to stay in Edinburgh for a few days, I'll agree to it. It'll give us a chance to spend more time together."

She arched a brow. "Has anyone ever told you how maddening you are?"

"All the time. You know how I deal with it?"

"Please tell me," she said with an exasperated sigh.

"I ignore them."

"Of course you do." She glanced around. "I need to

find the doctor. I want to know if you're to be moved and if you can have anything to eat."

"That would be nice. I'm quite famished."

"As am I."

"'ll be back in a minute."

She patted the back of his hand before turning to go and find the doctor. After scanning the car, she found him with someone else. A young man approached her as though knowing what she needed.

"Can I help you, milady?" He was about nineteen or thereabouts with carrot-red hair and the most amazing green eyes.

"I was curious if my husband can be moved. He's hungry and I'm sure he could use a good hot cup of tea."

He nodded. "Yes. I've found a shirt and coat for him. As soon as I help him dress, he may leave. If he's careful." He passed her a small bottle of laudanum. "He may need this later. To help him sleep and for the pain."

"Thank you. I'll let him know what's going on."

"You're welcome, milady. If you go to the next car, they're serving sandwiches and other simple fare."

"That's most welcome," she replied. "Any idea when we'll head to Edinburgh?"

"No, but I'll find out for you," he said shaking his head.

"Thank you."

She put the laudanum in the pocket of her skirt and returned to where Augustus was now sitting up on the table.

"They're looking for a shirt and coat for you to use. After that we'll go find something to eat."

"Excellent."

"Just take care, Augustus. You're injured and you need to take care."

"Yes, wife," he snorted.

Beatrice shook her head. "That's not funny. I should have never told you about that."

"How else would you explain your presence?"

"I'm very persuasive."

"You are that."

She yielded to the young man she'd spoken to a few moments before to let him assist Augustus with dressing. Turning, she walked over to the windows which were still covered and pulled one of the blinds open. Outside it was still raining and there was a montage of people scurrying about. She wondered if they were still tending passengers or if their job had changed. By the light of day, despite the gray skies and rain, she got an eyeful of the carnage of what had happened the night before. Mangled cars everywhere, bits and parts scattered like toys. The track had been blocked by pieces of trees, rocks and whatever else the robbers could find. It was a wonder anyone had survived.

"Are they taking a different route? It seems to be taking far too long, don't you think?" Beatrice asked folding her hands in her lap. She was still wearing the clothes she had on when they left London. Dirty and damp, she pretended not to notice.

Augustus smiled. "We're not far."

"Then I suggest you sleep. You need to regain your strength."

"Hardly worth it right now. I'll sleep once I've had a hot bath and a change of clothes."

She looked out the window. "Do you keep a change of clothes at the townhome?"

"Yes. I never know when I might find myself having to spend the night," he replied, arching his brow. "I believe you'll find some of my sister's clothes there as well. I'm sure she won't mind."

"That's good. I thought we should stay in town for a couple of days. Let you rest for a little while."

The thought that she was concerned about his well-being touched him. "I won't argue with you."

"Good because it wouldn't do you any good."

She was trying to revert to the Beatrice the businesswoman who didn't have time for personal relationships. He'd seen a different side last night and today, and he was determined to crack her hard exterior once and for all.

Augustus realized while he was being tended to by the doctor that he was enamored with this woman. He wanted her for eternity and would move heaven and earth if that's what it took to win her over.

"I don't know what you find so amusing, but you need to get it out of your mind and rest."

"I have no idea what you're talking about," he snorted. He averted eye contact with her, afraid his eyes would give him away. His mother and aunt always said the eyes were windows to one's soul and he wasn't quite ready to reveal himself to Beatrice.

"The weaving mill I'm purchasing is about an hour outside town. I thought I might pay them a visit while we're in town."

He nodded, his eyes shutting, unable to stay open. "So you've said. That would be nice."

"I'll send a message to the man in charge and arrange it."

"Hmmumm. Really Beatrice, do you ever think about anything outside of business?"

"Yes, of course I do."

"Give me one example."

"I was worried about you and your injuries," she snapped.

"Nice to see you care."

She shifted on the leather seat. "You're impossible."

"Perhaps. Why don't you close your eyes and try and relax? Don't worry so much. I'll be fine. If I need you, I'll wake you."

She shut her eyes. "Maybe it won't hurt for just a few minutes."

He watched as she rearranged herself into a more comfortable position in the corner of the seat. Though she was disheveled Augustus found his body reacting to her in ways it hadn't in quite a while. He shook his head. How pathetic. How could he have lustful thoughts about her and what he'd like to do with her when he was injured, and she was exhausted? Still he couldn't deny what his body wanted.

Soon. Once he regained his strength. In the meantime he would continue accordingly. He would go to great lengths to win her over and he was halfway there, regardless of what she said. Beatrice, he was learning, was unsure of how to act when it came to all things romantic. He would change that, and soon.

He found himself considering marriage to this woman and the thought didn't scare him nor did he try and dismiss it. All he had to do was win her over, convince her he wasn't after her money, but her. He wanted her for his wife and the mother of however many children they would have. By God, he would have her.

He watched her sleep a few minutes before giving into what his body craved. Sleep. But no matter how many times he tried to shut his mind down he found his thoughts coming back to Beatrice. She had proven herself after the robbery, helping to see to the safety of the other passengers while putting her own needs aside. Most women would have shrunk into a corner, seeing to their own needs and those of their immediate circle of family or friends. Beatrice acted on instinct, and hers was to take care of others. No wonder she was such a good businesswoman. She'd had plenty of practice, seeing to the needs of her sisters and her brother, putting her own dreams and needs aside until everyone else was tended to. She was selfless.

Augustus wasn't a fool. He knew he still had to prove to her he was able to take the opportunity she'd given him with his whiskey and make it a success. He had no doubt about his product. Soon he'd be able to pay her back. From the early sales projections he would be able to pay for the shipping, taxes, and warehousing of the second shipment on his own. It would be tight, but he would do whatever it took to make a go of this on his own.

He needed to get her mind off business while they were in Scotland. Once he'd given her a tour of the distillery and she visited her mill, he would make a point of taking her on some outings. There were lots of things to see in Edinburgh and on his estate. He wanted her to relax and let the real Beatrice shine. He doubted she'd taken any time off since inheriting her empire, and that had to change. He would once again suggest she look at hiring someone to assist her. He understood her hesitancy at doing so. She was a woman who wielded a great deal of power in more than one way. He would help her find someone. Someone she could trust and feel comfortable with.

ARRIVING in Edinburgh Augustus wasn't surprised to find his valet waiting on him as he and Beatrice stepped from the train. Augustus had sent him on ahead knowing his majordomo preferred to make the journey a couple of days before Augustus traveled, knowing he could manage without a valet for several days.

If he was shocked by their appearances, he masked

his feelings well. "Milord. Milady if you'll follow me, I have the carriage waiting."

"Thank you for meeting us," Beatrice said as she began walking in the direction of the carriages lined up nearby. She had sent her maid on before her.

"I got word of the accident early this morning."

She nodded and took charge. "Lord Augustus was struck by a bullet fired by one of the robbers. Though the bullet went straight through, he is still going to require rest. Let me know if he doesn't comply with the doctor's orders."

Augustus thought he noticed a faint smile come across the man's lips. It was highly unusual for anyone to dictate to him how he lived his life, but he'd make an exception for Beatrice. Not that it would do any good to do otherwise.

"The family physician will come to look at his lordship once he's settled in."

"A hot bath and change of clothes is all I require," Augustus said.

"And his lordship will be staying in bed to rest for the next couple of days at least," Beatrice said knowingly and with some authority.

They had arrived at the family carriage and Beatrice ascended as though she were lady of the manor. Augustus joined her with some assistance from his majordomo.

The curtains were pulled to ward out the damp weather, making it dark inside the carriage. Beatrice made no attempt to open one of the curtains but instead settled back in her seat.

"Once we've both bathed, I'll send for the physician. After he's finished, you need to rest."

"I'd really like to eat before he arrives."

"I'll see something is sent to your rooms."

"Yours as well. The housekeeper will probably put you in the lilac room. It overlooks the gardens. I think you'll be most comfortable there."

"As long as I can take a hot bath, eat, and change into something clean I'll be happy."

"You need to rest as well, Beatrice. You look tired."

"I will, I promise."

He wondered if she would or if she were merely trying to make him happy.

After riding in silence for much of the way, the carriage slowed and finally came to a halt. The door opened and a footman assisted Beatrice from the carriage. He followed her, fussing over being helped down.

Climbing the stairs to his suite of rooms he left Beatrice in the capable hands of the housekeeper before turning and entering the peace of his chambers. Quietly he walked through the sitting room and into the dressing room where a bathing chamber with a large copper tub sat, filled with steaming hot water. Never in his life had he remembered being so excited for a bath. He felt as though he were caked with mud and grime and couldn't wait to scrub it all off, though with his shoulder injury, might go a little slower than usual.

His clothes were ruined but he borrowed a shirt and jacket. He stripped and climbed into the tub, and sat back in the hot water sinking up to his neck. It stung his wound, but he didn't care. He then sunk even further down so he could wet his mud-caked hair. Sitting up, he reached over and picked up a cloth and cake of wintergreen scented soap and began the task of washing himself. He took his time with frequent breaks to rest.

Augustus was about finished with his ministrations when he looked down at the bath water, now discolored from all the dried-up dirt and who knew what else. He thought of Beatrice and wondered how she was getting along. He smiled. Probably giving orders. That was one of her many traits he loved. She wasn't afraid to voice her opinion, and like everything she did, Beatrice did it without malice. She always tried to be fair. It was just her way of getting her point across and being a woman it could sometimes be hard. It wasn't impossible for her. She tried to think things through before speaking, knowing words could be hurtful. He knew she learned that while his sister had been courting her brother. Beatrice made it be known what her thoughts were on the matter. She smiled, if he remembered correctly, as she went out of her way to snub Cora. That had all changed once she saw just how much the pair loved each other. Maybe with some luck the two of them would find the same sort of love.

All he had to do was convince her, which he didn't think would take much effort. Not after their shared experiences. He just needed to go slow and let her think it was all her idea. Being in charge was what Beatrice thrived on.

His majordomo entered the bathing chamber. The man seemed to have a sixth sense and knew Augustus would need some assistance, which he gladly took. After drying himself with some help he began to dress, scoffing that the man had laid out a nightshirt and nothing more. It meant he was overruled by his trusted man and Beatrice. He might as well submit to it at least until the physician arrived. He would eat now and once the doctor left, he would sleep. There had been little if any since they embarked on their journey north. Once he awoke, he would see about getting dressed. He hated lounging about and besides, it was only a through and through shoulder wound. Nothing life threatening.

"I can sit up and eat," he announced as his man pulled back the covers on his bed.

"Very well, milord. Would you like a tray or to sit at the small table in front of the windows?"

"Table," he replied. "You know how I detest crumbs in my bed."

"I saw that some cheese, bread, apples and chicken were brought, along with some wine."

"What? None of Cook's fried pies?"

"Of course I didn't forget, milord. I know how you love them."

He padded across the room in his robe to the table where the simple meal sat waiting on him. He sat on the upholstered chair and sighed. As he picked up a hunk of cheese, he wondered how Beatrice was faring.

"Is Lady Steele comfortable? Does she have everything she needs at her disposal?"

"Yes, milord."

"Excellent. Make sure she's well taken care of. She's important to me."

"Yes, milord. If there's not anything else, I'm going to check and see if I can find out when the doctor will be arriving."

He shook his head. "I don't need a physician."

"You do, milord. Someone with expertise needs to assess what the doctor did at the scene leaves no room for infection."

"I'm sure he did his best. The man was overwhelmed by it all. Anyone would be," he said, picking up a piece of pungent Stilton cheese. "But since no one is going to listen to me, go see what you can find out."

Augustus turned his attention back to the table but found himself thinking more about Beatrice than the food in front of him. No matter what he did, he couldn't get her out of his mind. They'd shared a horrid experience together and despite it all they worked together quite well.

~

BEATRICE AWOKE WITH A START. She had fallen asleep! Recalling that after her bath she had put on a dressing gown as she waited for the lady's maid assigned to her to return with the dress chosen for her. She had picked at the food brought to her, eating only the apple slices before lying down on the large comfortable bed. It was nothing too pretentious, fruitwood from France whitewashed as most of the furniture was. The lines were soothing.

The last thing she remembered was covering herself with a light blanket, telling herself she was just going to relax until the maid returned. According to the clock on the white mantle it had been close to two hours ago.

Panic set in because she never slept during the day. There was no time for such luxuries. That, and she was determined to be there when the physician came to check Augustus's wound. He had insisted she needn't bother herself with attending, but Beatrice knew if she wasn't in the room, and there was anything wrong, she would be the last person Augustus would want to tell. He would want to protect her.

Practicality told her he was fine. The bullet had gone all the way through his shoulder. She sighed and shook her head. She was being ridiculous.

Walking over to the corner she pulled the cord letting the maid know she needed help to finish dressing. Then she would go in search of Augustus. No, she would find his majordomo and see what she might pry out of him. Augustus would simply sugar-coat things but his man, well, he might be more honest with her.

Depending on how Augustus was, they needed to make plans for their stay in Edinburgh. If he had to rest, she would go on and take care of things without him. The journey to his estate needed to be worked out. The entire reason she'd come to Scotland was to see his distillery and to watch as the first batch was readied for delivery back to London. So many details, but that was half the fun.

She hadn't realized until the robbery how much she needed to get away from the stresses of work. It was exhausting some days. Trying even, but she loved the challenges. Now she had a new challenge – Augustus.

She was indeed attracted to him. They'd shared something unique and it had drawn them closer. She found herself wanting to spend time with him. Time not devoted to business, whiskey, or travel. She wanted the closeness she felt whenever he was near. He was attracted to her, that much she knew, and she felt herself drawn to him as well.

Could she trust him and her heart to enter a relationship with him? The interest he'd shown her was a noted change from before. He seemed to have matured. His circumstances had been forced on him and he was humbly learning how to deal with what life dealt him. He wasn't one of those peacocks who never listened, thought she was in way over her head, and made it known she'd be better off letting a man handle her business affairs. Not Augustus. He listened to her suggestions.

Egad! Was she softening her thinking on him and men in general?

She smiled. They had worked together well after the derailment. Perhaps they had both changed. She would give him the benefit of the doubt and see what transpired between them. She had to admit he was handsome, witty, and smart, even if he doubted himself at times.

He was a lot like her. When she gave her heart she gave it fully, and Augustus seemed to share that trait. Falling in love for either of them was a lifetime commitment. Was she ready to make such a serious commitment?

The lady's maid assigned to her, Agnes, took that moment to reappear, dress in hand. It was a rich plum colored cotton day dress with black piping and lace. Despite plum not being among her favorite colors, she was pleasantly surprised at how nice it looked on her as Agnes fussed with the buttons on the dress sleeves and the front.

"Do you know if the doctor has come?" she asked glancing at herself in the mirror.

"Yes, milady. He's come and gone. His lordship will be right as rain. Just needs to rest and let the wound heal."

"Knowing Lord Augustus that won't happen. Not after today. By tomorrow he'll be giving orders and overseeing his affairs," she said. She smiled, knowing she was right.

"Yes, milady."

"I'm going to check on him and make sure there isn't anything he needs."

She would visit with him, and afterwards, go in

search of the library to find a book. She could read out loud to him to help him pass the time. It would be a nice, quiet way to spend the afternoon. She hid a smile from her maid as she thought how some would view her visiting Augustus in his bedchambers as inappropriate, no matter how long they'd known each other. Then again, when had she ever listened to what polite society had to say?

After asking her lady's maid where Augustus's suite was, she marched out into the hall. She found it was just as the maid told her. Across the hall and two doors down. Standing in front of the closed door she drew in a breath and contemplated how she should act. Deciding she was being silly, Beatrice knocked on the door and waited for his majordomo to appear. Instead it was Augustus who opened the door. He was wearing a white nightshirt under a robe of dark blue. He looked delectable, but tired.

He looked her up and down with what she detected as a smirk. "Bea, I see you found something to wear."

"Yes, the maid did. I'll have to thank your sister next time I see her."

Grinning, he opened the door wider. "Would you like to come in?"

"Yes. I was informed I slept through the doctor's visit, and I'd like to have heard what the man had to say."

"Ah, that explains why you weren't here when he arrived. I thought perhaps you were bathing or dressing."

She let out an undignified snort. "Hardly. Though I love a hot bath I see no reason to spend hours in a tub. I was more tired than I thought. I sat down on the bed and fell asleep."

He led her over to the hearth where a fire was crackling and gestured to one of the two damask chairs. "It seems we are both worn out from last night's adventures."

What was he doing? Trying to drag this out with useless conversation about the infamous train robbery or was he avoiding telling her what the doctor had told him. A knot formed in her stomach as she wondered which it might be. Surely the wound hadn't gotten infected that easily. Augustus was certainly not acting delirious from a fever. He was his normal self as far as she could tell. Still she worried.

"Yes. A lot's happened. You need to go to bed or that wound won't heal properly."

"Bea! The physician said I'll be fine and that I'm lucky the bullet went straight through like it did. I just need to rest today and do what I can to protect it until it heals."

She arched her brow. "You aren't just telling me that, are you?"

"Of course not."

"That's good news then."

"It is," he agreed. He glanced over at a table in front of the windows. "Have you eaten? Cook sent far too much."

"A tray was sent but I didn't really touch anything before falling asleep."

"Come then. There is some rather savory roast chicken, some Stilton, apples, and you must try one of Cook's amazing fried pies." He held out his hand to help her out of her chair.

"That all sounds delicious. I think I will. I didn't realize how hungry I am until you started describing what's on the table." How long had it been since she had anything substantial to eat? The basket on the train? No wonder her stomach was grumbling.

They walked over to the table together. She hadn't noticed he never let go of her hand until he pulled out a chair for her. For the first time in a long time she didn't admonish herself for doing something a young woman shouldn't. She rather enjoyed his closeness.

"There's only one plate so I'm afraid we'll have to share," he said.

"Or we can nibble off the serving plates and not bother with formality." So unlike her. She would have never made such a bold suggestion before, but Augustus made her feel comfortable and at ease. She could be herself. He accepted her for who she was. She liked that.

She reached for a piece of chicken and bit a piece off and followed it with a taste of Stilton. The two together were divine.

"I trust you like it?" he asked taking a piece of apple and biting down on it.

"The cook is to be commended. The herbs of the chicken are perfectly paired with cheese."

He motioned to a bottle of red wine. "Would you care for a glass? It is excellent."

She nodded. "We'll share, though given your shoulder, I'm not sure if it's good for you to have any."

"It'll numb any discomfort I have."

He poured the wine, and she took a liberal swallow. He was right, the wine was very good. She silently ate a little more of everything on the table. It was a comfortable silence. She could feel his eyes on her and dared not look at him. If she did, she would give herself away.

"How about these infamous fried pies? What flavor are they?"

"There are some apple and pear," he replied. "Would you care to split one of each? That way you can taste both."

The pies were delicious just as he'd claimed. They were also very juicy and as she dabbed her mouth of the excess, she found him watching her with great interest. In that instant she thought if he did not kiss her, she would die. Well, perhaps not die, but she had a sudden urge that he needed to kiss her.

As he pushed his chair away from the table, he picked up the wine glass and emptied it. By the naughty grin on his face he was having the same thoughts.

She wiped her mouth once again. "What? Did I get apple or pear all over my face?"

"No, not at all. I was just admiring you."

"Whatever for?"

"For being yourself. You're the only woman I don't have to pretend I'm someone else with and can be who I really am."

"Because I've seen you at your worst and I know who you really are, and it doesn't scare me. In fact it intrigues me," she said.

Beatrice who was sitting next to him, made a bold move. She had been wanting him to kiss her all afternoon. The tension in the room was thick but still Augustus made no move. She leaned into him and kissed him squarely on the lips, ending the kiss almost as quickly as it had started. Perhaps now he would know what she wanted.

He obviously was not expecting her boldness but made no attempt to stop her. He was so taken with what happened he smiled sillily at her.

The afternoon was spent in playful sparring and further lively discussion. Upon finding a book on the

Roman army's rise and fall, Beatrice began reading to him until he fell asleep.

~

BEATRICE WAS STARTLED when she found Augustus at the table in the breakfast room eating and glancing over a small pile of newspapers which sat all neat and perfect to his left. The night before she'd left as he slept and figured today, he would stay in bed and recuperate. While he rested, she would go out to one of the many dress shops and try and find herself a couple of changes of clothes. There was no telling where their luggage was, and she couldn't impose on her sister-in-law by borrowing anything else from her wardrobe. Instead he was sitting at the table, deep in thought.

He peered up at her as she prepared to sit. "Good morning. I trust you slept well?"

"I did," she said. "What are you doing up and dressed? I would think you would take advantage by stealing another day or two of rest."

"And I'd go crazy if I did. No, I thought this afternoon we'd meet with a man I'd thought about hiring for distribution here, Glasgow, and surrounding areas. And you?"

"I was going to go to one of the dress shops. That's all."

"There's a lot to see in Edinburgh."

"Yes, I know but it appears the weather may have other ideas."

She quickly wondered what happened to the man she'd had such an enjoyable time with the night before.

He speared a piece of sausage. "How about I send a message to this fellow and see if this afternoon or tomorrow will work. If he can't do today, I could accompany you and we could enjoy a leisurely afternoon."

She avoided answering his questions. Or were they mere statements? "When did you wish to leave for your estate?"

"Tomorrow afternoon or the following morning. Why?"

"There's much to do and this robbery business has slowed us down."

He shook his head, smiling. "And nothing must be decided today. Everything will be there tomorrow."

She said nothing as a footman placed a plate in front of her with eggs, sausage, and toast. "You're right. Why don't you send a note to this man you're thinking of hiring and we'll plan accordingly?"

Augustus set his newspaper aside. "That was easy. Are you sure you're feeling all right?"

"Perfectly. However, I am concerned you might be trying to do too much too soon."

"I'm fine, but thanks for asking. What else would you like to do while we're at my estate and readying the shipment of whiskey?"

"The stag. I wish to see that magnificent stag I keep hearing about."

"Hmmm, I'm sure we can manage that as long as he doesn't elude us."

"Perhaps the weather will show us favor and we could go on a picnic," she said.

"And if it doesn't, we can make our own inside."

Surprisingly she found herself hanging on his every word. Such silliness. Or was it? Her body had already betrayed her more than once when Augustus was around. She decided then and there she wouldn't fight it anymore because she craved his touch and his closeness. She was pretty sure he wanted the same, but how was she supposed to go about getting the message across to him? She hadn't a clue.

Maybe she should be the aggressor? She was confident Augustus was feeling similar feelings and didn't have the slightest idea what else to do. No, that wasn't right. He was a man. Men always knew what to do.

He began to push his chair back. "I'm going to send a letter over to Mr. MacRae and see if I can find out when he can meet."

"Very well. I need to write Sebastian and let him know we're fine. I'm sure he's heard about the robbery by now."

"Yes, and I'm surprised we haven't heard from him."

"Would you care to meet in say an hour or should I go on to the dressmaker and you can meet me there once you've heard back from Mr. MacRae."

"That sounds like a plan,," he said picking up a newspaper. Newspapers made a perfect way to hide when one didn't want their face read. And he didn't want Beatrice to try and read his. She was too observant.

In true Scottish fashion, the weather the next day had turned from a beautiful sunny day to a dark, wet, and dreary contrast of itself, reminding Beatrice of the night they spent during the train wreck. Still, as the carriage turned down the oak-lined drive to the manor Augustus called home, she envisioned herself living there. A couple of weeks ago she would have dismissed such thoughts as silly. She had no plan to marry--at least no time soon. There was too much to accomplish with her many businesses. Perhaps with success she might consider such a move.

She was also frustrated by Augustus's lack of interest. She couldn't read him. Once upon a time she had been able to know his every thought, but he had turned standoffish since their arrival in Edinburgh. She tried to tell herself it was nothing more than the experience they shared. Perhaps she should take matters into her own hands rather than wait on him. At least if he rejected her, she could stop spending hours wondering what she'd done to make him distance himself. She'd tried to run every scenario over in her mind but came up with nothing.

The carriage came to a halt in front of the stairs

leading up to the house and a footman quickly opened the door, holding an umbrella to keep her from the rain. She descended and quickly she found herself inside the great hall. She handed her cape to the butler just as Augustus entered, shedding his hat and greatcoat.

"Come let's get warm while your maid unpacks."

She nodded and followed him into a well-appointed drawing room, done in dark green, cream and gold. "I'd forgotten how lovely this is."

He walked over to the blazing fire in the hearth and stood before it, warming himself in front of the flames. "I took the liberty to order tea," he said finally.

Something snapped in her. She was going to get to the bottom of whatever was going on with him, and she was going to do it now. Talking with him wasn't working and she knew something daring was needed if they were to advance their relationship. She boldly approached him, taking a cleansing breath at what she was about to do. Rejection never occurred to her.

She approached, standing mere inches from him. He was looking into the flames pretending to be unaware she was so close. Then he turned slightly, and Beatrice cupped his face with both hands and kissed him squarely on the lips. It took only a moment before he was hungrily responding to her advances as he pulled her against his rock-hard body. He kissed her in a ravaging kiss, his lips moving hotly over hers, urging them to part for him. His tongue tangled with hers, the stroking deepened, possessing her as if he owned her. As he invaded her mouth, she dropped her hands from his face and wrapped her arms around his neck desperately trying to hold on.

This was unlike any other kiss they'd shared in the past. This one was full of raw lust unlike anything she'd experienced before. Moments later when they untangled themselves from the grip of passion, they were breathless and panting.

"What brought that on?" he asked.

"I've wanted you to kiss me for days and all you've done is ignore me, so I decided to take matters into my own hands."

"You certainly did that," he said. "I haven't been ignoring you, Bea. I've been unable to trust myself or my feelings when I'm around you like this."

"How do you mean?"

"I want to take you upstairs to my bed and make you mine."

"You do?"

He stared at her as though he couldn't believe her naivete. "Where have you been living? The jungles of India? How could you not know the feelings I have for you?"

"I...I don't know what to say," she said. "My only excuse is I've gotten myself too caught up in my business to take notice."

He arched a brow and smiled. "Now that we've got that out in the open, don't you feel better?"

"Yes, I have to admit I do."

He reached for her hand and clasped it in his larger one. "I do also. And to make things official how about if I ask your permission to court you?" Beatrice was finally relaxing and letting her heart lead her feelings. She no longer thought of him as the rake he once was like she proved the night she pushed him in that pond.

"I would like that. Very much."

He gestured with his free hand to a comfortable dark green couch in front of the fire. "Come, tea should be here shortly."

"I hope you asked for some of your cook's delicious shortbread," she said, smiling shyly. "I remember it quite well."

She was overwhelmed by all the feelings running through her body. Her experience with men on a personal level was limited. She'd always taken care of everyone else around her, denying herself the same sort of happiness their siblings found. It was her turn now.

Several minutes later a tray was brought by one of the footmen under the supervision of Augustus's butler. It was conveniently set on a table in front of them, leaving Beatrice free to remain warm in her spot in front of the roaring fire.

"So what do we do now?" she asked innocently.

"We enjoy our tea. Things will progress naturally now, Bea."

She passed him a cup of tea before preparing her own. "Just promise me you won't ignore me again."

"I promise, sweet. I could never ignore you. Not when I know you want me as much as I desire you."

She did feel a lot more relaxed and at ease now. She'd always been outspoken and putting her cards on the table was how she'd succeeded so far in a man's world. And somehow, she was going to have to be able to separate her business and personal life. She and Augustus had business together and she couldn't let this budding romance get in the way of any deal they may have struck. This was something she'd thought about, and thought she had worked out in her mind. But had she really? She couldn't let her heart get in the way. That could prove disastrous.

She would restrict business to her deal with Augustus that she'd already made, she'd observe how he ran things at his distillery and move forward accordingly. Matters of the heart had to wait for more appropriate times.

"When is Mr. MacRae arriving?" she asked. Augustus had found the man at his home in Scotland and extended an invitation to tour the distillery once they arrived.

"Tomorrow morning."

"Good. That will allow me time to catch up on some correspondence," she said.

He waggled his eyebrows. "Unless you'd like me to give you a tour of the house."

"Hmmm...are you trying to distract me?"

"Yes. I can tell no lie, though I would think you'd be eager to explore."

"There isn't any correspondence that can't wait," she thought out loud. "But I should like to change clothes before we do anything else."

He set his teacup back on the tray and grabbed a piece of marmalade cake, one of his favorites. "Very well. Why don't we meet in the hall in say an hour?"

She nodded and gifted him with a smile. "I would like that."

An hour later when she came back downstairs, Augustus was nowhere to be found. A footman quickly informed her he'd gone to his study. She shook her head in disbelief at how easily he'd lost track of time, and how naïve she'd been putting off matters which required her attention.

She knocked on the door and entered without waiting for him to acknowledge her. "Did you forget about me?"

He glanced up from a paper he'd been reading. "Of course not. I would never do that." Without a word he was on his feet and at her side so quick it made her head spin. He grabbed her shoulders, his eyes like fire.

A long moment passed and neither of them moved. Beatrice let out a groan as he pulled her against him and kissed her in a demanding kiss, his lips moving hotly over hers, urging them to part for him.

She clung to him relishing the taste of him in her mouth, his tongue tangled with hers. He deepened the kiss so thoroughly she felt faint. His hand moved down to her breast, cupping the fullness, making the nipple harden. After working the buttons, he parted the fabric and slid his hand inside. His palm abraded her nipple.

Augustus groaned as he kissed her throat, pulling the pins out of her hair. He slid the bodice of her gown off her shoulders, baring her to the waist. She did not try and stop him when he lowered his head and took a nipple into his mouth. She trembled as his hand then moved lower, shoving her skirts up. In a matter of seconds he had stripped her bare and pulled off his clothes. He eased them both down on the sofa, his hardness pressed against her thigh.

His hands caressed her breasts, stroking them. She whimpered when he moved lower, cupping the mound of her sex, his fingers lacing through the hair at the apex of her legs.

"Augustus..." she moaned when he parted the slick damp folds at her core and slid a finger inside her.

He took her in a savage kiss and in moments she was on fire for him as he stroked her damp passage again.

"I'll try not to hurt you. I promise to make it good for you."

She nodded as he spread her legs and settling his lanky frame between her thighs, he kissed her again while his fingers stroked her, and he eased his hardness inside. He didn't stop until he reached the barrier of her innocence. He plunged deeper and she cried out, the sound muffled by his lips.

A shot of pain fled through her. As quickly as it came, it was gone. He loomed above her, resting on his elbows, holding himself immobile by sheer will. "Are you all right? I tried not to hurt you."

"Yes, the pain is gone."

Slowly he began to move, his hips rising, easing himself out, his buttocks flexed and he dropped deeply back in. Sinking in until he filled her. She could feel every hard inch of him, the heavy thrust and drag of his cock. Her body trembled as she arched upward taking him deeper. Her hands gripped his sweat slickened shoulders. The heat in her loins fanned out through her. Warmth coiled in her belly, her body burned. In and out, faster, harder, deeper until the pleasure was unbearable.

"Augustus!" she cried out as she shattered into a thousand pieces. Pleasure overtook her as she clung to him. Augustus's body tightened above her. She heard a groan rumble from his throat as she felt the last of his hard driving thrusts.

He pulled out and she felt something warm on her stomach. After a few moments, he spoke. "That was beautiful, Bea."

"Yes," she managed to say.

Not a word was said for a moment. "Come," he said. "We need to get dressed."

She looked down as she began to gather her clothes, noticing her legs speckled with her virgin's blood. He realized her dilemma and walked across the room, returning with a damp cloth and towel kept behind a screen near his desk. She accepted them as he turned and walked away, giving her some privacy.

She joined him a few minutes later, perfectly

dressed and her hair smoothed into a bun at the back of her neck. "I would love to go exploring...unless you're too exhausted."

"Never." He took her gently by the arm. "Bea, I feel I must apologize. This wasn't planned. I envisioned our first time as more romantic. Please forgive me."

"Goodness, Augustus, no need for apologies. I thought this was very romantic. I'll never forget this, and I'll cherish the memory for the rest of my life." She kissed him on the cheek. They had been through a lot together and for the better part neither had faltered. Four years apart had been what they had needed to mature and grow. Now it was time to take the next step. Their lives had been changed forever and Beatrice had no regrets. Whatever reservations she had about him had almost faded away. She knew at that moment she was going to marry this man.

12

One thing that could be said about Declan MacRae was that he was punctual. He showed up at the front door of the manor fifteen minutes early, holding a brown, leather-bound notebook in one hand. He struck Beatrice as an odd man. Very much Scottish with his carrot-red hair and the freckles he'd never outgrown. He was average height and build--nothing that set him apart from other men. That is until he opened his mouth and began answering Augustus's questions about whiskey. The man was a wealth of information from the process harvesting the grain and making it into whiskey, the history of distilling in Scotland, to who and where to sell to in Edinburgh and surrounding cities, leaving Beatrice impressed.

She hadn't intended to be here, but Augustus insisted, knowing her keen eye for business and the questions needing to be answered. A lot of business, especially in the whiskey industry was done on word of mouth and who knew who.

"What other qualifications do you bring, Mr. MacRae?"

He arched a brow and looked her up and down

carefully considering how he should answer. He certainly hadn't been expecting her to ask that question or any other. The man expected her to stand quietly by and let Augustus lead the meeting. Unbeknown to Mr. MacRae, that wasn't in her nature.

"My family lived on the west coast of Scotland. My father ran a decades old distillery. I learned from him among others."

She would make inquiries of course to make sure what the man said was true. Augustus simply would take the man at his word. Word of mouth had its drawbacks and she hoped she was wrong, but there was something about this man that didn't ring true. He was too anxious, wanting to know things she thought weren't appropriate for someone not yet employed by Augustus.

"You have no problem with seeing to the distribution of a new distillery's product over running the process?"

Again he stared at her as though she had two heads. "Yes. The fact that the first batch is so good will be an easy selling point."

She smiled graciously and turned her attention to Augustus who had been standing next to her observing them. "Why don't you take Mr. MacRae to the distillery. If he's going to be your Scottish distributor he should see where it is made." She turned her head ever so slowly back to Mr. MacRae. "Mr. MacRae. It was wonderful to meet you. I hope you and Lord Talisker can work out all the details."

Out of the corner of her eye she thought she caught Augustus desperately trying not to smile.

"I'm sure we will. It was nice to meet you, Lady Beatrice. He dismissed her just that fast and turned his attention to Augustus.

Once out of the drawing room Beatrice made her way back upstairs to her rooms as fast as she could. Mr. MacRae may not approve of women being involved in anything outside domestic duties, but he'd never met someone like her. As much as she wanted Augustus to find someone to handle his Scottish distribution. She wasn't sure he was who he said he was.

Sitting down at the small white writing desk she took a piece of paper out of drawer and began to write a letter to John Winters. He was an investigator of sorts Beatrice had used quite often. He had an uncanny ability to find out things about people they'd rather keep hidden. A very good skill to possess for someone like her. Being a woman in business she quickly learned not to take people at face value. Especially men. It was amazing to her how many of them thought women were inferior.

She didn't want Augustus to hire the man and later find out something unsavory about MacRae that could damage his fledgling reputation as a distiller. He might not be happy with her if she did find something, but in the end, she was certain she could make him understand how important it was to check a person's credentials. After all, she'd made inquiries into Augustus's business dealings before committing to him completely. Making sure he hadn't gotten himself back into debt.

Rereading what she wrote and satisfied, she readied the missive for delivery and decided to go in search of the butler herself rather than give it to her maid. Not that she didn't trust the girl. This was too important, and her maid might take her time getting it into the hands of the right person.

Sealed envelope in hand she didn't have to go far to find Augustus's butler. The man was in his office going over what appeared to be a schedule of some sort. Seeing her he immediately stood as she entered his domain.

"Lady Steele, may I help you?" he asked, not accustomed to guests coming below stairs.

She held up her letter. "I need this to go to London immediately. Do you have someone who can take care of that?"

"Of course, milady," he replied reaching for the envelope.

"Thank you." She was going to mention not saying anything to Augustus but decided against it. It would raise suspicions and if it came up, she would simply say she was checking on something. Not a total lie, just not the complete truth.

Beatrice smile and turned to leave. She decided she would take a walk in the gardens while Augustus was occupied. Walks had become even more of a way of life in London than in previous years. Beatrice found them an excellent way to think through problems, getting her out of her offices to enjoy the fresh air. The air was cool and crisp still as she made her way to the garden that ran behind the house. Acres of well-manicured bushes and beds of Rosebay Willowherb, Foxglove, daisies, and poppies along with magnificent roses stood well-tended for all to enjoy.

She could be happy here if she and Augustus married. Smiling she reminded herself she was getting ahead of herself. Up until the train robbery, the two had been vastly at odds about almost everything. But she found her feelings had changed since then as she learned the real man he was. It took turning himself around from the rakehell he once was to the man he was becoming for her to even consider a future with him.

~

AUGUSTUS FOUND himself having difficulty paying attention to the questions MacRae was asking as he showed him around the distillery. He knew he was going to hire the man, he knew whiskey and the market, especially the market here in Scotland well. His thoughts, however kept wandering back to Beatrice and how elegantly she'd responded to MacRae's obvious distaste for women in business.

On their walk to the distillery the Scotsman let it be known that a woman's place outside the home was limited and they shouldn't wander into areas of finance and contracts, let alone putting together complex business deals. Augustus listened to the man rant, saying nothing until they finally sat down in the small office he kept and poured a taste of what the man would be selling.

He swirled the amber liquid. "If we're to do business MacRae, you need to know that Lady Beatrice will be an integral part of all this. Not the day-to-day operations, but in other areas. She has quite a head for business and has never led me wrong. In other words, I trust her to a fault. So if you have a problem with that, we need to work it out now."

MacRae sipped his whiskey before uttering a word. "I have no problem with that as long as I'm reporting directly to you."

"Then we have a deal?" Augustus asked. He swallowed the contents and placed the glass on the table.

"Yes."

"Excellent." He breathed a sigh of relief. Apart from the man's viewpoint on women's place in the workforce they could get along. They shared a mutual bond for good, well-made whiskey, and that's all that mattered. Everyone was entitled to their opinion, but some needed to be kept private. Beatrice had an interest in all this and he would continue to be an open book with her. Even if other men didn't understand.

He spent the next two hours giving the man a tour and discussing a marketing plan for introducing his new brand onto the Scottish markets. If MacRae truly didn't know of his connection to the family brand he masked his recognition well and Augustus offered no explanation. Family dynamics were not an outsider's concern. Though if MacRae asked him about it he would answer with his standard reply. That he and his father had differences of opinions.

"I'm sure you're aware the market here and the one in London are vastly different," MacRae said as they were leaving the building.

Augustus thought it an odd statement. Why would the man make a statement about something like that? Was he sowing a seed that he was interested in expanding to London? Or was he simply making conversation?

"Yes, I am. That's why I plan to have a man there with extensive knowledge of it all."

"If you don't mind my saying my lord, I would be far more suited to the London market."

He shook his head. "I have someone in mind already. He's been able to get my brand into two clubs that wouldn't give me the time of day because I'm so new."

Judging from the look on MacRae's face he was having a difficult time not showing his disappointment in this news, but he pursued.

"That's where you need to let them know of your affiliation with the family brand. It can't hurt."

Trying not to look shocked by the man's boldness,

he stared down at the floor for a moment to collect his thoughts. "I want to stand on my own two feet. Show that I'm just as capable of producing the highest quality whiskey. Once they taste my brand they'll be convinced."

"Still..."

"I don't want to mix the two. If someone happens to ask, of course tell them the truth."

MacRae arched a brow. "Which is?"

"As I told you. I decided to branch off on my own," he replied. "That doesn't mean the two companies won't merge at some point in time."

"It shouldn't be too hard to explain, especially once they've had a chance to taste your fine product."

Augustus smiled and the two walked outside into the sunshine. He had promised to take Beatrice riding this afternoon, and as soon as he was rid of MacRae he would. As they walked back to the house and the man's carriage, they discussed what would happen next. Augustus wanted a contract drawn up by his solicitors in Edinburgh to make sure everything would be in order from the start. Before he went to the solicitors, he would run it by Beatrice and make sure he wasn't leaving anything out.

MacRae had come highly recommended, but Augustus couldn't ignore a gnawing feeling in his gut that warned him to beware. The man seemed too interested in whether he had representation for the whiskey in London. In fact, looking back MacRae seemed too interested in that market and not the one in Scotland.

He shook his head as he watched the carriage disappear. Maybe he was overreacting. MacRae might be able to handle both markets. There were some distilleries that used only one person as their distributor.

His father was one of those. But the brand had been around for generations and was well known and respected for producing high quality whiskey. It sold itself.

He turned and headed inside to find Beatrice. On a day as nice as this one she would be outside. In the gardens most likely. That was where she seemed to spend time when she came for her brother's wedding. He remembered it was also a way for her to find peace and quiet away from her sisters. She would lose herself in his father's gardens, taking a book or embroidery and enjoying the fleeting Scottish good weather.

She didn't make the time these days. She was too busy, but he was determined she would find the time. She wouldn't last long if she didn't find a way to empty her mind of all the daily business. He worried she was taking too much on. Before he said anything he wanted to observe her more. He hadn't been around her all the time until this trip and he could be mistaken.

He saw her on a path in the gardens behind the house bent over examining some of the many flowers. He felt his cock twitch as he took in her beauty. What was it about seeing her in unusual situations? His lust was already making him want to take her by the hand, find somewhere hidden from view and make love to her, just as he'd done in his study.

Upon hearing his footsteps on the crushed shell Beatrice turned, smiling. "Mr. MacRae gone? So soon?"

"Yes."

She straightened up and neared. "So are you going to hire him?"

He nodded. "Yes, though there were a couple of things about him that bothered me."

"What were they?"

He kissed her on the forehead, taking in the smell of oranges and vanilla. "He seemed to have a great deal of interest in being the distributor in London instead."

"Maybe you should check him out a little more thoroughly."

"I plan to do just that. I also thought you might have the perfect people to do just that."

"I already have," she said. "But otherwise you liked him?"

"Yes, his knowledge is above reproach. I have no doubt he'll do a fine job. It's just his unusual interest in London I found odd."

"I contacted someone I use to investigate MacRae. He'll check all the usual things out about the man and the parts of his life he may not want people to know. And I'm having him check what the man's connection to London is."

"Thank you."

She smiled warmly. "No need. I want to see you succeed, Augustus."

They began walking down the path in silence. As they did, Beatrice wrapped her hand around his arm.

"Would you like to take a ride this afternoon?"

"Yes, but you'll have to have patience with me."

"Why's that?" He knew she wasn't as passionate as his sister about horses but did seem to enjoy riding.

"I'm only a passable rider."

"Don't worry. I know the perfect gelding for you. He's well-mannered and gentle. You'll be fine."

"Very well then. When do you want to go?"

"After lunch. You can change and we can meet in the front hall."

"Excellent.."

"You're quite efficient you know."

"So I've been told."

They walked for a few moments in silence until she stopped and peered up at him. "I've forgotten to ask, but how's your shoulder and your wound? You never complain about it."

"It's doing much better, thank you. No need to complain, I was lucky."

"Yes, you were extremely fortunate. I hate to think what the circumstances would be if it had hit you in a different spot."

"I try not to think of that."

"I'm surprised your father or sister haven't inquired as to your well-being."

He glanced at her sheepishly. "Did you mention something to Sebastian, because I haven't told either about the incident."

"Why wouldn't you do that, Augustus? I'm sure they would want to know."

"I just didn't feel the need to recall the whole unfortunate accident."

"Accident? It was a train robbery!" she exclaimed.

"And I'm sure they've heard about it."

"Tell them, Augustus or I will. They're your family and deserve to know."

Shaking his head as they reached the terrace stairs leading to the French doors of the drawing room he stopped. "I promise I'll mention it to my father next time I write him."

"Good. As long as you do, I'll hold off making mention to either Sebastian or Cora." The edges of her mouth turned up as she began to climb the concrete steps.

"Has anyone told you you're a demanding young woman?"

"All the time, but it is needed if I'm to succeed in a man's world. Besides, you love it," she said over her shoulder as she continued.

"One of your many captivating traits."

They reached the top where they found luncheon laid out on an iron table. "I take it this was your idea?" she asked.

"Actually, no. The staff knows I prefer to take my meals here when the weather is warm. There are too many months where I must dine indoors."

"It looks lovely." She found cold roasted chicken, a variety of smoked meats, fruit, and crusty white bread. She hadn't realized until now just how hungry she was.

"Afterwards we can change and take that ride."

"Yes, and I'll write to London."

He watched as a footman helped her as she sat down before he joined her. "Would you care for a glass of wine?"

She shook her head. "Thank you, no. Lemonade is fine."

13

"Cora and Sebastian are throwing a dinner party at Brookshire and I believe Theodora and Matilda are going to be helping her," Beatrice announced the next morning, waving the invitation in her hand as she entered the breakfast room.

Augustus glanced up from his newspaper and grunted. "Your sisters will do fine. Cora will make sure they are well supervised."

"Sounds like mischief to me."

He folded the newspaper and set it to one side. "Why would you say that?"

"Think about it Augustus. I'm sure they and everyone else knows I accompanied you to Scotland. To them the real reason is not important; the fact that we traveled all this way together is."

"I see. I didn't think you cared about what others thought."

She set the invitation on the table to her left and nodded for the footman to set her breakfast in front of her. "I don't. I just know my sisters and how they like to meddle."

That much was true. She and Augustus were getting along so well and what she wanted was to allow their relationship to grow, and without outside interference.

"It's not for a week," he said. "We'll be back in London and if memory serves me right Brookshire is in Kent, is it not?"

"Yes, why?" She glared at him suspiciously.

"No reason other than we wouldn't have to stay overnight."

"Are you suggesting we arrive together?"

He grinned. "Why not? By now they know we traveled here together."

She arched a brow and picked up her fork. "I certainly didn't tell them."

"Will your brother require that I speak with him?" he asked trying to keep a straight face.

"If I can come here, alone with you, without Sebastian's permission, I sure don't need his permission for us to court."

The edges of his mouth pulled up. "Don't forget your maid. You traveled with your lady's maid."

She picked up a forkful of scrambled eggs and took a bite. They were light and fluffy, not scorched. Among the best she'd tasted. "Yes, let's not forget her."

"Sebastian's blessing would mean a lot to you, wouldn't it?"

"Of course it would. Now what's going on today?"

Changing the subject from family, which was personal, to something else made matters easier. Though she loved her family dearly, they just didn't understand her.

"I have men coming to load the barrels headed to London."

"Where they'll be stored in Edinburgh until we leave tomorrow?"

"No. They will take the wagon to the station right

before we leave here. Our train leaves in the morning and they'll be loaded onto a car first thing."

"You seem sad to leave. Did you want to spend more time here? I can always change my plans."

He shook his head. "No need. As much as I'd love to stay, I need to get this whiskey to London and on to market."

"Yes, you do. Besides, you can return again before summer ends."

"I can."

"I forgot to mention that when I wrote my contact about looking into MacRae, I told him I'd be returning to London and to send anything to my office."

She spread marmalade on top of a piece of toast and watched him. He was in good spirits but sensed a moodiness about him. She decided it was all the talk of family. Though he was doing so much better on his own, she knew he missed the closeness he and his father had once shared. Hopefully they'd make amends before too long and could heal whatever gap had come between them.

"As this is our last day, would you like to go on a picnic? I can ask Cook to put a basket together and we can take the gig. I know the perfect spot."

"Where?"

"You'll see." He grinned.

"Very well. That sounds like an enjoyable way to spend part of the afternoon."

He pushed his chair back and stood. "Excellent. I'll go speak with Cook and go to my study to finish my correspondence and go over the estate ledgers."

"While you're doing that I'm going to sit here and finish my tea before I go tell my lady's maid she'll need to pack for our departure."

The trunks she'd brought from London were eventually found at the wreckage site and sent on to her. It was more than expected given the carnage. When she'd seen the destruction when the daylight broke it was far worse than she first thought. They had all been fortunate more lives had not been lost. The robbers had not been caught, but from what Augustus had been able to find out the band of robbers were getting sloppy in their attempts. Police and other officials were combing the land looking for these men. This incident had been their most brazen and the first one where an accident occurred. The sooner the police caught them the better for everyone.

With her tea growing cold, she headed upstairs to her rooms. Her maid was humming a tune somewhere in the dressing area. She made her way in the direction of the sound, startling the girl as she entered.

"Lady Beatrice, I wasn't expecting you. Is there something I can help you with?"

"Yes. Get everything ready. We'll be heading back to London in the morning. Also, I'd like to wear the apricot muslin dress if it's ready. I'm going on a picnic with the marquess."

"Yes, milady. The dress is ready whenever you want to change."

"I'm going to finish some correspondence first. I'll find you when I'm finished."

"Yes, milady."

Turning on her heel Beatrice walked out of the dressing room, through the bedroom and across the small sitting room to the small writing desk. She sat down and reread her sister's invitation. Pulling out a sheet of paper she wrote her response, short and to the point, telling her she'd be in touch with them once she returned to London.

Her second letter was to her assistant, Mrs.

Hughes. She once again informed her of her return and to have everything in order and ready for her. She needed no extra time to rest or catch up on anything. She needed none of that. She had businesses to run and needed to bring herself up to date on what was happening with each.

If it hadn't been the matter of the train fiasco, she would have made time to visit the mill that weaved cloth. Next time she would, and there would be a next time. Until Augustus paid her back, she would be involved in his distillery. Besides it was a good diversion and way to spend time with someone whose company she enjoyed. She learned she relaxed when she was with him. A far cry from a couple of years earlier.

She smiled, recalling the time she pushed him into a certain countess's pond after overhearing him brag to a friend he was going to compromise her if he had to. He certainly hadn't expected it. That had been the last time she'd seen him. She mused they'd both grown up and changed since then. Hopefully for the better.

Beatrice had no regrets about being with him intimately. And though they hadn't had the opportunity for further dalliances, a shift in their relationship had happened. Yes, they shared kisses and intimate touches, but that was all, causing her to wonder if he was trying to save her from gossip among the staff. Because after all, staff, no matter who's they were, gossiped.

Not that she cared. She had no time for idle gossip.

14

Though she was happy to be home, Beatrice found the eerie quiet of the house unsettling. She had thrived in the tranquility of being alone for the first time in her life. Now she wished to share her life and adventures with someone, but for now her only comfort would be in sharing her life in her diary.

The trip to Scotland had been a business trip but had turned into something far more than simply moving Augustus's shipment of whiskey. For the first time in a long time she relaxed as she found herself enjoying long walks, picnics, and riding. As unexpected and unplanned as it was, she had to admit she and Augustus were forming a relationship that was more than that of simply business partners.

She shook her head and strolled to the study, asking the butler to have tea brought to her while she went through a large stack of correspondence sitting on the desk. Mrs. Hughes knew her well enough to know she wouldn't come into the office as soon as she arrived but knew she would want to go through her mail. And there was a lot of it. It would keep her busy for several hours and keep her mind off anything else.

Beatrice sat down behind the large oak desk and

picked up the correspondence. She sorted it accordingly into three stacks. One for personal, one for invitations and one another for business. The latter she would go through last. It was easier to get personal matters taken care of right now. Her mind wasn't ready.

Letters from both her sisters awaited her, each admonishing her for having not told them that she and Augustus had been on board the train that had derailed. They had heard the news from their brother, Sebastian and were both angered to have learned the news that way. It hadn't been that she didn't want to tell them, there had been other things going on and truth be known she hadn't wanted to tell them because they'd have worried and probably been on the first available train to Scotland.

She smiled as the subject of the dinner party was brought up. Each had made mention of it wanting to know what she planned to wear, how long she was staying, when she would be arriving. They were both excited to spend time with her and their letters were so similar in contents it made her wonder if perhaps they'd written them together.

A letter from her childhood friend, Eloise caught her attention. Her friend had married Viscount Travers two years ago in a lavish London wedding. The pair had departed for a long worldwide wedding trip, which included the pyramids and India. It seemed they were on their way back to England as Eloise was with child.

While she was overjoyed her friend was going to be a mother, Beatrice didn't find herself with any profound feelings one way or another. She had chosen to put off marriage and motherhood after raising her sisters. That became even more apparent once she inherited from her aunt. All her attention was required. She was daring to go into areas dominated by men; men who wanted to see her fail and she was not going to give them the satisfaction.

She had kept the news of her growing business ventures to a minimum when she wrote Eloise, knowing her friend would not understand nor would she approve.

Putting aside the pile of personal matters needing to be addressed, she quickly went through the invitations that had accumulated while she'd been away. Thankfully, Mrs. Hughes had sent regrets to those she received while out of town. She read each invitation after those and marked on the outside whether she would go or to have her regrets sent. Mrs. Hughes would do the rest. Right now she didn't want to spare time to spend an evening at a ball or theater. She first had to catch up.

A knock on the door shifted her attention as the butler and footman brought in a tray with tea. There were also several plates of sandwiches and cake. She hadn't eaten since early this morning and seeing the food made her realize how hungry she'd become.

"Cook thought you might be hungry," the older man said.

"Tell her thank you."

Once again, she was alone.

~

BEATRICE WENT DOWN the stairs wearing a deep purple silk gown with lavender piping. As she got closer to the entry hall she noticed Augustus was clad in a dark charcoal gray suit and crisp white shirt. It was nice to see something on a man other than black. She and

Augustus were going to attend the affair at Brookshire together. There was no need to take two carriages since they were going to the same place, and besides it wasn't as though they hadn't traveled alone together before. Her uptight sisters would simply have to accept it.

"Are you sure your sisters haven't invited single, eligible young men to this soiree?"

"I'm sure they have, and that's their problem. They know how I feel about the two of them trying to play matchmaker."

"You realize when they see us arrive together, they're going to draw their own conclusions."

She smiled. "Let them. It's not as though we're trying to hide whatever our relationship is."

"Something we need to discuss at some point, Bea."

"What do we need to discuss? I thought we were both comfortable with this."

"But what is this?" he asked.

"Are we courting? Are we nothing more than friends? Are we lovers? I'm afraid not even I am sure what our relationship is."

Knowing he was frustrated and not wanting to ruin the evening she reached across the carriage and took his hand. "We're all three," she said. She noted the carriage had turned down the drive leading to Brookshire. "Let's be ourselves and enjoy the evening."

"Fair enough, though I will admit it's going to be hard."

She arched her brow and smiled. "Remember we'll be leaving together. All the way back to London."

"You are a wicked, wicked woman, Beatrice Steele."

Smiling she peered out the window as the carriage

came to a stop in front of the huge, granite manor house. It stood three stories tall. Dusk was upon them, making it hard to make out the finer details of the structure as torches had been lit which cast a dim light on the manor house.

The door opened and she descended with the help of a footman. She hesitated a moment, waiting on Augustus to join her. They climbed the stairs leading to the massive black oak front door and were about to the last step when Theodora flew out of the house to greet her guests.

Her sister blinked, staring in disbelief as she realized Beatrice had not arrived alone. Beatrice on the other hand tried to keep a smile off her face knowing she'd shocked her prudish sister. She wondered where Cora and Matilda were. Surely they would be out in a moment to greet them.

"Beatrice. Augustus. I wasn't aware you would arrive together."

Beatrice handed her cape to the butler before answering. "I'm sure I told Cora. We thought it best to share a carriage since we were both coming from London."

"Of course."

Augustus greeted Theodora who took them to greet the other guests in the drawing room. She and Augustus shared a private look between them. Beatrice had accomplished exactly what she wanted. She shocked them.

"It's such a pity you couldn't spare more time. I've got so much planned," Theodora said.

"I don't have time for house parties. Perhaps another time."

Her sister gave her a disappointed glance and turned to her guests, introducing her and Augustus.

Beatrice was gracious and engaging to each person. Even though she had arrived with Augustus, Theodora went out of her way to personally introduce Beatrice by herself to men she obviously had invited in hopes of making a match for her older sister.

"Do you know how foolish you've made me look?" Theodora hissed as she took Beatrice's arm and led her away from the others.

"How have I made you look foolish? You are the unmarried young woman helping your brother's wife host a party. Augustus and I merely shared a carriage ride together."

"You knew I was inviting eligible young men in hopes you might make a match."

Beatrice shook her head of blonde curls. "I have no need in you or anyone else making me a match. I'm quite capable of doing that on my own."

"Are you telling me he's calling on you?"

"That's really none of your business, Theodora."

"You are!"

Beatrice said nothing for a moment, collecting her thoughts. Augustus had been right. They shared something together but had yet to put a name to it. "When there is something to tell, you, Matilda and Sebastian will be the first to know."

"What of Cora?"

"Her too, and her father as well. Until then, stop reading things into my sharing a carriage with the man."

"Hmph."

"He's also become a business associate, Theodora. I've been warehousing his whiskey when he ships it from Scotland."

"Yes, and Sebastian says five years is far too early for whiskey."

"That is Sebastian's opinion and he's entitled to it. I can assure you Augustus has had no complaints."

"Not yet."

As much as Beatrice wanted to continue this discussion, her brother and sister-in-law had guests and several were watching them. "We should return to the guests."

Theodora nodded. "Yes, of course."

"You're happy here?" she asked as she looked around the room. The dark green wallcovering made the room look even darker than it was. In her opinion there was nothing cheerful about it. The house was a secondary of Sebastian and Cora's, closer to the race tracks. It gave a place for the family to gather when Cora had horses racing nearby.

"Yes, of course I am. Why do you ask?"

"No reason. I just know how you love town."

Beatrice prayed the evening would go by quickly. It wasn't that she didn't love her sisters, she just disliked being the center of attention. She knew everyone, at least the women were aware the reason for the party was not just a festive evening. But then there never was just one reason when it came to society. Someone always had an alternative motive for what they were doing.

They had just settled into mindless conversation with a group of the women when the butler announced dinner. She held her breath to see if Theodora was going to have everyone go in according to rank or if she would be informal. She saw that she'd chosen who Beatrice would sit with, the seating arrangement was informal. She was placed between an older widowed viscount and a newly minted earl.

As she was seated, she gazed up and down the table before she found Augustus seated next to a young woman she remembered to be the daughter of a baron and another she didn't know. If she didn't know better, she would take the woman to be an actress, but her stiff sister would never allow such a person to attend, making her wonder what the redheaded woman's story was and more importantly who was Augustus to her.

Sebastian was at the head of the table with Cora seated to his right. Matilda was among friends at the opposite end of the table.

His eyes locked with hers and he flashed her a quick smile before being drug back into the red-head's conversation.

"I understand you run a business your aunt left you," the Earl of Canton said.

"Yes, I do." She decided not to elaborate on the number of businesses as one was enough to send most men off on a tangent about women in a man's world, and the earl was probably no different.

"I have an excellent man of business. I'm sure he could find you someone with excellent credentials to run it for you."

She arched a brow and sat back to let the footman take her soup. "And why would I want to do that?"

"Running warehouses is a man's business. Not something well-bred young ladies should be part of."

"Really? Because I happen to enjoy what I do immensely."

He sputtered for a moment having not expected her to be anything but compliant. "You might say you enjoy it but, in the end, can you keep it a success?"

"Yes, I can. I've already proven that with all the businesses my aunt left. All are running smoothly, and I've even been able to purchase a couple of new ones."

"You mean there's more than just the warehouse?"

"Yes. Warehouses, textile mills, railroad car manufacturers, and later this year a department store."

Canton sniffed. "Then you'll never find a suitable husband."

He turned his attention to whoever was seated on his other side. He ended the conversation thinking he had the upper hand. Not that she was in any way interested in the likes of him.

She noted Augustus taking it all in with a grin on his face. Goodness, he'd best hope the young lady he was conversing with thought he was paying attention to her.

"I'm sure you will hand over the reins once you've married and your husband has gotten you with child," Viscount Thigpen drawled.

"I may hire an assistant, but I can assure you my lord I'll never relinquish control."

"You don't want to marry and have children? I thought that's what all women wanted."

"I do, just not now," she said quietly. The viscount was no better than Canton.

"Some will think you on the shelf and you'll never find a husband."

"If that's what they want to believe then so be it. I'll not be dictated to and told when and who to marry regardless of what the ton says."

"You're a fascinating woman, Lady Beatrice," he said as the next course of lamb was served.

"Thank you."

"It would take a strong man to bring you in line. You have too many silly notions of women's rights I can see. I'm sure spending some time at my estate outside York I could make you see the error of your ways."

She set her knife down. Sebastian would never agree to a match with this absurd man. She was so angry at this moment she might actually stab the man with it. "Fortunately for me that will never happen as I have no intention of marrying. At least for now."

The man cut a piece of lamb and chewed thoughtfully. "Lady Beatrice. I came here looking for a wife. One that can bear children. I find you quite refreshing. It is my intention to speak with your brother, the duke and see what sort of arrangements might be made."

"Though I'm flattered, my lord. I still have no intention of marrying you." She decided to try something bold, something she probably shouldn't. If it got the viscount out of her life it would be worth it. "You do know the Marquess of Talisker and I are close friends, don't you?"

The man sputtered, but quickly pulled himself together. "Talisker? Why he's poor as a church mouse. Lost all his money gambling I heard."

"You heard wrong, my lord."

"Why would your family not mention this when I arrived?" He asked.

"Why should they? As I said we are close friends."

"Really? Why might that be?"

She was on shaky ground. "That's not important. I accompanied him to Scotland and it was quite the adventure. The train we were on wrecked because of robbers, then once we arrived in Edinburgh we went on to his estate."

"You, a single young woman traveled alone with a man?"

"Yes, why wouldn't I? Technically he's family since my brother is married to his sister."

The viscount leaned over making sure she didn't miss what he had to say. "As I said before, you need a strong husband to tame you, and it is my intention to do it."

"And you my lord are sadly mistaken if you think I'd ever marry you."

He had not been expecting her to be so forthright and was having a hard time dealing with it and did so by going back to his meal and ignoring her. She breathed a sigh of relief as she looked anywhere else. Towards the head of the table, she noted Theodora glaring at her in a most disapproving way. She smiled back before turning her attention to the lamb in front of her.

This evening was a disaster so far. Her sisters had deliberately set it up so she'd meet men in search of a wife, and she was not going to play a part in it. It was time she and Augustus decide what way they wanted to take their relationship. At least with him, he knew her, respected her and her decisions. More than the other men she'd spoken with this evening.

Her sisters might be perturbed with her, but that wouldn't last long and once they understood Augustus was who made her happy, they would accept him with open arms.

AUGUSTUS KNEW the moment in climbed into the carriage behind Beatrice he was going to have her. They had played a game of seductive cat and mouse all evening and now he was going to do everything to convince her they belonged together, and he was going to enjoy it.

He sat down next to her and as he waited for the carriage to turn onto the main road, he closed the curtains, giving them complete privacy. Turning towards her, he couldn't help but grin at the seductive smile she wore on her face. He slid closer to her.

Untying the pretty bow that tied the top of her combinations, he slid the silky, lacy fabric off her shoulders. Her breasts were firm and tight round full ones. He cupped one breast before leaning forward and licking it.

He felt her heart beating swiftly as he nuzzled her skin as her nipple came to attention. She gasped. He suckled her gently before drawing one nipple between his teeth. Her eyes half closed, she reclined on the cushioned seat, breasts bare, legs spread for him in the lamplight. Beautiful.

He kissed between her breasts before moving his way down. He enjoyed himself, tasting her skin.

She pushed open his shirt. "This is better."

His next kiss was hot, hard, and taking. He undid the buttons that held her pantalets closed and moved the cotton down her legs. He parted her legs and bowed over her. Beatrice jerked as he closed his lips and tongue over her most intimate place. Her knees bent, her legs coming up as she rested her feet on the seat. She was open all the way to him.

She furrowed his hair as he continued his strokes and pulls. She wanted him and was coming apart, but Augustus continued until she could hardly breathe. The only thing in the world was the two of them and the dark fire spreading through her body.

"Augustus..."

She wasn't sure what she begged for, only that she wanted him near. Inside her.

He pulled his trousers past his knees. His shaft long and hard. She reached up and closed her hand around him, not hiding her pleasure.

He groaned as she squeezed, his cheeks flushed,

enjoying what she did to him. A few moments later he removed her hand from him and lifted her up off the seat.

He moved between her thighs, his tip touching her opening as she ached with need. His breath came fast as he dove deeper and deeper inside her. She was so damn tight and as he kept sliding in and out of her, he realized he never wanted it to end.

She was making beautiful noises in her throat. He felt the scrape of her fingernails on his back.

"Beatrice..."

She touched his face looking straight into his eyes. Neither said a word as he felt his finish coming. Too soon, but she was squeezing him hard, sending pleasure pulses up and down his cock.

"Augustus. What is happening?" She flew apart into a million pieces as her climax took her.

He growled as he slid out of her and wrapped a handkerchief around his hardness and spilled his seed.

He sat next to her after handing her the undergarments scattered on the floor. Neither said a word as they caught their breath.

"Now what?" she finally dared ask.

"What do you mean?"

"Us," she said as she put herself back to rights.

"We've had this conversation before. After the time in my study, remember? Do you wish to court?"

She laughed, taking his hand. "I think we're past courtship, don't you think?"

"I don't understand."

"Augustus, this was fun. Wonderful even, but let's not get ahead of ourselves."

Suddenly his heart ached. "What? You wish to be my mistress?"

"No, I'll not be your mistress. I'll never be any man's mistress."

"You'd marry me?" he asked in disbelief.

"I love you, you fool. I have for years."

"I love you too, but I've misread everything. What a fool I've been."

"We'll figure it out. I'll find an assistant to help me with my work. We can work on getting your single malt established. Most importantly, we'll be together. Perhaps then we can talk marriage."

"You have this all figured out, don't you?" he said.

"Of course I do."

He laughed. "How long are you talking?"

"I don't know. I can't put a time on something like this."

"Then I don't think we should be spending as much time together as we have. People are sure to talk," he said.

"Augustus, please."

"No, you're right. I need to get the distribution set up, you've got all your endeavors. We both need to concentrate on business before we make any decisions regarding each other."

There were a few minutes of quiet, the only sound was the carriage creaking as the horses plodded along down the road. He glanced over at Beatrice to find her eyes closed. He smiled even though his emotions were going from sad to angry. She was still the center of his life. And here she was. She was sated and had given into her body's response. He found his own eyes growing heavy and minutes later joined her.

Augustus opened his eyes sometime later, being awoken by the change in pace of the carriage. Slower and on cobblestones. They had reached London. He hated having to wake her. He hated for their night to end. Turning to her he found her staring back at him.

"We're here aren't we?" she asked.

"I'm afraid so."

She sighed. "I need to be at my best. I have a meeting with the solicitors tomorrow."

"Something going on?" he asked.

"No. Just our normal quarterly meeting."

"Ahhh..." he replied. "Busy day then."

She said nothing, just gathered her things and readied herself to exit the carriage.

The carriage came to a stop. They'd reached Beatrice's home.

"I guess we're here," she finally said as the door opened, and a footman lowered the carriage steps. The young man held out his hand to assist her to the ground. She stood and waited on Augustus to join her.

"Yes." It was quite late. Dawn was not far off.

"Aren't you meeting with a potential man to sell your whiskey tomorrow?"

"Yes. Why?"

"No reason. If you're free this afternoon, why don't you stop by the office and you can accompany me to see how work is progressing on the department store."

"I would love that."

"You can tell me about your meetings."

He nodded. "It's late. I should go."

"Take my carriage."

"I can walk."

"No, not at this time of night. You'll use my carriage. My man will drop you right in front."

He hated the idea of anyone seeing where he lived. Even though there was nothing wrong his rooms, they were in a respectable part of town and the rooms were nice for a bachelor like himself.

"Very well. I know better than to argue with you," he said. He left the carriage and held out his hand to assist her down.

"You'd better," she teased.

He took both her hands. It was time for him to leave. If he didn't, neither of them would be sleeping the rest of the night. Not that they would mind, but there would be time for long nights.

"Then I guess this is good night," he said.

"Sleep well, Augustus. I know I will."

"I have no doubt I will. I'll see you soon."

He leaned over and kissed her on the lips before he turned and climbed back into the carriage after telling the coachman where he wanted to go. The door shut behind him, and Beatrice stood at the bottom of the steps watching the carriage disappear into the dark.

15

"How was your dinner party?" Harriet asked as she began to button the buttons on the back of Beatrice's dove gray colored cotton day dress.

"It was interesting."

"Are your sisters trying to find you a husband?"

"Yes, even though they promised me different."

"Was there anyone interesting?"

She told the girl briefly about the two horrid men her sister had sit with her at dinner.

"Not a good match for you. You need to find someone like Lord Augustus. You've worked through your differences and seemed to get along so well."

She nodded, looking at herself in the looking glass. "Yes, we do. I suppose we've grown up."

"Maybe he's the one."

"He might just be," she said with a smile. "Right now though I have a meeting with the solicitors to prepare for."

"You look beautiful in that color if I may say, milady."

"Thank you. If you wouldn't mind, make sure the garnet gown is pressed and ready for tonight."

"Are you going out, milady?"

"I'm not sure at the moment."

"I'll have it and the emerald green ready."

"Thank you. Now, I must be going. I don't want to be late."

Beatrice took one last look in the mirror. Satisfied with what she saw, she turned and hurried out of her rooms. She accepted her cape from the butler after slipping on her gloves. He opened the door and she headed down the stairs. The day was gray, with rain in the air. She could smell the dampness and hoped it wouldn't last.

Once at her office she was greeted by two men from her solicitor's firm. She asked them to wait while she settled in. Divesting of her cape, gloves and hat, Beatrice gathered what paperwork she knew she needed, a journal she always took meticulous notes and asked Mrs. Hughes to send the men in. She was ready, though it took all she had not to let her mind wander as the men began to go over the previous quarter's figures. But as hard as she tried her mind wandered back to the night before and Augustus.

Since she was always focused on the task at hand, she found herself miffed that her thoughts were wandering to places it shouldn't during a meeting. She'd worked too hard and there would be plenty of time for distractions. But right now she needed to focus. She also needed to find someone she could trust with the running of her empire when the time came for her and Augustus to marry and go on their wedding trip.

There was much to be done, and she would handle it all as easily as she always did. Her feelings for Augustus needed to be contained, and she wondered if they'd always interrupt her train of thought.

The meeting went on for over an hour, until Mrs. Hughes came to the door. She apologized profusely for the interruption, but Beatrice could see the woman was frantic and whatever it was was important. She excused herself, leaving the solicitors sitting in front of her desk.

"I apologize for interrupting your meeting, milady," Mrs. Hughes said.

"That's quite all right. What is it?"

"The work site. The department store. It's on fire."

Beatrice stared at her in disbelief for a moment. "Who told you this?"

"The foreman sent a boy to tell you."

"Where is the boy?"

"He said he couldn't stay. He was needed back at the site."

"I thought no one was working today. That the workmen had varnished yesterday and were letting it set."

"Yes, milady. The damp weather makes it take longer to completely dry."

"Then how did this happen?" she said to no one in particular.

Remembering her solicitors were in the next room, she urged Mrs. Hughes to send someone to the site and see whatever information they could. She'd go herself after she finished up.

There was no way she could hide this from the two gentlemen. It would simply be sooner than later. Taking a deep breath Beatrice re-entered her office.

"I'm sorry to keep you waiting. I have no details, but I just received word that the construction site for the department store is on fire."

"That is dreadful news, milady," the first man said.

"It is, but I'm hopeful it's under control," she said. "I hope you gentlemen don't mind if we postpone the remainder of our meeting?"

"Under the circumstances, not at all," his partner said. He nodded as he rose from the chair he'd been sitting in. "Let us know if we can be of assistance."

"I will."

As the men left Beatrice rushed to put on her cape. Despite Mrs. Hughes pleas that she stay, Beatrice pushed past her and out the door. She had to see this for herself. She tilted her head to tie her bonnet in place and when she did she could see a thick black plume of smoke rising just a few blocks away. Exactly where the work site was. All her fears had suddenly become reality.

She fought her way through the crowd which was gathering at the end of the block. Fire brigade had put up barriers at either end to keep the curiosity seekers out of harm's way. But she wasn't just anybody, and she needed to speak with someone in a position of authority.

Ducking under the barrier she tried to make her way to a small group of men, one barking orders in the direction of a maze of men in a futile attempt to save the building. He saw her and motioned her back. When she made no attempt to do so and continued toward him, he strode over to her in three long steps.

"You have no business here, milady. I must insist you return to the other side of the line."

She peered up at him. He wasn't a particularly tall man, but from the grip he had on her arm, Beatrice concluded he was powerfully built.

"This is my store!"

"Was your store. I'm afraid it's a total loss, milady."

"I demand to know how this happened!"

The man continued to haul her to where the crowd was. "I don't know how this happened, but I'll be looking into it as soon as the fire is out. Now go back home. This is no place for a lady, and I promise to send word once the fire is out."

He was leaving her with no options but to obey him. He was right, there was nothing she could do and standing here watching her dreams be destroyed in front of her was more than she could bear. She nodded, told him who she was and where he could find her. With that she turned and left, fighting her way through the growing crowd as hot tears streamed down her face.

The store, had been her project from its inception. Not only had she overseen every detail of the building and what materials were used, she approved every item that would grace the shelves. Now it was up in flames. Luckily inventory was being stored in one of her warehouses, so that wasn't ruined. But now she had an entire department store sitting in crates and boxes. What to do with all of that didn't matter so much right now. Finding out how this happened needed to be her priority.

She took one last look at the black smoke still billowing from the fire before entering the door to her offices. Mrs. Hughes fussed over her telling her she'd been foolish to get that close to a dangerous situation. She assured her assistant that she was unscathed and as far as she knew no one else had been injured. As she handed her cape to Mrs. Hughes, she could smell the odor of the smoke. Not only did it permeate her cape, but her dress and hair as well.

With all that was going on she wasn't about to go home to change. She kept one or two changes of clothes here in the office in case she needed to freshen up for meetings or had a luncheon engagement where she needed to be dressed a little more formally than she normally was.

"I can't tolerate the smell. I need to change," she announced.

"Very well," Mrs. Hughes said as she led the way to the small room where Beatrice kept a small bed and personal effects. The older woman began to unbutton her dress.

"It's ruined," Beatrice said as she tried desperately to keep her emotions in check. "All that hard work gone in the blink of an eye."

"I'm sure it was just a unfortunate accident."

She shook her head, the smell of the fire still permeated in her locks. "I can't think of that right now."

Mrs. Hughes being ever the peacemaker took Beatrice's shoulders from behind. "Be thankful no one was hurt. All that has been ruined was just a structure. It can be rebuilt, if you so choose."

"Thank you," Beatrice replied. She reached up and patted the older woman's hand. "Thank you for reminding me of that."

"Now let's get you changed."

Beatrice nodded and stepped out of her dress. "Yes. I need to be ready in case I have visitors."

"I'm sure you will once the fire is put out."

"The battalion chief promised he would."

Mrs. Hughes nodded and handed her fresh combinations and stockings. Once she'd put them on she stepped into a dove gray muslin day dress Mrs. Hughes had chosen for her, knowing she would want to change after visiting the fire. The woman had always known what she needed sometimes before she did.

She sat in a straight back chair and pulled on boots before looking in the mirror. She could still smell the smoke.

"Don't I have some perfume? Something to rid the burnt smell in my hair."

A FEW MINUTES later she returned to her office and strode over to the windows and peered out at the busy street when a familiar voice spoke from behind.

"I came as soon as I heard," Augustus said.

She swung around, grateful to him for coming in her time of need. She had dreaded being alone while she waited for news.

"It's awful. Completely destroyed."

He neared, putting his hand on her shoulder. "Please tell me you haven't been there?"

She nodded and peered into his eyes. "Of course I have. I went as soon as word arrived. I was dismissed and he told me someone would pay a visit as soon as the fire was out."

"It's no place for a woman, Bea. It's dangerous."

"So I've been told," she bit out. "Still it's ruined. A complete loss."

"Come, let's sit down. Surely between the two of us we can come up with an alternative plan."

He guided her to a dark blue wing-backed chair and motioned for her to sit. She lowered herself and once she was settled, he walked over to the bell pull.

Mrs. Hughes appeared, making him wonder if the woman stood outside listening. He ordered tea for them before sitting in a matching chair next to her.

"You can rebuild," he said.

"Yes, but that takes time. I have an entire warehouse filled with merchandise. By the time I rebuild, the clothing will be out of season."

"How's that?"

"Winter. I bought for winter. Now what do I do with it?"

He sat back and pondered her dilemma. "You could sell it to one of the other department stores, or even specialty shops."

"Yes, and I'll have to discount all of it. I'll lose a small fortune."

"Better that than losing it all."

"True."

He leaned forward. "Or you could give it away. I'm sure it would be appreciated among those less fortunate."

"I hadn't thought of that. I need to think it through."

"Orphanages, children's homes..."

"That would take care of children, what of the adults?"

"Same. I'm sure parishes would welcome any donations."

"Let's come back to this. I need to find out what started the fire and what it's going to take to rebuild."

"Can you think of anyone who might deliberately do something like this to try and ruin you?" he asked.

She shook her head. "No one comes to mind."

"Have you crossed anyone?"

"I image someone isn't happy with me. I'm a successful business owner who also happens to be a woman. Yes, there are quite a few men who think I should still be at home embroidering rather than making such important decisions."

"Think about it. Write their names down. Discreetly of course."

"You know it might simply be a horrid accident."

"Do you believe that? You told me your workmen were quite diligent with safety."

"They are."

"Good. Now we wait for word," he said.

Mrs. Hughes opened the door bringing with her a tray laden with sandwiches, fruit, cheese, cake and of course tea. She set it down on the oak table in front of Beatrice and Augustus, then turned and left.

Beatrice began to pour for both of them while Augustus filled a plate. She smiled wondering how long since he'd had a good meal.

"How have you been? Any luck with potential clients?"

"Yes, I'm making progress."

"Good. What about MacRae?"

"I've made a decision. The whiskey is only five years old. Barely mature enough for some establishments. So I've decided to hire someone here in London and my distillery manager and I can cover Edinburgh and rest of Scotland. At least for now. I still must find someone here in London, but MacRae isn't the man for the job."

"Wise move. I have yet to hear back about him, but there's something about him, and I can't put my finger on it."

"He's too anxious. In spite of my telling him a couple of days ago that I wished to go in a different direction he's written to me twice wanting to know my answer."

She passed him a cup and picked up the other for herself. "He is too anxious, and you need to know why. I think you're making a smart move; handling Scotland yourself with your distillery manager."

"Thank you."

Setting her cup down, she glanced at him. "I need to apologize for the way I acted before. If I hurt you, I'm sorry."

"No need. I understand. It's a lot to take in."

"It is. I was overwhelmed. So I thought perhaps we could just see how things progress and not force it."

The corners of his mouth turned upward. "I think that's an excellent idea."

She beamed, picking up a piece of marmalade cake and placing it on a plate. "Here. You must try my cook's marmalade cake. It's one of my favorites."

"I thought seed cake was your favorite."

"It's a hard choice between the two, especially after you taste the marmalade cake."

Food was always a safe topic, and right now she needed a safe place. If she didn't, she was sure she would go mad. Too much was happening. Thank goodness, Augustus had appeared when he did.

Augustus was alarmed at the sight of Beatrice when he first entered her office. Her face was racked with worry, and why shouldn't it be? She had just had news that her largest project to date had been destroyed in the blink of an eye by a fire, which was still raging from what he understood. He was not surprised to learn she herself had gone to the site, hoping to learn something, anything. Being a woman she'd been quickly dismissed.

It was the moment he laid eyes on her, standing by the windows of her office he decided he would do everything in his power to help her out. It was the least he could do. She'd been so accommodating to him in his own time of need. Now he would help her.

She knew as well as he did that the building was a complete loss. Could she rebuild once the debris was cleared away? More importantly, would she rebuild?

If someone was out to ruin her by deliberately starting the fire, they had no idea who they were dealing with. Beatrice would come out on top no matter what the result. Rebuilding would take time and a lot of what she had in one of her warehouses needed to be used quickly. Not because it would turn bad, but because it was winter clothing, and by the time she rebuilt customers would be looking for spring fashions. She also had food coming in and it would have to be distributed or sold quickly so it didn't go bad.

Maybe she could put together a proposal and sell to a competitor. She might break even with such a move. There was plenty of merchandise for doing both. Giving it away was perfectly well and good, but it would take a lot of time to put together a list of charities. He knew little about such matters. It was always something his mother, aunt, and sister tended to. Seeing that tenant's children had at least coats and shoes for the winter months.

He waited as she poured him another cup of tea. "I have a thought on the clothing," he said as he sat back with his cup.

"What?"

"If you must give it away, make sure your tenants and their families have warm clothing for the winter. Once they're seen to, give some to your parish for distribution to other families in the village."

"I'd need to speak with my brother. It's not my place since he's married, and I have no country estate yet."

"True, though I can't see Sebastian refusing such a project."

"Why couldn't we do the same thing on your estate? Or even your father's estate. Perhaps your father would let you as well. You are going to be duke one day."

"You wouldn't mind?"

She shook her head. "I'd rather do that. I'm afraid my sisters will want to be involved and the entire matter could get out of hand."

"You do have a valid point."

"Once I hear the scope of the loss, I'll pull out my books on what was ordered and how much. We can make a list of where to help, and how much each will need."

"That sounds logical," he said.

"Any extra I'll divide to charities here and in Edinburgh. Maybe even Inverness."

He nodded. "Scottish winters can be brutal. It will be most appreciated no matter where you send it."

Beatrice sighed. "You do realize once word gets around my brother is going to want to be involved."

"Why? The store is your project. Your money, your building. Why would he want to intrude?"

"Out of concern."

He'd never thought of her family like that, but he knew there was animosity between her sisters now that Beatrice had become rich in her own right.

She stood and began pacing the room. He knew her well enough to know she hated waiting. Her life was an ordered one. If it wasn't she wouldn't be as successful as she was.

"You need to sit. You aren't going to make the fire officials appear any quicker."

"I know that. I just want to know what's going on. Instead I'm sitting her like some naughty child who's being punished for something they didn't do."

"Would you like for me to go and see what I can find out?"

"No, it would do no good."

"I could see if the fire is under control or out," he replied.

"It's too dangerous."

He groaned. "It's not as though I'm going to break through the line and put myself in harm's way."

"I know you wouldn't, but still it's a dangerous place to be. When I left the police were moving the crowd even further back."

"You may be right. They may have cleared the area for blocks in case another building caught fire."

"I hope not. I couldn't bear to live with that," she said.

"Don't go there, Bea. Be thankful your workmen weren't working today."

"You're right. It was simply a skeleton crew. Varnish had to dry first."

"There you, see? Something good."

"Yes, of course. I am grateful the men weren't working."

"Would you like another piece of cake?"

"No. Thank you," he said.

A knock on the door brought Mrs. Hughes in.

"The fire chief, Mr. Thornton is here to see you, milady."

"So soon?" she said to no one in particular. "Show him in."

Moments later a man she recognized from the street in front of the fire appeared. By the look of his attire, he obviously wasn't there for a social call. He wore a filthy canvas jacket; his shirt had also become covered in black soot along with his canvas pants.

"Mr. Thornton. Thank you for coming," Beatrice said sweetly.

"Lady Beatrice. I apologize for my appearance, but

I thought you would like an update on the situation." He glanced over at Augustus.

"No need to apologize. This is my associate the Marquess of Talisker. You may feel free to speak in front of him."

He shifted his weight before speaking. Beatrice imagined he was exhausted. "I hate to be the bearer of bad news, but it's a complete loss."

She nodded. "I anticipated as much. The building was quite engulfed when I saw it."

"It was. The speed of the fire leads me to believe an accelerant, perhaps the varnish itself was used. That would explain why it burned so quickly and so hot."

Beatrice glanced at Augustus out of the corner of her eye. He was sitting back listening to everything the chief had to tell her. She sucked in a breath and formed her next question in her mind.

"Do you believe the fire was set deliberately?"

"I won't know until my men, and I can get inside and look around, but yes. I suspect arson. The fire could not have burned like that without some form of help. Someone helped get it going."

Rather than answer, she countered with her own question. "How long before my own people can go in for a look around? I know my insurance people will need access to process my claim."

"I'll let you know, but no more than a day or two."

"Thank you."

"I'll leave you now, Lady Beatrice, milord. I need to get back."

"Yes, of course."

"I'll be in touch," he said before turning and walking out of her office. The door shut behind him and she turned to Augustus.

Saying nothing she sat back down in her chair, trying to grasp what she'd just been told.

"Who would do such a horrid act?"

"As we discussed earlier, a rival, someone who has a problem with you and doesn't want you to succeed."

"I'm surprised Mr. Thornton didn't ask me if I had any ideas as to who might have done this. If indeed it was deliberately set."

"You should make a list of potential suspects. We can weigh what each one has to gain by getting your store out of the way."

She arched her brow. "I won't be deterred. I will rebuild and open as I planned. It may take longer, but it's going to happen."

Beatrice rose and walked over to her desk, sitting down with a fresh piece of paper in front of her. There was no time to wait. The quicker she had answered the faster she could get to work. No one was going to deter her.

16

Beatrice was shocked when two days later Mr. Thornton deemed the fire an unfortunate accident. No mention of arson, the fire being deliberately set, but an accident. He drew his conclusions that an open can of varnish had been knocked over near a lantern, thus causing the fire. Two days earlier he'd been certain it was arson, causing Beatrice to believe this quick turnaround meant someone had gotten to Thornton. He'd been paid off. Someone had offered him money and rather than turn it down and look the other way, he accepted a bribe.

She wasn't angry. She'd halfway expected something like this to happen. Mr. Bottoms, who owned the building next to hers had never been happy with the idea of a woman as a business owner. Businesses for women were limited to dress shops, and things more feminine in nature. But that made no sense because a week ago they'd seen each other at a luncheon and he walked up to her and told her how impressed he was, and that he shouldn't have misjudged. So if not Bottoms, who?

She had her suspicions about MacRae after her discussion with the investigator. She herself knew

MacRae wasn't happy Augustus hadn't hired him. The man wanted far too much. She had learned that MacRae's own home in Aberdeen had gone up in flames two years ago and had been a total ruin. If he did indeed set fire to his own home, he did it to avoid having to pay a debt. The bank had wanted the house and its contents are partial payment.

Though what the investigator had discovered was not enough, the man had also learned MacRae had been seen near the construction site before the fire ignited.

Or was her imagination working overtime? But it rarely did. Her intuitions were usually right.

Everything was humming along despite the news. Her insurance man had visited the site the day before, she and Mrs. Hughes were pouring over invoices and orders. Once she had that she could better decide about dispersing the clothing. Augustus had sent word to his father, telling him what had happened, and what Beatrice was leaning towards doing. She had done the same, writing Sebastian. Unfortunately, he and Cora had left for Berkshire again to ready one of their horses for an important race. Royal Ascot would be upon them, and it was Cora's dream to have a horse of hers race there. Despite the change of residence she would get word to her brother.

Clean-up of the site would begin in the next few days and she'd been told it would take several weeks to remove all the charred debris from the fire. Then and only then could they proceed with rebuilding the entire store. Last time she at least had a structure to work with. Now she had to start from the ground up.

An architect, who worked alongside the one who designed the interior of the previous site was being brought in to come up with a rendering and ideas of the new and improved department store of the future Steele Department Store.

Sitting back in her leather desk chair, Beatrice closed her eyes. Only for a moment, but it was long enough to fall asleep. An hour later she awoke abruptly, reprimanding herself. There was no time for sleep during the day when she should be working. She would just go to bed earlier or curb her evenings out for the next few nights. People depended on her, especially now. There were men who became unemployed because of the fire. These men had families to support and feed and she couldn't let any one of them down.

A noise at the doorway caused her to look up. Augustus stood there, his arms folded, watching her.

"You need to go home, Bea. You're exhausted."

"It's bad enough I fell asleep here while there's so much to do."

He strode across the room. "You can't do everything yourself. Let me help."

She shook her head. "I couldn't ask you to help. You have a distillery to run and whiskey to sell."

"That's why I have an excellent man in charge of the distillery who can handle orders up north. If someone wishes to make a purchase, they know how to reach me."

"I'm not sure what you could do."

"What about the merchandise you want to give away in Scotland? I could make inquiries with my estate manager and my father's man."

"The local parish priest?"

"Yes. Him too."

She arched a brow, sat back in her chair and considered his words. "Very well. You may use that desk," she said motioning to a small oak desk set off to one side, against a wall.

Grinning he nodded his appreciation. "I'll send word to each of the estate managers and the priest."

"Don't tell them too much. I don't want someone getting greedy."

"Good idea," he replied. "What about Sebastian's estate?"

"Let's take care of your people first. Winters are far worse in Scotland than here."

He slid into one of the chairs in front of her desk. "We can revisit after we've finished with the people in Scotland."

"That sounds more than fair."

"I'll let Mrs. Hughes know you'll be working here, helping me on a project. Give your correspondence to her and she'll see to the rest."

He nodded, his eyes danced with mirth. Beatrice chose to ignore it.

"I'll get right on it. The sooner I send it off, the quicker we can head north."

"I wasn't meaning for you to start this very moment, Augustus. Tomorrow would be fine."

"No time like the present."

"I'll get the inventory of what was purchased. Look at it and make a list of what we should take," she said, "and not just for the children. Everyone."

"That's more than generous, Bea."

"Don't be silly. The adults need coats, shoes, and other things just as badly as the children. Parents often forsake themselves for their children and end up suffering."

"You amaze me."

As he watched she rose from her chair, flustered by his compliment. "I'm doing nothing more than what any good person would do. Let me find Mrs. Hughes and have her come in. See what you need, and she'll provide it for you."

He stood and watched her walk past him and out the door. He turned and made his way to the desk she'd told him he could use. It faced the wall, but at least it was near her. She was exhausted and couldn't continue without some help. Though the fire had one good outcome, it had opened another which was not. The rebuilding of the store. Beatrice had put in endless hours overseeing this project and she'd been so close to opening. She would; just not when she wanted.

As Augustus was settling himself at his new desk, Beatrice found Mrs. Hughes and let the older woman know what she'd charged Augustus with and why. She also asked her to make sure Augustus had what he needed.

"That's an excellent idea, milady. He's right; winters are colder. Doing this will take care of everyone before the seasons change again."

"That's what we decided."

"The young man has potential. He'll make a fine duke one day and someone a wonderful husband."

She nodded. "He will, but don't let him hear you say that."

Mrs. Hughes bit out a laugh. "By someone I was meaning you, Lady Beatrice. If you don't act, someone else will realize that and snatch him up in the blink of an eye."

"We're friends, nothing more. Besides I don't have time for such nonsense as a husband."

She didn't and that was her doing. For now she was perfectly fine with how things were between her and Augustus and her life. She was in love with him, but how would that work? The last thing she needed right now but as long as they worked together... Once they distributed items bought for the store, she would distance herself. She had helped him with getting his whiskey to London and now he could manage without her. It was time.

"Tell that to someone who doesn't know you like I do. I can see you watch him when he leaves and how you pace the floors when he's due to arrive."

"Mrs. Hughes, please make sure he has whatever he needs, that's all."

The older woman rolled her eyes but nodded. "Very well."

"Thank you," she said. She turned and walked back to her office.

"Would you like me to see to lunch for the two of you or will you be going out?" she heard Mrs. Hughes call out.

"Something simple would be nice."

She continued through the door. Augustus was already hard at work, writing a letter. He'd removed his frock coat and had rolled up the sleeves of his white shirt. She caught herself staring at his forearms, something she normally wouldn't do. She remembered from the times they'd shared how strong he was. Beatrice caught herself before he turned around.

"Mrs. Hughes is going to bring us lunch."

"I had thought we might go out and get fish like we did that once."

"And if we do that, we might take longer than we should, and nothing would get done. At least this way you can write your letters and I can finish up with mine. Afterwards we'll make lists."

"You are a hard taskmaster, Bea."

"Mrs. Hughes was just telling me the same thing."

He turned back to his desk and continued with his letter, saying nothing. Probably for the best. He didn't need to read things into them being together or working together. Their indiscretions, as she liked to refer to the time they had been together, led her to believe Augustus might still hold out some hope for them. Maybe one day. Mrs. Hughes might be right. Perhaps it would be best if he found someone else. Her body told her otherwise.

What was she going to do?

AUGUSTUS STUDIED the paper before him, the words running together once again. He hadn't thought being in such close proximity to her would have such a profound effect on his ability to work, but it did.

This was a list of the inventory in one of Beatrice's warehouses. As he ran down the paper, he made a mark next to items with his pen. These were shoes, coats, all clothing he knew would be appreciated during the brutal winters of Scotland.

By the end of the week he and Beatrice would once again be on a train, bound for his estate in the north. Crates would accompany them to their destination and once there he imagined something would be organized to distribute the clothes and other items. They hadn't discussed how they would pass out the many items, but Augustus was sure Beatrice had the details already worked out in that pretty little head of hers.

Setting the pen aside, he turned to face her. She sat writing something, her head bent in concentration.

"Have you made a decision on how the clothing will be distributed?" he asked.

Her head came up, her eyes focused on him. "I have a couple, but I'll decide once we arrive. Do you have a secure place to store everything?"

"I have a place in mind at the distillery. It's not being used at the moment, but hopefully it'll be storing whiskey next year."

"So it's large enough?"

"Aye. Plenty."

"I hope you're ready to get your hands dirty, milord." She flashed him a smile and his heart melted.

"I'll be ready to do whatever it takes."

"Good because we'll need all the help we can get. We'll need strong men to move about the crates."

"No problem. I've sent a note to my estate manager."

"Then we'll be ready to leave at week's end?"

His weight shifted in his chair. "Yes."

17

The pair arrived in front of Augustus's manor house, ready to work. The weather was anything but cooperative. The rain started in the middle of the night and had been relentless, reminding him of the last time they'd visited. Fortunately, this time there had been no train robbers along the way.

Beatrice had worked out the details of what would be taken, while Augustus sent word ahead to both his estate and distillery managers outlining what he needed. Beatrice and he decided upon leaving London that they wouldn't finalize anything until they were in Scotland.

"It's still as lovely as always," she said as the carriage came to a stop and she peered out the window.

"I'm glad you approve," he quipped.

She ignored his comment as though she hadn't heard it, but Augustus was sure she had. No way she couldn't have.

"I feel quite at home here."

He jerked his head away not wanting her to see him flush. Men didn't do that, but with Beatrice anything was possible. She had his emotions all over the place, and he wasn't sure how much longer he could deal with such strong feelings.

He decided before they left London that he would take charge of whatever this was between them. By the time they returned to London either they were going to be betrothed with a wedding date decided or he would end this once and for all and sever ties with her. She kept him tied up in knots and he wondered if she had any idea of what her mere presence did to him. This couldn't continue and he was fairly sure they could never just be friends.

"Augustus?" he heard her call out.

Immediately he ignored her, pretending not to hear, and stepped down from the carriage. A footman held an umbrella, holding it over him as he offered his hand to her. She descended and stared up at him.

"What is wrong with you? You're acting strangely."

"Nothing is wrong," he replied. "Shall we get out of the weather?"

Taking the umbrella from the footman he escorted her up the steps to the front door. Handing the now wet umbrella, he removed his great coat hat, handing them to the butler and watched as she did the same. She started to say something, but he silenced her quickly.

"I have some things I need to see to. I'm sure you want to rest and change after such a long journey."

He dared not look at her and instead spun around on his heel and headed to his study. He needed solitude, somewhere away from her. Even the perfume she wore was distracting. He'd found his cock had been hard more times than not during the train ride, and it was all because of her. She had ruined him for all other women.

A fire was burning in the hearth as he entered the

study. Immediately, he strode over to the edge of his desk and poured himself a whiskey. Drinking it straight down, he poured another before finding a chair near the fire. He sat down and scrubbed his face with his free hand. Once he collected himself, he'd go through whatever correspondence sat on his desk. Anything to keep his mind off Beatrice.

After that he wasn't sure how to spend his time on such a dreary day. He could go and make sure everything was being unloaded and stored properly. Tomorrow he and Beatrice would begin to call on tenants and their families, much like his mother and grandmother had done in years past. Seeing what each family needed. If they had time they'd move on to his father's tenants, who one day would become his. Once completed Beatrice would decide the best way to distribute clothing. It was a monumental task, but together they would make it happen.

$\sim$

"I KNOW you don't care to spend long times in a saddle, so I thought the gig would be better suited," he said leading her down the front steps of his house.

"Thank you for remembering."

Before she could ask a question, Augustus handed her up. "I thought we'd start with the tenants on my estate. If we have time, we can begin visiting those on my father's land."

"Yes, why don't we concentrate on your estate first. Tomorrow we can make the rounds of the ducal estate." The two estates weren't that far from each other, perhaps a mile. Also his was a lot smaller than his father's and therefore had fewer tenants.

"Yes, it would keep things better organized," he agreed.

He climbed up beside her and picked up the reins and clucked to the dark bay.

"I brought a notebook to write everything down. Family name, how many children, age, and sex."

"You are meticulous, Bea. No wonder you've become successful in such a short amount of time."

"My organization skills are only secondary. The business was successful when I inherited."

"And so modest," he countered.

She shook her head, the dark blue bonnet hiding her face. "Is your estate manager going to meet us?"

"No, he has more important matters at hand, but he got word out to the tenants to expect us. Besides I think we can handle this ourselves."

"Yes, we can."

"What about your father's estate?"

"I've sent word to his estate manager and told him what we're doing, and that I'd be in touch when I knew when we'd be visiting the tenants."

"And the parish priest?"

"I thought I'd wait until after all our tenants are taken care of. The church can get a little greedy when it comes to donations."

"Augustus!"

"Tell me I'm wrong."

The edges of her mouth turned up as she studied him. "No, you're not. But there is plenty to go around."

"I know, but I take care of my own first."

"An honorable thing to do," she replied.

A short time later he turned off on a smaller road. A whitewashed cottage came into view and as they neared two children, a boy and a girl dropped what they were doing and rushed towards them.

They had fiery red hair and appeared to be about ten years old.

He noted Beatrice smiling at the pair as they rushed up, but it quickly disappeared when she realized he was looking at her. Rather than say something he jumped off the gig and walked around the front and helped her down.

As they did a woman appeared from inside the cottage. She smiled recognizing Augustus, wiped her hands on her dress and neared.

"Milord, this is an unexpected pleasure. Mr. Macintosh told me you'd returned."

"Mrs. Macintosh, may I present Lady Steele," he said, swinging his gaze to Bea.

"A pleasure Lady Steele."

"Mrs. Macintosh," Beatrice said extending her hand.

"What may I help you with, milady?"

"The marquess and I are collecting information from all his tenants."

"Won't you both come in for a cup of tea?"

"I'm afraid that won't be possible," Augustus said. "We plan to visit all the tenants today, so we have a full day. Perhaps another time."

Beatrice continued, briefly telling the woman what they needed and why. A hint of a smile crossed her face as Beatrice pulled out her notebook and began writing in it.

Beatrice looked up briefly and began asking the woman questions about the family's needs and explained why. It turned out Mrs. Macintosh had five children in total. The two oldest were helping in one of the fields while the youngest was a mere infant.

"Bless you, milord, milady. We worry every winter about how we can make sure the children stay warm."

"Put your mind at ease. You won't have to this winter," Beatrice said closing her book. Noting Augustus was subtly trying to end their visit, she added, "It was wonderful to meet you Mrs. Macintosh. We'll be in touch."

She climbed back into the gig with his assistance, waving to the family as they drove off. Seeing the Macintosh family only strengthened her belief that she should give the excess she had to share with those in need.

"Ready for the next?"

She nodded. "Yes."

He clucked to the bay, and they made their way back onto the main path leading to yet another cottage.

"How do you think we should distribute the items? Have you been able to give it some thought?"

"Taking everything to each family will take time. Days. I thought we have the families come to the house. That way what they need will be waiting on them. We can also send them on with some food stuffs I had ordered. There's enough cheese in one crate to give each family a wheel."

He smiled. "You amaze me."

"How?"

"You care."

"Of course I do. I remember going with my mother in the autumn to visit with the families and handing out cheese and smoked meats. They were most appreciative of any help."

"Yes, they are."

"I have the means to give back, so why not? Everything would sit in a warehouse and could possibly spoil. This way needy families will be prepared for the winter."

"Any man would be lucky to call you wife."

"Where did that come from?" She said with wide eyes.

"Just an observation."

"I have no intention of marrying any time soon as we've discussed many times."

He knew it was time to stop. Her attentions were with the families and were not receptive to anything that did not relate to them. His intentions while they were here would be to pursue her, talk with her. He wouldn't push her, and marriage would not be discussed unless she brought it up.

For now, he had to be satisfied with sitting next to her in a gig.

He observed her out of the corner of his eyes noting she'd closed her notebook and was looking off into the distance, deep in thought. What was she thinking about?

18

Exhausted from their long day, Beatrice returned to her rooms and took a long hot bath while she thought back on what they had accomplished. Tomorrow they would do it all over again. This time on the duke's estate. She knew his father wasn't in residence now and wondered if Augustus had even been in touch with the duke.

It had been a successful day, but she had second thoughts about her decision to accompany Augustus to every tenant. Some saw her presence as confirmation that she was betrothed to him. Why else would she go with him? It took Augustus explaining it was Beatrice's generosity that made it all possible.

He was handsome enough, had a heart of gold and would make someone a good husband. He had had feelings for her for years. She just wasn't sure she was ready for such a change. Marriage, motherhood? When would she have time for her own ambitions, the businesses she'd worked so hard to build?

She needed to keep her distance, but could she? For now, that was the best solution she had, but she knew he didn't make it easy to resist him and didn't want to.

She went down the stairs in search of Augustus.

To her surprise she found him in the red drawing room. The room was one of his least favorites because it was darker than other rooms, even on sunny days. She walked to the deep gold damask couch. He sat down next to her rather than one of the nearby floral print chairs. His nearness overwhelming her as she ached for him to touch her. She admonished herself for wanting such. Still she was on edge, wanting his fingertips to graze her skin. The air was thick and heavy with desire. She was doomed.

"I'm not going to bite," he said.

"I never thought you might." Truth be known she wanted to feel his teeth nipping at her flesh, his lips on hers. She wanted him desperately. She had to kiss him. She angled her body toward his and drew his mouth down to hers with both hands as she kissed him demanding more.

He wrapped his arms around her, drawing her closer. This was what she had been waiting days for. She relaxed as he drew her onto his lap, determined not to let her go.

He kissed her back and parted her lips with his as she slid her tongue into the velvety depths of his mouth. He tasted like wine and musk. She kissed him as though her life depended upon it. He had pushed up her skirts when he moved to hold her in his lap. Beneath the fabric she could feel his cock stand. He was hard and she ached for him. Longed for him to make love to her.

Breaking the kiss he feathered kisses down her throat. She could feel her pulse beating rapidly. She gasped as he opened his mouth and gently sucked the smooth and supple skin on her neck. She tipped her head back, wanting more as his fingers worked swiftly to get her out of the bodice of her dress, unlace her corset, revealing here chemise.

Suddenly she stiffened. "The servants, Augustus. This is neither the time nor the place for this."

"Bugger the servants," he growled. "They know better than to interrupt me unless it's urgent or life threatening"

"If, you're sure."

He sighed, looking up at her. "Would it put your mind at ease if I got up and locked the door?"

She shyly nodded. "Yes, please."

The door was locked within seconds and he returned to her only to find she'd pulled her chemise down. Her breasts spilled out, her pink nipples were pebbled and begging for him.

He lowered his head and took one into his mouth and began sucking. She ran her fingers through his hair pulling him closer as he drove her mad. A hand found its way under her skirts, as she parted her legs for him. He found her heat, dipping a finger over her entrance.

"You are wet for me," he whispered as she writhed in his arms. His touch brought her to the edge, but no further.

"Augustus..."

He blew on a nipple and pressed a finger inside her heat. "What do you want, my dove?"

She wanted to come. They both knew it as his fingers worked on her needy wet flesh.

"You know what I want," she said, rocking against him. "Please Augustus."

His fingers fluttered over her pulsing heat, using his thumb to stimulate her further. Then suddenly he withdrew his hand from beneath her skirts as he showed her the wetness on his fingers. "Look how much you want me," he said licking her juices from his hand.

"Stop teasing," she panted.

"I can taste how much you want me. Do you want me inside you? Do you want me to fuck you, my dove? Say it."

"I want to come. I want to feel you inside me."

He shifted her on his lap and lifted his kilt. He rarely wore trousers when in Scotland and right now was one of many reasons not to wear trousers. His cock was thick and rigid and the tip already seeping.

He helped her so she faced him with her legs spread and guided her into position. Clutching her hips he guided her down on his aching cock. They moved together as one. She rocked against him claiming her pleasure.

"Go ahead and take your pleasure."

Without hesitation Beatrice began moving harder, faster, riding him. Their bodies joined, he slid his hand between them and found her mound of nerves. It was all she needed, crying out, her hips grinding on his cock wanting more as she shuddered her release.

Restraint slipping away from him, he groaned with pleasure. "I'm going to come."

His hands on her hips he began to lift her off his cock. He didn't want to spend inside her. Not yet, not until they married. To his surprise she angled herself, so he went deeper. It caught him off guard and he spilled inside her before he could stop himself. If he could have quit. He kept thrusting and rocking her atop his cock to empty every bit of himself inside her. His release was so fierce he was left gasping for breath.

Beatrice collapsed against him. Her breathing and the pounding of her heart were as deep as his. At last she found where she belonged, and his name was Augustus Keats.

~

INHALING her scent and holding her close in his arms, he listened to her breathing as it subsided to a normal rhythm along with his. Augustus knew this was the woman he was going to spend the rest of his life with. He'd known that since the night she pushed him in the countess's koi pond. *Mine.*

They would marry. Quickly. Here in Scotland. Even now she might carry his child, possibly his heir and he was unwilling to allow that child to come into this world a bastard.

No one would think twice about their hasty decision. Both he and Beatrice were known to be headstrong, breaking all the rules of polite society. If nothing else people would wonder what took them so long.

He snorted and she raised herself off his chest to gaze into his eyes. "What is so funny?"

"Us."

"You find us and what we just shared funny?"

His hands cupped her cheeks. "No, no, you misunderstand. What we shared was the most incredible thing I've ever experienced. No, I had a thought about how unconventional we are."

"How's that?"

"You're an unmarried woman, traveling with a bachelor, staying without proper chaperone with said gentleman at his estate. We've broken every rule in polite society."

"I'm also considered old by some. On the shelf.

You know what I think about the ton and their ridiculous rules."

He bussed a kiss on her cheek. "You're anything but old, and we're perfect together."

She lifted herself off his chest and sat up. "What are you saying?"

"You know my feelings for you, Bea. I love you. I want to make you my marchioness, my future duchess."

A slight grin crossed her lips. "Are you proposing?"

"I suppose I am. Would that be so bad, being married?"

"No."

"You hesitate. What's the problem?"

"I've worked so hard to get where I am; to grow my businesses in a relatively short time. I've expanded into areas that complement each other. I'm proud of what I've accomplished. A woman marries, she belongs to her husband, and everything she owns becomes his as well. I'm not willing to give it all up. I won't give it up."

He shook his head, an errant lock of hair falling over his eye. "I wouldn't expect you to."

She wriggled her way off his lap and onto the cushion next to him. She smoothed her skirts before turning her attention back to him. "It's so easy for you to say that now."

"I'm serious, Bea. Marry me."

"Just answer me this, why? Why now?"

"I was planning on proposing while we're here. Our love making just made me realize I can't wait."

"May I at least think about it?"

He nodded slowly. What was she up to? Why the hesitation. "You may be carrying my child as we speak Bea, and if you are I will not take the chance my future heir is born a bastard because you're trying to prove something."

"I'm not trying to prove anything. I merely asked if I could think your offer over. It would be a huge change for both of us."

"Beatrice, do you have any idea of my feelings for you? You are constantly in my thoughts. Night and day. You're the object of all my desires and you are the core of my existence. I love you with all my heart," he blurted. "But yes, if you must think it over, go ahead."

"Thank you," she whispered, leaning over, and kissing him on the cheek. "I promise to have my answer soon."

Soon? Now would be the optimal time. Not tonight, not tomorrow. He'd just bared his heart and soul to this woman, and he wanted an answer before she left the room. But Beatrice in all her stubbornness was determined to have her way, have the last say in the matter. He would let her, but in the end, he hoped she would see things more clearly and would agree to become his wife.

~

"Good morning," he said. He pushed back his chair and rose from his spot at the breakfast table, greeting her with a dazzling smile.

She walked towards the sideboard filled with delectable items and made her selections. Fruit, sausages, eggs, scrambled to perfection, toast and cheese all caught her eye. "Good morning," she said feigning her attention to the food in front of her.

"Are you ready to meet my father's tenants? Our future tenants?"

She pretended not to hear the last sentence. That

would be exactly what he wanted her to do. Make a remark about it. She sat down and accepted a cup of chocolate the footman poured.

"Yes."

Her cheeks blushed recalling how she melted in his skilled hands. He was utterly beautiful in a masculine sort of way. From the angular contours of his face to those lips that begged to be kissed. And she couldn't forget his muscular arms and legs. The man was not one to sit inside like a lot of his peers. He was perfection.

"Did you sleep well?" he asked, his tone polite but teasing.

"Quite well." A lie. She'd tossed and turned alone in her bed wishing he were beside her. She picked up a piece of toast and began to spread butter on it. "And you?"

"I slept well enough, though I won't lie, I longed for you. My cock ached to be inside you."

She glanced around the room, making certain no footman lingered. Luckily, they were alone. Thank goodness.

"You're an incorrigible rake."

"Yes, and it's one of the virtues I'm most proud of."

Shaking her head, she ignored him. He was testing her, wanting a hint on what her decision was. Instead she would let him charm her with his pretty words and actions. She'd made her decision, but she was not about to give it to him so easily. No, he would have to painfully wait for her answer.

She noted no newspapers in sight. Unusual as most men spent this meal hidden behind the well ironed paper. "No newspapers?"

"I read them already. Didn't sleep as well as I normally do, remember?"

"Yes, you mentioned."

They ate in silence though Beatrice could feel his eyes on her as she finished the last of her sausage. She usually never ate much for breakfast, but quickly recalled how the fresh air made her unusually hungry.

She caught him out of the corner of her eye as he was finishing his cup of tea. He pushed away from the table and stood. "I will meet you out front at the gig as soon as you're ready."

"Very well. I need to get my notebook first."

"Whenever you're ready."

She watched as he walked outside and down the stairs to the waiting cart they would use again today. It was a comfortable way to ride. The gig kept her close to him, something she craved.

"Another productive day, wouldn't you say?" She asked. They had just finished visiting with the last family on his estate.

He nodded, his eyes never leaving the road. "Yes, very productive."

Augustus had been brooding the entire day and she knew exactly why. She had yet to give him her answer regarding love and marriage. It wasn't that she didn't want to tell him how much she loved him, she just didn't want to be expected or forced to do it before she was ready. It wasn't as easy as saying the words. There was a lot to consider, decisions to be made. She wasn't some doe-eyed debutant who agrees to the match and leaves her dowry to her father and fiancé to settle. She would be going into this marriage with more than a dowry and she and Augustus needed to sort everything out ahead of time.

"Is there somewhere special you'd like to go to enjoy that basket of food your cook sent along?"

"I suppose we could go to the orchard. It's on the way back to the house, just off this path coming up."

"That sounds wonderful."

Approaching the crossroad, Augustus turned to the left. Almost immediately, the scenery changed. Rows and rows of trees appeared. Apple trees still bearing a few apples. He steered the horse off the path towards a row of trees and stopped.

"This should suffice." He pointed to a tree. "We'll eat there. It's shaded nicely and isn't as rocky as some of the other places."

"What sort of tree is that? It looks different than the apple trees."

"Pear," he said as he hopped down.

Coming around the front of the gig, Augustus helped her down. Grabbing the basket, they walked to the tree.

"I'll leave you to get things organized while I take care of the horse."

He nodded and turned to walk back to the gig. She watched him for a few moments before turning her attention to the basket. A tartan blanket sat on top and she quickly unfurled the cloth and smoothed it.

Finding a bottle of wine, she placed it to one side of the basket and pulled out meat pasties, they were flaky just like she remembered. A wedge of cheddar cheese and fried fruit pies rounded the meal out. Simple fare, but very delicious.

As she watched Augustus approach she noted a pear in one hand. He passed it to her and sat down beside her.

"I'm hungry."

She passed him a plate. "We can't have that, can we?"

He poured her a glass of wine and handed it to her. She quickly took a healthy sip, nervous about what she wanted to accomplish today.

She waited until she offered him a fried pie. They were a favorite of his and the cook evidently knew it by the number of golden pies that sat on the plate. He immediately took two. Beatrice bit into one and returned it to her plate.

"Augustus, I know I left things in the air, and I want to address them."

He arched a brow. "Very well. Continue," he said as he finished off his first pie.

"Matters of the heart have always been difficult for me to discuss with anyone. I know in my heart of hearts my deep feelings I have for you. It's just difficult for me to say them."

He nodded. "I know."

She fidgeted with her napkin and looked him in the eye. "I do love you, Augustus, with all my heart. I think I fell in love with you that night I pushed you into the koi pond."

He grasped her hand. "I love you, Beatrice. Thank you for overcoming your fear to tell me. I will always cherish this moment."

"I'm not through, silly man."

"What do you mean? There's more?"

She nodded. "Wasn't there more than one thing I needed to think through? If there isn't then, I'm done."

Augustus arched a brow, one corner of his mouth tipping up. "Have you considered my marriage proposal?"

"I have. There is much to be considered by your

proposal." She could tell he was holding his breath waiting for her answer.

"Go on."

"All the other matters will fall into place. Marrying you is far more important than anything monetary. So yes, I will marry you."

He leaned into her and kissed her. "I love you, Bea. You've made me a very happy man."

"There is a lot to be considered. I would like to be married quickly. I see no reason to have a large wedding, I've never wanted one."

"Whatever you want. Just name it."

"Sebastian needs to be informed. I thought I could write him telling him of my love for you and my desire to marry you. You can write him and either ask him for permission or tell him we're to be married. Perhaps by the time the news reaches him we'll be married."

"Do you think he'll be amenable to that?"

She nodded and smiled. "Yes. He knows of the three of us, I am the one sister he has with whom he doesn't need to worry about."

"That is true."

"My biggest fear has been the fact that in spite of the recent marriage acts, technically everything I bring into our marriage becomes yours."

"You know you don't need to worry about it. Perhaps with Sebastian's help we can figure something out."

"That was my hesitation, but I decided my love for you is more important. I trust you and know we can come to some sort of agreement on how they're run and by whom."

"I think this calls for a toast," he said pouring them each another glass of wine.

"We better make it quick. I don't like the look of those skies." She took a sip of wine. "Does the weather always change so quickly?"

"Always," he replied. He swallowed the remainder of his wine. "Can you manage with packing this back up? I'll tend to the gig."

She bit back a smile. "Go. I am fine."

Fortunately for them, the rain held off until they arrived at the house. But as they were making their way up the front stairs, the downpour began.

~

"THESE JUST CAME FOR YOUR GRACE," his butler said placing a small silver tray on the table next to him.

Sebastian glanced at the handwriting on the top letter. He recognized that handwriting. It belonged to his sister, Beatrice. He glanced up at the older man. "Thank you. That'll be all. I will let you know if a reply is immediately required."

He finished his cup of tea and waited until the door closed. He picked one up and tore open the envelope with the opener sitting on the tray. It was from Beatrice. She told him after careful consideration she had agreed to marry Augustus.

Yes, he knew that must have been a huge decision for his sister, but common sense prevailed. She would be quite happy with Cora's brother, and he would treat her well. The idea of her marrying anyone else had never crossed his mind. He'd sent quite a few off with their tails between their legs once he figured out it was Beatrice's money they were in love with.

The second letter was from Augustus asking if he had permission to marry Beatrice. He mentioned she didn't want a large wedding and if he didn't mind, she wished to get married with just the two of them present.

That was amenable with him. He and Cora would host a ball in their honor instead. Knowing Bea, she would protest, but it wouldn't last long. He sat back in the dark blue damask chair and reread both letters. Bea was worried about her own businesses and Augustus made mention of wanting to speak with him about it. They would become her husband's but they both wanted some sort of assurance that if anything happened everything would revert to her. Quite easy if she were to become a widow. He'd have to speak with someone more knowledge in the legal aspects of such a transition.

There was time for that. Right now, he'd pour himself another cup of tea before retiring to his study to pen a letter to each of them.

He looked up as he heard the door open once again. This time it was Cora, who had obviously just come from the stables, judging by her dress. She wore britches, an oversized shirt and boots. Her hair was pulled back in a queue. She smiled in his direction. No one would ever guess she was a duchess. His duchess and one he was quite proud of.

"Who are these from?" she asked as he kissed her on the cheek. He would forever associate the scent of horses with his wife. It smelled so feminine on her.

"One's from Augustus and one's from Bea. Care to wager what they're about?" He asked with a sly grin.

"What's the wager?"

"Ah, you're interested. Good."

"You didn't answer my question."

He arched a brow. "No, I didn't because you already know the answer and wagering with you isn't a good idea. Especially if you're right."

"Very well. They wrote you to tell you they've fallen in love and wish to marry."

"How do you do that?"

She smiled seductively. "Do what?"

"Know something before I've even told you."

"Easy. Why would they both write you at the same time?" she replied, adding. "We've both known they were in love, it just took a while for them to figure it out."

He passed her the letters after she sat down in a chair adjacent his and watched as her eyes ran back and forth reading what each letter contained.

"You're going to agree, aren't you?"

He nodded, giving her a lopsided grin. "Yes. Bea has never cared that a fuss be made over her. I thought we could host a ball in their honor at some point in time."

"Don't forget our earlier wager," she said reaching forward and pouring herself a cup of tea.

"How could I forget? You were right. They fell in love."

"I'm happy for them."

"As am I. With that said I need to retire to my study to write out my replies to each of them."

He stood to his full height and picked up the two letters and walked out of the room, barely hearing what Cora was saying to him.

A week later Lady Beatrice Steele and Lord Augustus Keats stood in the drawing room of his Scottish estate and were married by special license. The only witnesses to their nuptials were his butler, housekeeper, and the vicar's wife.

It was a typical dreary, rainy Scottish day. Though Augustus wanted nothing more than to whisk his bride upstairs to his bedchamber, Beatrice had other ideas. She'd extended an invitation to the vicar and his wife to a small wedding breakfast. Her way of thanking the man in addition to the payment he gave the vicar and sharing with him her plan to donate a large amount of clothing and other items.

They had finished passing winter wear out to all the tenants of both estates. Servants from both were also included and after keeping aside a good stockpile there was enough to donate to the church.

He could be patient. This was Beatrice, the unrelenting businesswoman at work, and he would not interfere. She knew what she was doing and understood this was a way for her to make her place in the community. She was going to make an extraordinary marchioness and future duchess.

Once their guests left, he would take her by the hand and lead her to his bedchamber where they wouldn't be disturbed until morning. He set it up for a fruit, bread, along with a selection of smoked meats and cheeses to be laid out in his private sitting room. Dinner would be served later, with a simple knock at the door letting him know of its arrival.

He would show her go slow, not wanting to scare her. The last encounter had been in the heat of the moment, and he wanted to show her there was another world to the art of lovemaking, one she'd not yet been shown.

"His Grace must be very proud of you," Mrs. White, the vicar's wife said, pulling him out of his erotic thoughts about his bride.

"How's that?" Augustus blurted out.

"What you and your wife are doing for the community. Seeing everyone will be warmly clothed for the upcoming cold months."

Neither he nor Beatrice had told their families about her idea. Beatrice feared letting too many people know would be a recipe for disaster because everyone would have their opinions on how the matter should be handled. How the clothes should be distributed, who should get what. Beatrice had shown she was perfectly capable of such a task. Not that he ever harbored any doubts.

"My father wouldn't be surprised I suppose. Her Grace, my late mother, did much the same thing when she was alive," Augustus said.

"Yes, she did," Mrs. White said. "She would be very proud of the caring man you've become."

Augustus nodded. "I would like to think so. I also wish she could have been here to share our happiness."

Beatrice reached out and covered his hand with her smaller one. "I'm sure she's quite proud of you."

Once again, his bride had rescued him from an uncomfortable situation. It's not that he minded remembering his mother or even talking about her, but today things were more emotional, and he didn't deal with his emotions well. His father had done his best in helping his two children through the grief of losing their mother, but the devastation of losing the love of his life proved too much and it was left to their aunt to guide them.

The wedding breakfast soon finished. Vicar White and his wife thanked them before heading back to their house adjacent the kirk. Though the couple usually walked most everywhere they went, Augustus had seen one of his carriages readied to pick up and deliver the pair back home. It was a small gesture, but it was the least he could do for a man whose wife feared wagons, carriages and horses. He wondered briefly what might be behind it.

He stood next to Beatrice right outside the front door and watched until the carriage disappeared down the long drive and out of sight. At long last he was alone with his wife. The words sounded strange as they filled his thoughts. He led her into the entry hall, took her hand and without a word took her upstairs to his bedchamber. Knowing Beatrice as well as he did, he knew she was slightly nervous and when she was nervous, she tried to steer away from what was making her uneasy by talking or finding things to take her away from what made her that way.

Having dismissed his valet, Augustus opened the heavy oak door leading to his bedchamber. Beatrice passed him, giving him the slightest glance complete with the hint of a smile. He shut the door behind them and watched in awe as his bride looked around these new surroundings. She ran her fingers delicately across a small bronze statue of a horse his father had given him one Christmas.

The rooms were large as they should be for the master of the house. The sitting room was done in shades of blue, his favorite color. The shades were lighter and more cheerful than the foreboding dark blue silk wall coverings in the bedchamber.

"Have you never been in a man's bedchamber before?"

"Only Sebastian's and he doesn't count."

He watched her as she continued to wander the room. The weather outside was miserable, dreary, and cold, and the rain could be heard pelting against the windows. Ending up at the sideboard filled with ham, cheese, thick chunks of bread, jams, pastries, and fresh fruit she smiled in approval. "The cook thought of everything."

"As they know not to disturb us, they thought this a perfect way to see to it we were fed."

"I agree. I doubt we'll need to leave your rooms until tomorrow."

He approached her from her right, picking up a bottle of wine and poured two glasses. "I thought to save the champagne until later. Unless of course you'd like some now."

"Let's wait."

He nodded. "As you wish. Wine it is."

"Thank you." She accepted the glass, their fingers brushing. Neither wore gloves and the contact was electric.

He raised his glass to her in a toast. "To my beautiful bride," he said softly.

She raised her glass. "To us."

There was no denying there was an intimate tension between them. They had made love before, but things were different now. They were husband and wife. He yearned for her but quelled his urges feeling she needed to grow comfortable with the idea.

She turned to him, glass empty, a gentle glow settling over both. He refilled her glass.

"Why are you so nervous, my dove?" Augustus knew she really wasn't, but she tapped a finger on her glass which meant she was at least apprehensive.

"I'm not. Why would you think I am?"

"It's not uncommon for a bride to be nervous," he said.

She took a sip from her glass and smiled. "But I'm not just any bride."

Beatrice was right. She wasn't a demure bride on her wedding day. That word didn't exist in describing his bride. Still, she, like women before her knew what lie ahead. Regardless of the fact they'd made love before. This time would be different.

"No, you're not and that's what I love about you. You're unlike any woman I've met. Don't ever change."

"I have no intention of ever changing. Not for you or anyone else, so you needn't worry." She finished her wine and set the glass on a nearby table.

He was at her side in one swift motion and offered his hand. His fingers tightened on hers. "Like I said I don't want you to change. Ever."

She stared at his hand for a moment, knowing everything was about to change. He led her towards the bed which was perched on a pedestal overlooking the windows. He paused and turned facing her.

"I'm going to get you out of every piece of clothing and into bed where I'm going to make love to you, and we're not going to stop until we both fall asleep from exhaustion."

He ached for her, and he teetered on the edge of self-control. He wanted to feel the wetness between her legs, wanting to slide inside her and fill her with his cock. All he wanted to do was to be inside her and fuck her.

Their clothing strewn on the floor, they fell into bed their limbs entwined in an erotic embrace. He didn't care, she had told him she wanted him, wanted him to make love to her.

His mouth found hers and he kissed her deeply, showing her how desperately he needed her. Her tongue moved with his, decadent. He never wanted her to stop kissing him. His cock hard, he settled between her legs where he could feel her lush, wet heat. It would take only a shift of their positioning for him to slide into her wet passage.

He felt as her hips writhed against him, seeking more. The kiss grew deeper, more carnal. His lips never left hers as he palmed her breast, biting the taut nipple into a tight peak. He caressed down her tender flesh over her stomach until he reached her entrance.

He groaned as his fingers slid inside her, finding her hot, wet and ready for him. Her hips jerked as his finger swirled over her clitoris as she cried out and came apart.

This was what he'd waited for. Her body beneath him, jerking for more. This wasn't enough. He craved to taste her on his tongue. Kissing her all the way down her curvaceous body, he smoothed his palms over her soft thighs as his lips found her sweet spot.

He sucked, flicking his tongue lightly over the engorged bud.

He almost smiled, realizing she wanted more as she arched into his face. He licked her thoroughly before burying his tongue in her heat. She strained for more. He knew to take it slow. She would need to be introduced slowly to some of what he had in mind. He didn't wish to scare her off, but at the same time he wanted her to learn to enjoy.

He thrust a finger inside her, sinking to the knuckle and added a second. He watched her as she raised her hips to take him deeper. He worked her; in and out, showing her no mercy until finally she stiffened beneath him as an orgasm thundered through her.

Settling himself between her thighs he lowered his body to hers, his weight on his forearms. He feathered kissed along her cheek and taking her mouth as she moaned beneath him.

"I'm going to make love to you now," he said.

"Yes," she whispered. "I want you inside me."

He guided his cock and thrust. It felt right, her heat wrapped around him as his cock filled her. They began moving together in a perfect rhythm, which turned frantic. They lost themselves in a frantic, unending kiss. "You feel so good, my dove."

"I never imagined it could be like this," she rasped as he moved faster, harder.

He thrust faster, sliding through the slickness, coming undone. He threw back his head and cried out her name as he pushed deep into her and filled her with his seed. He continued to thrust until he'd completely emptied himself inside her. Spent and still joined, he held himself still, his heart beating wildly.

Finally, she wrapped her arms around his neck and kissed him soundly. "I love you."

The three words he could never hear enough. Not from her, his perfect wife.

20

"It is time for us to return to London. I cannot be away from my businesses any longer," she announced while they were in bed the next morning. Augustus had risen earlier, finding a tray ladened with a simple, but hearty breakfast at the door. Together they had eaten, quite naked, on the floor before the fire. Only a sheet had covered her.

"I thought we agreed not to discuss business for at least two days," he countered.

"I'm sorry, but it's hard for me not to."

"Then when we do return you shall hire someone who can take care of the simple things when you are away. We've discussed this and now is the time to act."

"Yes, and the sooner we return the quicker that can be accomplished."

He leaned over to kiss her. "Tomorrow. We'll discuss it tomorrow. Not before then. You promised me two days, and I'm holding you to it."

"You're not going to give me a choice, are you?"

He shook his head. "No. This is our time. We may not have this much time alone, without distractions for a long, long time."

She smiled coyly. "You drive a hard bargain, husband, but I'll live up to my end."

"Thank you. That's all I want. One more day alone with you."

"What do you have planned for today?"

He waggled his eyebrows. "I thought we would stay in here. I'm sure we can find something to do."

She walked over to the large windows overlooking the gardens. Rain still pelted the windows, the day dark and gloomy, but she was determined not to let another gray day ruin anything. "It doesn't look like the weather is going to cooperate anyway."

Augustus neared, the heat of his body warming her as he stood close. "I should have asked earlier, but would you like a bath?"

"That sounds heavenly."

"I thought you might like it."

She turned to him. "I noticed the tub. You've renovated?"

"Yes. I've upgraded the water closets and bathing chambers in here and the marchioness's suite."

"Do you plan to do the entire house?" She was referring to the guest room he'd put her in when they first arrived. While it had been comfortable, it was not near as lavish as his rooms.

"Yes, eventually. I had to slow down renovations a couple of years ago."

She knew what he was referring to. When his father and brother lowered his cut from the distillery significantly. "We'll see it gets restarted. We will be spending a significant amount of time here so we might as well be comfortable."

"How?"

"We're married, silly. You did inherit a dowry when

we wed. There is plenty there to do all the renovations and then some."

He nuzzled her neck and pulled her close. "I had completely forgotten you had a dowry."

"We'll have to go to London for you and Sebastian to sign the papers. While we're there I'll find an assistant."

"That's all I ask."

"I'll still be hands-on, but it'll allow us to return here for the summer."

"Have I told you how much I love you?" he whispered.

"Constantly."

"Come, while we're on the subject of renovations, allow me to show you the marchioness' suite. I took the liberty of having your things moved yesterday."

"Has it been renovated?"

"Only the bathing chambers. You are free to do whatever you like to make it your own."

"You may show me after I've bathed."

"I thought we'd bathe together," he said.

"You're too big to share a tub with."

"You haven't looked closely at mine," he smirked.

"You are aware your mind stays focused on one thing?"

"Really? What might that be?"

She playfully pushed him away. "You're incorrigible."

"I thought you liked the rakish side of me," he teased.

"Yes, but only in private."

He tried to look hurt at her words, bottom lip protruding from his handsome face. "Your wish is my command, milady. Now, come. Let me show you your new chambers and after that we'll bathe."

Taking her by the hand Augustus led her to a door to one side of his chamber and opened it. He gestured for her to walk through and followed. There was a low fire in the hearth and fresh flowers decorated tables throughout the room.

She walked about, just as she had in his chambers before turning to him. "This is very nice. I'd like to freshen it up with new wall coverings and paint..."

He cut her off. "Do whatever you wish. Whatever makes you happy."

Beatrice took his hand. "I believe you said something about a bath?"

AUGUSTUS MOVED BEHIND HER, his hand brushing hair from the nape of her neck as Beatrice laid her cheek on her knees at the first touch of the sponge as water flowed down her back. He snaked an arm around her from behind and pulled her back into his embrace. The sponge was momentarily forgotten as he slid his hands to cup her breasts. He kissed her neck as she inhaled. He pressed his fingers between her legs, and she opened at his touch.

He laughed softly. "Minx."

He cupped her, Beatrice's hips rocked as his fingers did their dance until her climax rose. He slowed his movements and laughed as she growled in frustration. When she went over the top, he held her close. He crawled out of the tub and lifted her slippery body and kissed her deeply. Her hand covered his cock which was hard, and thick.

"Augustus."

"Let me love you," he rasped.

Legs apart, he knelt in front of her. Her head went back as he pressed his mouth to her. His tongue was a hot pressure, parting her opening and delving inside her. Beatrice's fingers got lost in his hair and held on. He knew how to use his tongue and mouth. He knew how to drive her insane.

Moments later he was holding her across his thighs, his erection pressing into her bottom. He kissed her as he slowly eased her onto him, holding on to her hips as he entered her. She drew in a breath as he settled her onto his cock.

She began to rock on him. He pushed into her as she gasped with pleasure. He grasped here hips and drove into her harder. He came too soon, his body shuddered. His fingers found where they were joined, rubbing, and teasing her to climax. His touch sent her into a frenzy as she pulled him deeper into her heat.

"We're good together," Augustus said softly.

"We are, but we can't stay in this position on the floor forever."

"I don't see why not." He gathered her against him as they both caught their breath.

"Augustus."

"Yes, what is it, my dove?"

"I'm famished."

He threw his head back and roared in laughter.

21

The journey back to London started out wet and dreary in Scotland, but by the time they were in central England the sun came out from behind the clouds. Beatrice had been anxious to return as soon as possible. This had been the first time she'd been away for pleasure since inheriting her aunt's businesses. While her husband slept, she found herself making notes and lists, unable to sleep herself.

Augustus had sent word ahead to his staff to have the marquess's London home cleaned and readied for him and his bride. Bea had instructed Mrs. Hughes to see her things were moved and more staff was hired. Her husband had not lived in the home for a number of years due to financial reasons and the staff was minimal, and she knew it would take a good many more people than were on hand to clean and ready the house.

She pondered what their families would think of their marriage given the way they had wed. Not that it mattered. She'd never really wanted a lot of fuss with a lot of people present, flowers galore, social events that went along with planning a wedding. The thought made her nauseous. Between her sisters and

Cora, things would have quickly gotten out of hand. She had no regrets. None.

She and Augustus would host a dinner, inviting immediate family members as soon as they settled in. Sebastian insisted on doing something for them though, there was no telling him no. He was the great duke and everyone around him knew what he wanted was what would happen.

Regardless of who he was, she'd sent him a letter informing him of their wedding and to ready any paperwork surrounding her dowry for her and Augustus to finalize.

While she left that to them, she would go to her offices and catch up on business. Hopefully a more concrete explanation as to what had caused the fire at her unfinished department store would await her, and plans could be finalized to rebuild.

Everything had to be done in a fortnight. She promised Augustus that as he wanted to spend the fleeting summer in Scotland and not the dirty air of London. What was left undone, she would complete in the north. She needed to find office space for whomever she chose to act on her behalf when she needed. She'd never give up that control. All pertinent paperwork would go with her and whomever she chose would have to be comfortable with that.

There was so much to do in a short amount of time, but she thrived on the thrill of meeting deadlines and accomplishing things men deemed too difficult for a woman to comprehend.

Feeling someone staring at her, she looked up from her list and saw Augustus awake and watching her keenly. "I know we're headed back, but can't you just relax a few more hours?"

"I'm sorry. This is important. I've never been away from my responsibilities this long."

He shook his head. "And we agreed you would learn to delegate."

"I will. I just want to make sure everything is in order for whomever I find." Not entirely the truth, but it might put his mind at ease, and get him to stop smothering her. That would ease as they settled into their new lives. Especially once she hired a manager.

"I'll hold you to it," he said. "We've been through a lot lately. I only want what's best for you and what's best for you is that you not work yourself to the bone."

"I promise."

It would do no good to get frustrated with him. She'd made him promises in the heat of the moment during those private times at his home and intended to keep them. She just needed time to reorganize.

She put her pen down and gathered the papers, shuffling them and returning them to the case she carried. She smiled. "Better?"

"Much." He leaned over to kiss her. "Thank you."

"Mrs. Hughes was going to make sure the carriage is waiting when we arrive." Augustus had been trying to skimp and just like his London home, thought it was a frivolous expense at the time when he was trying to prove his whiskey was as good, if not better than the rest.

He had sent his majordomo on ahead, assuring him he could manage for a few days without him. His clothes and personal effects would be moved from the rooms he had rented to his home.

"I wonder how long we'll have alone before our families descend on us?" he said.

"Can we not think of that? There is so much we need to do before they invade our privacy."

"They mean well. I'm sure they're in shock at what we did." He pulled her over to the leather covered seat he sat in across from her. His arm around her, he pulled her close.

"Which is precisely one of the reasons we married in Scotland."

"Hmmm. Agreed." He spread his legs and glanced out the windows trying to gauge where they were. Damn he hated wearing the Englishman's clothing. He did so because it made him appear as civilized as one of them, which he was. Some of them still thought a Scot was as untamed as his ancestors. They were barbaric and could never fit in with modern society. They were so mistaken.

"I was surprised to see you wore trousers since you claim they're not nearly as comfortable as a kilt."

"They're not."

"Personally, I've gotten used to seeing you in a kilt."

"It's still not practical in some circumstances in London or even England in general."

She giggled into her gloved hand. "So you try and conform?"

"Aye."

"It must be very hard for you, brawny Scotsman you are."

He arched a brow, gazing down at her. "Are you mocking me, wife?"

"I would never do that."

"Good because you'd best get used to the idea your husband is still thought to be uncivilized by some. Title or no title."

"Your father is respected."

"Yes, but he's not me."

"No, he is not. No one could ever be you."

FROM THE MOMENT Beatrice stepped over the threshold of her husband's London residence, she felt at home. Renamed by Augustus, Talisker House stood out from those surrounding it.

Standing on the black and white marble floor of the grand hall in the Palladian-style house, Beatrice stared in awe at the fresco painted on the domed ceiling above. A large, polished wood table with hot-house flowers greeted them. She handed her cape and gloves off to the butler as she took everything in. Yes, she could understand why Augustus hadn't wanted to stay here on his own. The place was far too big for one person, but by the time she got through with it, the house would be a showplace fit for the Prince of Wales himself.

"You haven't said anything," Augustus said from behind her. "I take it you like what you see?"

"You never told me how magnificent the house was."

"That's because I've only spent about a week here. I closed it up and haven't been back until now."

She turned to face him. "I need to see all of it, but I think with a little work this will be a home we can be proud of."

"I leave the details to you, milady."

"As we won't be in residence long, most of the work can take place while we're gone."

"You're thinking too hard, my dove. Would you like to see your chambers?"

"Yes, but only if you show them to me," she said coyly.

"Wicked woman."

"You have no idea."

She turned to the butler and requested a light repast be sent to Augustus's rooms. However, first she wanted to bathe and change out of her navy traveling outfit.

"Come," he said taking her hand and leading her to the staircase.

~

"Your majordomo told me you were here," she said eying the dark wood paneling dotted with portraits and landscapes. This wouldn't do. Never. The room looked as though his grandfather might step out from a dark corner.

"I have a pile of correspondence needing my attention."

"Couldn't it wait until morning?"

He nodded. "Perhaps. Most of it can, but there's a letter from your brother. He wants to meet with me tomorrow."

"Really? Where?"

"At his home. Late morning."

Beatrice lowered herself into the straight-back wooden chair in front of his desk. It was uncomfortable, but that was the idea. Not to let anyone get too at ease. "I imagine he has the papers regarding my dowry."

"Yes."

The air was thick. Unusual because neither of them usually had a problem talking to the other. "Should I accompany you? I'm sure the girls will want to see me."

"You're welcome to come, but I, um, thought you'd have plenty to catch up on at your office."

"I do but considering the circumstances of our

marriage it probably would be a good idea if I accompanied you. I can send word ahead to Mrs. Hughes, informing her I'll be later than normal."

"As you wish. I'm sure your sisters and Cora will be happy to see you and are impatiently waiting to hear all the details."

He kissed her on the cheek.

22

Augustus followed his brother-in-law into the study of his London home. His desk was neater than his own. Outside of that, the room was not much different from any other peer's study. Dark and forbidding. He gestured for Augustus to take a seat on the opposite side of the old mahogany table which had two neat piles of papers at one end and another next to two empty chairs.

"I won't sit here and pretend to be shocked by the route you and my sister took. She's always done things on her own terms, and quite frankly I don't blame her."

"The idea of planning a wedding was something she had no interest in."

"I will insist, or should I say your sister insists we hold a dinner in honor of your marriage. Just family, no one else."

"I think Beatrice will be amenable to that," Augustus said drumming his fingers on the wood.

"There is one thing I think you should know before we move forward."

"What's that?"

"Our sister, Theodora seems to have developed

feelings for your friend, Sutton." Edwin Beesley, the Earl of Sutton. One of his nemeses. One who gladly took his money when he was down.

"What? No!"

"He came to me to ask permission to court her."

"And have you? Surely not."

"I have given him permission, but informed him I would be watching him closely," he said. "I can't be positive, but Cora seems to think they've been secretly meeting. This was a way to perhaps dissuade that."

"He can't be trusted. The only reason he's doing this is because it's a way to goad me."

"Perhaps. I thought together we might see what he's up to," Sebastian said. He picked up a stack of papers and lay them in front of Augustus. "If he hurts Theo, he's going to regret the day he met her. I won't have it, and I know Bea won't either."

"You forgot one thing."

The duke arched a brow. "What's that?"

"He and I have a past and if he hurts my wife's sister, I'll see him ruined." Sutton and he used to run wild in London. Endless nights of drinking far too much, gambling, and visiting brothels were among their vices. Sutton had gambled away all his cash and anything that wasn't entailed. Never had he told a soul his friend's circumstances, wanting to help him through a dark part of his life. In spite of that, Augustus knew his friend hadn't given up all his old, reckless ways. If he hurt Theo in any way, he would contact some mutual friends he knew Sutton owed money to. He would convince them to call in their loans and Sutton would find himself groveling.

"Good."

Sebastian leafed through his own papers. "This is Beatrice's dowry." He began to go over each point of the document. Her dowry was more than he imagined and with it he could accomplish a lot. The London house could be renovated, and most importantly he could pay off the remainder of the money Sebastian had used to pay off his gambling debts.

Augustus sat and carefully read each page before setting it aside. "I do have a couple of items I'd like to address while we're alone."

"What's that?"

"I wish to pay back the remainder of my debt to you."

"That's commendable. We can speak with your father about how to handle this because I know you want me out of the family business."

"Not necessarily, although bringing my father into our discussion is wise."

"I'm listening."

"I would like for you to remain as an advisor. I have my own distillery now which takes a lot of work at the moment. That said, I would like to propose merging mine into the family business at some point in time. As another brand. Separate but under one roof. I think we could all profit from this. It would strengthen both enterprises." While he wanted to create something on his own, there were other ways it could be done. The family distillery had been around for generations. He was starting out and clients knew that. Merging the two made sense. It would give his brand the respect it deserved.

"I like the idea, and I think your father will also. What does Beatrice say?"

"I haven't told her."

Sebastian grinned knowingly. "Does she intimidate you?"

"Sometimes. This however is something I need to

do on my own. It'll allow me to focus my time elsewhere."

"Yes, there is a vast distribution system set up," he said. "On the other hand, you've worked hard for this. I hate to see you throw it all away."

Augustus shook his head. "I won't be. I would like to be as involved as I was before."

"It's going to be hard with Beatrice's businesses being here."

"We've discussed this in great length. She is going to find someone to do the day-to-day operations. She knows I'll be needed in Scotland. This way will allow her to still run her empire, but without some of the headache."

"You'll be able to work on both distilleries."

"Yes. I think it's the perfect solution. So does, Bea."

"I'm glad she's in agreement."

Sebastian rose from his chair after both he and Augustus signed the dowry paperwork. He poured two glasses of whiskey and handed Augustus a glass. "I think a celebration is in order."

Augustus accepted the crystal glass. This was overdue. Sometimes though you had to go through bad things before you could see the light and the good. "I'll drink to that."

They toasted their wives, the whiskey's future, and anything else they could think of. Augustus was glad there were no hard feelings for his brother-in-law the duke. He was a good, fair man, and would not stand by and watch anyone do harm to his family.

The only person he needed to make amends to was his father. That would not be easy for either of them, but maybe between Sebastian, Cora, and Beatrice they might help make things go smoother. He and his father had not been particularly close, but maybe now with him and Beatrice living close by they might begin to get to know each other once again. He needed to take an interest in things that mattered to his father. The older man loved hunting and fishing, and he needed to make an attempt to learn from his father.

"We were all impressed with what Beatrice did after the fire. How she's donated all those clothes to less fortunate families."

"Everyone on my estate and my father's benefitted first. The remainder of what was shipped to Scotland was donated to the village parish."

"She will make you an excellent marchioness, and a duchess when the time arrives."

He nodded. He was extremely proud of his bride. She was unselfish and would give her last piece of bread to someone more in need. Sebastian was right, she was the best thing about his life.

"I suppose we should join the ladies," Augustus said.

"Yes, though I wouldn't be surprised if Cora hasn't had someone keeping a close eye on the door." He chuckled at the thought. "I'll have my solicitors send anything else to you before you leave for Scotland."

Augustus grunted and tapped his fingers on the papers. "This is most generous, Sebastian."

"My father put it together. I just added to it because I was able. When you have three sisters to marry off, dowries can be important."

"One down and two to go, and I sincerely hope Theodora finds Sutton unacceptable for a husband. I would hate to have to see his ugly face at family gatherings. Thinks too much of himself, that one."

"Which was why Theo was attracted to him. That

and I believe she's trying to get a rise out of anyone who might disagree with her choice."

"It's not going to happen with me. I could have a word with Sutton, but it would only get back to her, and our lives would be made miserable."

"Yes, best to keep a close watch and let things happen as I believe they will."

Sebastian finished his whiskey, and put the papers on his desk, with Augustus's copy going into a leather pouch. He placed it in front of Augustus without a word.

"Please let me know what is still owed to you from my mistakes and I'll see you get the money."

"I will. Then we can sit down and make plans."

Both men headed toward the door. Augustus breathing a sigh of relief as Sebastian followed behind him. He sincerely hoped his father would be proud of how he'd turned his life around and by what he accomplished.

As Beatrice entered the salon of her brother's London home, her sister Matilda rushed to her side. Her younger sister had certainly blossomed since the last time she saw her. She was turning into a beautiful young woman. Gone were the gangly limbs and awkwardness. It hadn't been that long since she'd seen her sisters, but had she really paid attention to them or simply dismissed them because she was too busy with her business empire?

After they held onto each other in a long embrace, Matilda backed away smiling and began to pour tea from the service Cora had ordered. Her sister-in-law sat to one side, observing the interaction between the two sisters. Beatrice had never gotten the impression that Cora was jealous of the relationship she had with Theodora and Matilda. Cora had no sisters and had never voiced a longing wishing she had one. She was far more interested in her horses.

"You must tell us about all your adventures," Matilda said, handing a cup to Beatrice.

"Perhaps another time," she replied as she accepted the cup. "It would take up too much time, and there's so much to catch up on. I want to know what you and Theo have been up to."

"Are you and Augustus going to reside here in London?" Cora asked suddenly.

She regarded her sister-in-law with keen interest. "As soon as I find someone to assist me with my businesses, we plan on returning to Scotland. At least for the summer."

"Yes, summer is best spent in the country," Cora said.

"I was surprised to find you and Sebastian here. I know how busy you are."

"We returned when he got word you and Augustus were returning."

She nodded and took a polite sip as she looked about the room. It suddenly dawned on her. "Where's Theo?"

"She went shopping," Matilda offered.

"Alone?"

"I believe she was meeting her friend, Lady Flora Tatum at the milliner's shop," Matilda replied, but not before Beatrice caught her sister cutting her eyes to Cora, as though looking for help.

"I would have thought she would be here to welcome me back."

"She and Lady Flora have had this planned. Theo

has been invited by Lady Flora's mother to join them for a fortnight in Brighton Beach," Matilda said.

"Sebastian and I want to have a dinner for you and Augustus. Just family."

What that had to do with Theodora was unclear. Something was not as it should be. Sending her sister on holiday even with friends was a quandary. Sutton would follow and the two would secretly meet. Theo loved to disobey the rules.

Why was this conversation seemingly forced? The three of them had always had a good time when together, though both she and Cora had outside interests which most women didn't have, and they both tried their best to guide the two younger young women into fine, upstanding adults.

"I look forward to it. I know Augustus will as well," she said. "Has Theo caught the eye of any young men while I've been away?"

"The Earl of Sutton has been calling on her," Matilda blurted out.

"Really?" Beatrice asked. This would not be welcome news to her husband. Sutton had been one of the small group who encouraged Augustus to gamble with them. He would not be happy to hear his one-time friend was courting her sister.

"Sebastian is allowing this?"

"He's keeping a close eye on them," Cora said. She put her cup on a nearby table and rearranged her skirts.

"He'd better be. I'm surprised he's going along with this."

"Theo would just sneak off with him. You know how stubborn she is," Matilda said. "She had you as a role model. Going off to Scotland alone with a man..."

"That was different, and you know it. I'm older and I own businesses."

"Whatever you say," Matilda sniffed.

Wanting to distance herself from further confrontation with her sister, Beatrice decided the best way out was to change the subject. A lot of the time, Matilda was ignored or kept out of conversations because of her young age.

"And you? Is there a young man out there you fancy?"

"No."

"I find that hard to believe."

"I think it's because Sebastian intimidates them."

Beatrice smiled. Matilda was certainly astute and a good judge of character. Sebastian could be most intimidating. He was a duke after all.

"Well, we can't allow him to do that, can we?"

"No, but now you're married."

"That changes nothing."

"But you'll be going back to Scotland, and I'll go with Cora and Sebastian to their country estate."

"We'll arrange for you and Theo to come stay with us. I'm sure Cora and Sebastian would enjoy some time alone."

"I would like that, and I'm sure Theo will as well."

Theo would do whatever she was told. She might think she could win their brother over with her smiles and agreeable manner, but Beatrice knew her far better. Theo had always been the one who seemed to relish breaking all society's rules and shocking her peers. This wasn't going to be an easy feat. Theo was a young woman and a headstrong one at that.

The door swung open and in walked Sebastian and Augustus. Beatrice breathed a sigh of relief at the sight of the two men smiling and in seemingly good spirits. Sebastian must have been agreeable to her husband's suggestion the two distilleries merge at some time in the future. He'd mentioned his idea one evening, and she agreed it was worth mentioning to her brother. Of course it required his father's approval, but she'd assured Augustus his father would be most agreeable to have his only son back in the fold. Having Sebastian's backing would make things easier.

"Would you gentlemen like tea?" Cora asked.

"Thank you, no sister. I'm afraid my wife and I need to go as she's anxious to return to her offices."

"Yes, I'm sure she is."

"I told Augustus of the dinner you've planned? for them," Sebastian said.

"Yes, tomorrow evening."

Beatrice rose from her chair. "Tell Theo I'll expect to see her then."

"Sebastian assures me she will be there. Alone."

That certainly was good news. She had no desire to have to deal with a scoundrel like Sutton at a private family affair. She wanted to see Theo for the first time since her marriage to Augustus and for it to be a festive one where they could catch up. She knew she'd have to be discreet because Matilda was sure to tell Theo their sister wasn't happy.

"Good."

"And my father will be here as well," Augustus said with a grin.

"That's wonderful." She turned to Cora. "Forgive us, but we must rush. Please send me all the details."

"I will," Cora replied.

She and Augustus walked out into the daylight and climbed into their waiting carriage. Things had gone well. Better than either of them imagined.

23

Mrs. Hughes greeted them like a long-lost aunt might. The older woman talked non-stop, ecstatic over their recent nuptials, claiming she'd known this would be the ultimate ending to a fairy tale romance. She and Augustus exchanged knowing looks and accepted Mrs. Hughes good wishes.

Beatrice sat down at her desk, asking Mrs. Hughes for a light lunch, knowing Augustus was forever hungry. She had learned the man had an insatiable appetite and his needs went beyond the dining room.

Augustus sat in a nearby chair. "Tell me again who you have in mind to manage your businesses?"

"Mr. Henley from my solicitor's office. He keeps a keen ear on the pulse of the city. His advice has always been spot on."

"You don't think the firm might take issue with that? Would he be willing to leave? Leaving the firm is quite different from having your company as his only client."

"We discussed it a couple of times with both him and his boss, Mr. Whitefish. He was amenable to Mr. Henley taking me on as his only client, and we agreed on a monetary amount. Fair enough that Mr. Henley would have a substantial increase in his wages."

"You still didn't answer my question, Bea. Would he be willing to leave the firm?"

"Why do you ask?"

"If he left it might cause a conflict of interest. Perhaps not today, but down the road I can see where it would."

She nodded thoughtfully. "You may be right. I will speak with Mr. Whitefish before I make a final decision."

"Who else?"

"There's a Mr. Cunningham. He doesn't have much experience. He graduated Oxford two years ago I believe. I've heard nothing but good things about his abilities."

"Hmmm. Who else?"

"You don't approve?"

"I know nothing about the man."

"What about the gentleman who stopped by that one afternoon? The one who's just starting his own firm?"

"Mr. Lyons? I'm not sure. They would all be worth meeting with once again."

She'd already decided this would be the best course of action. Augustus would be present because regardless of her success, there were some men who still looked at women in a different light. She was fortunate that Augustus viewed her as an equal. He never tried to force his ideas on her. If he had one, it was always presented as a mere suggestion.

"Let me look at my schedule and I'll write each of them," she said.

"That will give you time to write out a list of things you wish to discuss with them."

She smiled and reached across her desk for the leather book where she kept her schedule. "Yes, it will."

Opening the book she ran her finger down a page while Augustus rose and began pacing the room. "May I say something that is not related to your search?"

"Of course."

"I don't like Sutton courting your sister."

"I don't think any of us do. Right now the best course of action is to speak with Theo on the matter."

"Of course. I just had to let you know."

She graced him with a smile. "Thank you."

He gestured toward the leather book. "Are your days full?"

"No, I believe I can meet with them over the next two days and decide. Whoever is not eliminated I shall meet with a second time. I want to make sure I've chosen the right man for the job and that I won't regret my decision down the road."

"When will you be ready to return to Scotland?"

"A fortnight at the latest, if I'm successful in finding a manager," she said. "Do you need to return sooner?"

"No. It'll give me time to go over my ideas for merging the two distilleries. Hopefully my father will be receptive."

"Don't borrow trouble. We've been over this. Your father is going to be proud of you, and with you repaying my brother, he'll see you've matured and learned from your mistakes."

"I apologize. I don't mean to be repetitive, this is a huge undertaking for all of us."

"You'll do splendidly. I have the utmost faith in you."

She turned her attention to a sheet of blank paper and began writing on it; afterwards adding her chosen day and time in her diary. While she was tending to that, Augustus pulled out his own small leather notebook that he kept in his coat and began making notes.. He needed to have everything ready for when he met with his father and Sebastian. His brother-in-law agreed with the idea, and he knew his father would look toward Sebastian for the final approval. His hated that his relationship with his father had become strained because of his foolishness and was determined to take this opportunity to repair whatever damage he may have caused.

His greatest regret was that his aunt wasn't here to see the changes he'd made in his life. She would especially be proud of his choice for a bride. Never one to push women on him, knowing he had to make his own decisions, she had on more than one occasion let him know how much she liked Beatrice, and what a fine duchess she would someday make.

24

Beatrice sat with Cora on a couch covered in a rich gold chenille fabric. They were engaged in a lively conversation with Matilda and Theodora about a house party one of Sebastian's neighbors was hosting at their country estate. The earl's estate backed up to Sebastian's and everyone was abuzz about this year's party as the countess always had a specific theme weaved into her affairs. This year it was sprites and fairies, and the girls were all amused at the thought of how the men would participate.

She was pleased at how much her sisters had matured. They weren't the giggly girls they once were and were on the cusp of becoming beautiful young ladies.

The drawing room door opened, and the butler announced a guest. Sutton. Beatrice quickly glanced at Theo who sat there with an adoring smile on her face. What was the scoundrel doing here when this was supposed to be a family affair?

"What is he doing here?" she hissed. "I thought this evening was for family only."

"It is, and I can assure you I didn't invite him," Cora said. Both women turned their heads in Theo's direction, but she was too distracted by the man to pay them any attention.

"Theo, would you care to explain yourself?"

"I don't see what all the fuss is about."

"The fuss is you invited him without Cora's knowledge, and you know how everyone feels about the cad."

"You've really become such a bore, Bea," her sister said as she watched Sutton cross the room to greet them.

Theodora extended her hand as Sutton greeted her followed by her sister. He saved Cora and Bea for last as he knew he'd pushed his luck. But the man was smart enough to know as long as he behaved himself, he would not be asked to leave. Theo knew this and was having a good time gloating about it.

He neared Bea and kissed the back of her gloved hand. "Lady Talisker."

Beatrice caught a glimpse of Augustus out of the corner of her eye, who was standing with his father and Sebastian watching events unfold. She focused her attention back on the interloper. "I don't like you Sutton, and if you hurt my sister in any way, I will hunt you down and castrate you for the animal you are. You can bet on it."

Theo gasped in horror while Matilda and Cora both hid their faces with either their fans or by turning their head to avoid chancing they would be caught practically laughing.

"Bea. You apologize this instant. That was rude and uncalled for," Theodora said.

"No, I won't. This was to be a family affair and you chose to ignore our wishes. I'm only saying what everyone else is thinking."

She waited for her sister to continue. Instead she

stood and linked her hand in Sutton's arm. "Come, milord. Let me show you the gallery. I think you'll find this one quite unusual as people aren't the only portraits displayed."

Sutton nodded. "I would love to."

He shot Bea an arrogant look as he led her sister toward the door. No one else said a thing which made Beatrice furious. Why was no one backing her up?

As soon as the couple was out of earshot she stood, shaking her head. "Am I the only one who thinks this inappropriate?"

Augustus sighed. Sutton, he knew was playing a dangerous game. "I'm afraid I'm to blame. You know the history between Sutton and me. The man's a scoundrel and will stop at nothing to embarrass me."

"Beatrice, you know Theo. If we force the issue, she'll keep seeing him out of spite. For now it's best to sit back and let things unravel." Sebastian said.

"And what if they don't? You know how stubborn and spiteful Theo can be."

"Cora and I will keep an eye on them," he replied.

"Perhaps Theo and Matilda could join us in Scotland for a time," Augustus suggested.

"No, that won't work. She'll see right through what you are all trying to do," Matilda said.

"She's got a point," Sebastian said.

"I think Matilda is right," Augustus's father said. He'd been standing silently watching everything unfold. "We should get through this evening without further incident. Speak with her tomorrow and let her know again how you all feel. But be gentle."

"Papa's right. The more we show our disapproval, the more determined Theo will be to further this relationship," Cora said.

"You're right, of course," Beatrice said. She looked

away from everyone and into the fire. She felt as though she was losing control, and the thought of that scared her.

Out of the corner of her eye she could see Augustus studying her, watching her every move. He'd come to know her far better than anyone else, even Sebastian no longer knew her in the way he once did. Augustus was waiting for her to disagree with his sister. Only she wouldn't. The old Beatrice, the one before her inheritance and before her marriage to Augustus might have, but she was determined to keep her thoughts to herself.

All she heard was the drone of others talking around her as she came to terms with how she must behave. Luckily the conversation had turned away from her sister and her uninvited guest.

"Bea," she heard Augustus whisper. She shifted her eyes to him as he stood in front of her, offering her his hand. "Time for dinner."

She nodded and put her gloved hand in his and rose to her feet. She smiled at her husband as she accompanied him to the dining room with the others.

As the footman pushed her chair closer to the table, she noticed that Theodora and the scoundrel were seated together. She knew her sister-in-law was rather informal with seating arrangements when it came to family dinners, but seeing the two of them together, Theo acting smugly like she'd won a battle was almost more than she could bear. Instead she chose to ignore her sister and direct her attentions to her father-in-law who sat to the left of her. She hadn't had much time to speak with him, this dinner being the first time since she and Augustus had married. She was determined to not only show the older gentleman how much she loved his son, but how much his heir had matured since their last encounter.

"You and my son have been through quite a lot," the duke said. His hair was silvered along the sides, giving him a distinguished look.

"We have," she said. The soup in front of her was a light asparagus soup which she remembered was one of the older man's favorites.

Why was the duke making her so nervous? No one ever did, but around him she could understand how Augustus and his father had had such a strained relationship.

She put her spoon down for a moment. "I'm sure you're aware I own several businesses which I inherited. As soon as I find the appropriate person to assist me with their management, Augustus and I will be leaving for Scotland."

"Do you have anyone in mind?"

"Yes, there are a couple I plan to interview. It shouldn't take long."

"Excellent," he said. "I must say my son seems to be thriving since he's met you. You gave him a chance when no one else was willing to."

Not sure what he meant, whether the duke was speaking of his son's personal life, or if he'd gotten word of the transaction that had initially brought them together. She decided staying neutral was her best course. As she was aware, many men weren't comfortable with women in a man's world of business. Her father-in-law could be one of those men. Though he'd backed Cora's horse training, the older gentleman may have other views on the matter. Cora was his daughter after all and from what she knew, he doted on her.

"We all have times in our lives we'd like to forget, Your Grace. Your son has an excellent head for business. I can personally attest to that and to the fact he's a most kind and generous man."

The duke nodded to let the footman know he was finished. "Spoken like a woman in love."

"Yes, I do love your son. Very much, but I also learned a long time ago that one must separate work from one's personal life. Especially in the case of a man and a woman."

Beatrice was not sure how to react to her larger-than-life father and redirected him into another subject. The duke was intimidating, but what duke wasn't, and Beatrice was determined to win her father-in-law over. With minimal convincing she hoped he would come to see his son had abandoned his foolish ways and was indeed serious about his own distillery. By the time she was finished they wouldn't be estranged any longer.

For the moment however, both men circled each other like two wary bulls. Only to her credit neither of them had charged the other.

HE'D KNOWN this evening would be a challenge. He knew his father would not be easily won over. Augustus had disappointed his father too many times in the past and didn't blame him. Perhaps now between Sebastian's help and his marriage to Beatrice his father would warm. His biggest objective to overcome was the urge to pummel Sutton. He was unsure what sort of game the man was playing, but he would be damned if he'd use one of his sisters-in-law in a game of revenge.

Beatrice was keeping an eye on the pair as well, as she was talking with his father. He needed to speak to his wife privately about his history with Sutton because what little he'd already told her was only the icing on the cake. She needed to know in case Sutton threw something out. He was cruel that way and had been the one who was reluctant to accept his money to repay his debts. Sutton was one of those who loved having something hanging between friends. Something he could use against them when it suited him. Toying with people was almost like a favorite pastime with him, and if he found out Sutton was playing with Theodora, Sutton would live to regret it.

Dinner was finished without further incident. The ladies retired to the drawing room for tea while the men remained in the dining room for brandy and cigars. Beatrice graced him with an amused smile as she followed Cora out of the room, Theodora and Matilda following.

"Is Beatrice ready for the move to Scotland?" Sebastian asked, pouring out four snifters of fine French brandy.

"As soon as she has hired someone to do the day-to-day running of her businesses we'll be on our way."

Sutton leaned back in his chair. "You need to nip that in the bud. You'd be doing her a favor before she bankrupts them all. Women have no place in running complex businesses."

Augustus arched a brow. "I must disagree with you, Sutton. My wife is far more capable in running a successful enterprise than most men."

"She has a gift few women have," his father said. "You ought not dismiss her so quickly."

"Yes, yes. Theo said her sister was ruthless. Bought

both she and Lady Matilda out for a pittance of what their portions were worth."

"Theo's always had a flair for the dramatic. In another life she would have made a fine actress," Sebastian said, trying to dismiss Sutton.

"Since we're discussing attributes or lack of them, exactly what is it you hope to gain by showing interest in my sister-in-law?" Augustus asked. He swirled the amber liquid in his glass as he awaited his answer.

"I intend to marry Theodora," Sutton declared with a smug look on his face.

Sebastian, always well-mannered and adept at showing little to no emotion was unprepared for Sutton's declaration. The sip of brandy he'd just taken, spewed across the room. "Does my sister know your intentions?"

"Of course she does."

"You do know you'll have to have her brother's blessing?" Augustus asked, referring to his brother-in-law. Sutton needed to be reminded his rank in all of this.

"And I intend to get the duke's permission to marry his sister. We wish to marry sooner rather than later," Sutton said smugly.

"You're awfully sure I'm going to give my blessing."

Sutton gazed at Sebastian with the same smug look he'd kept most of the evening. "While we would like your blessing, it is not necessary. Lady Theodora is of age and does not require it."

"The hell she doesn't," Sebastian roared. He slammed his glass down on the table. "It is time for you to leave Sutton. Come back when you decide to seek me out for permission to court my sister. Until then, you will have no further contact with Lady Theodora. Do I make myself clear?"

"Perfectly," Sutton replied. He finished his brandy, snuffed out his cigar and stood. "Gentlemen."

With that he turned and walked out of the room without another word, though Augustus couldn't help but notice the man was smiling. A smile he'd like to knock off his former friend's face but couldn't.

What was he up to? Augustus was certain Theo was just a pawn in some elaborate scheme Sutton was playing, and he intended to find out what. If unsuccessful, he would have to do it from Scotland, or better yet, speak with Sebastian about his fears. After this incident he had the feeling his brother-in-law would be doing his own investigation.

"Gentlemen, I apologize for my outburst."

"No need," both he and his father replied.

"If it weren't for the fact that Cora wouldn't allow the evening to be ruined by his unexpected presence, I would have asked him to leave before dinner."

The incident hung over the room as Augustus and his father tried to lead Sebastian onto other topics. Politics and hunting, but the duke's mind was somewhere else. Finally, Augustus suggested they rejoin the ladies.

Beatrice looked up from her place on a gold damask chair to observe him. He shook his head, noting Theo was looking for Sutton. When he didn't appear with the rest of the gentlemen, she began to storm out of the room. Sebastian took her by the arm and led her out.

"Did Sutton leave without saying goodbye?" Cora mused.

By now Theo could be heard as she loudly protested whatever it was her brother was telling her.

"Yes, I'm afraid he made a misstep and Sebastian asked him to leave," Augustus said.

"I'm afraid as soon as Sebastian returns, we must go as well. I have two appointments in the morning. With any luck one of the candidates will meet my needs and I can make a decision within the next day or two."

Augustus could feel her warmth as she stood next to him, having left her chair. She had a calming effect on him.. Perhaps once they returned to Scotland and all this was behind them, they could spend time exploring his estate and the land nearby.

"Are you all right?" she whispered.

"Yes."

Sebastian reappeared and made his apologies for leaving his guests. With that Augustus and Beatrice made bid everyone a goodnight and climbed into their waiting carriage.

Augustus joined her on the leather seat and took her hand. "I'd say with the exception of the disruption your sister and Sutton tried to cause, the evening was most delightful."

She squeezed his hand. "Yes, it was. Your father seems to be coming around. That pleases me as I'm sure it does you."

"It does, though these things take time. I'm sure it'll all work out."

"I only wish I knew what was going on with Theo. Her behavior was so unlike her. She knows better than to sneak off with that scoundrel. She was raised better."

This time he pressed a kiss against her palm. "Don't worry. All will work out. Sebastian and I will get to the bottom of this, my dove."

"I know you will. I only worry she'll do something foolish, and I pray she hasn't already."

"If anyone can bring her back around it's your brother."

She sighed. "True. I don't doubt my brother's abilities. He did an amazing job with us. I only worry there's something else going on and only Theo and Sutton know about it."

"Your brother, my father, and I also feel there's something we're not being told."

"Short of locking her in her rooms and making sure she's accompanied by her maid or someone else of Sebastian's choosing when she goes out, I'm afraid there's little more to be done. Except to trust her to make the right decision, but I'm not ready to do that. Not after tonight's affair."

"I have to agree, there is little more anyone can do."

He squeezed her hand. "Did I mention Sebastian gave me the name of a man you might want to consider speaking to about managing the businesses from here in London?"

"No. Why didn't he come to me?"

"I'm sure he would have. Anyway, the man's name is Timothy Collins. From what your brother mentioned, he sounds like he'd be a good match."

"Collins, Collins...I've heard his name before, I'm sure. Nevertheless, I'll see if he might be interested in at least coming to talk to me."

They rode in silence for a few minutes, the only sound was the hooves of the horses hitting the cobblestones. London was busy this time of night. People coming and going to balls, soirees, the theater. Soon the carriage slowed to a stop.

"No more talk of business?" he said.

"What did you have in mind, milord?"

The carriage door opened, and Augustus jumped down first and extended his hand to his wife "I have no words. I must show you."

She smiled, put her hand in his and descended the carriage. Placing her hand on his arm, he led her up the steps and into their home.

25

Standing in the privacy of their bedchamber, strong hands slid down her body, moving her closer, ever so close. "Augustus," she whispered, silently begging him to continue as each piece of her clothing fell to the floor.

"Have I told you how beautiful you are?" He asked as he scooped her up in his arms and carried her to the bed. With one hand on his chest she pushed him back, causing him to land flat on the mattress. He stared up at her with burning eyes, his lips parted with desire.

She straddled him, moving her hands to her belly and then far enough to cover her mound and touch herself. She brought one hand to her breast, pushing it up. "Is this what you want?"

"You know what I want," he growled.

Raising herself on all fours, she let her breasts sway just out of his reach. She lowered herself closer as his hands began kneading and caressing. He raised his head and took her in his mouth, his tongue flicked over the hardened nipple. He bit down, then suckled her, whipping her into a frenzy.

One of his hands left her hips, and gently pulled

her down until they were mere inches apart. Staring at each other. "Are you ready for me?" he growled.

She nodded.

"Let's find out if you are." His hand lowered, tracing down to her center. He moved slowly and deliberately, teasing her unmercifully. He touched her, swirling one finger against her soft flesh. Just that fast he slipped one finger into her passage.

"Augustus!"

He inserted another finger as she arched her back wanting more. "Yes, you're wet and ready for me, my dove."

His fingers slid out and his hands found her hips once again. He guided her down until his tip rested at her opening. His hands gently pulled her hips down on him, stretching her open to him. His hips arched as he pushed her down until she was fully seated on to him. Skin to skin. This was as close to being one a man and woman could be. His body began to writhe under hers as he fought for control as she began to move up and down.

"Augustus! Please..."

He grunted, his body bucked under hers. He could no longer control himself. It was too soon. They moved together until he heard a scream come from her as she fell apart.

Beneath her he exploded as he emptied himself into her and he called out for her. He gathered his arms around her and pulled her closer. They said nothing...just her lying atop him, still connected to him. Soon both breathed more normally, though Augustus refused to let her leave. Instead he rolled her underneath him and staring down at her he began to make love to her one more time. This time he was in control.

"Do you like this?" he growled sitting atop her, pumping into her wetness.

"Deeper, more," she panted.

He knew what she wanted, and he quickly withdrew, flipping her onto her stomach. He reached for two pillows and placed them beneath her. Then he reseated himself to the hilt without another word. He began to thrust into her as she spread her arms over her head and pushed back. His hands gripped her hips as he grew closer and closer to his release. He moved one hand around her front until he found her quivering bundle of nerves. He rubbed with his thumb, then pinched her. That was all she needed. She bucked against him as he released his seed deep inside her. He pulled back and thrust into her once again, still not finished. When he was quite sure he had no more to give, he lowered himself on her, his cock still inside her. His body began to relax. He could feel her breathing began to subside as did his. He never wanted this night to end. She was his life, his very reason for existing. No one else had touched him the way she had. He would do anything for her; never had he loved another like he loved Beatrice. They shared a oneness he'd never felt before.

~

BEATRICE WOKE up to the sound of her husband lightly snoring, his arm flung around her as he lay on his belly. The fire in the grate was long gone and she snuggled next to him for warmth before sitting up and pulling covers up over them both. He never moved.

It was dawn. She could see the faint light, not that from the streetlights, but from the sky peeping through the edges of the heavy drapes. The household should be stirring. Fires were relit for the day, though never in their bedchamber. It was one of her rules when she and Augustus first married. No servants were permitted to light fires or pull open draperies until they went downstairs for breakfast. She wasn't about to be in the middle of relations with her husband and have a maid enter to relight the fire, no matter how quiet she might try to be.

Her eyes grew heavy once again from having been kept awake most of the night. There was much to do today. She had meetings to try and find a suitable individual to see to her businesses from here in London. She needed to rise and bathe, but first she just wanted to enjoy the afterglow from their night of passion. It was the one time when the two of them weren't interrupted by the world outside, where they could be themselves. Never had she imagined some of the things possible Augustus continued to show her. She never thought lovemaking could make her feel so complete and so alive as a woman. She had never allowed herself to think about such things before. Her sisters had been her priority and she'd fully expected to become a spinster, especially after she and her sisters inherited their aunt's businesses and again when she bought them out and began to run everything thing herself. Now she found her mind wandering during the day to more naughty things her husband showed her. How he pleasured her and showed her how to pleasure not only him, but herself as well.

Finally, she sat up and swung her legs over the side of the massive walnut bed. Enough was enough. If she didn't rise now, her day would start late...no thanks to her very persuasive husband.

"Where are you going?" he muttered sleepily. He reached for her.

"To bathe and ready myself. Go back to sleep." She pulled her wrapper around her nakedness.

"It's too early. Come back to bed," he insisted.

She leaned over and kissed the back of his hand. "No, because if I do, you'll make me late for sure."

"Has anyone told you you're no fun?"

"Yes, you, every time you don't get your way. Go back to sleep. There's no reason for you not to sleep a while longer."

"Can't sleep without you," he said.

"Try."

"Mmmm."

Convinced he had drifted back to sleep she turned and made her way into the bathing chamber. She cracked open the taps and waited for the hot water before adding some of her favorite scents to the water. Vanilla and orange. She loved the scent because it was neither too floral nor too spicy. Nor did she wish a heavy, unpleasing fragrance.

As the water filled the tub, she found everything she needed. Towels, soap, a sponge. Laying it out on a table next to the bath, she pinned her hair up off her shoulders before stepping in. She lay back for a moment to enjoy the fragrant warm water. Baths like this were another of her favorite things in the world. When she'd been raising her sisters, a bath was the one place she could go to escape their chatter. Now she loved to sing or hum as she washed herself.

She had just wrapped a fresh towel around her when her maid appeared. "I'm finished. I'd like to wear the cotton periwinkle day dress today."

"Yes, milady."

"And I'll take breakfast in the small dining room. The marquess may be a while before he awakes."

The maid bobbed, turned and walked out of the

room. She would have everything laid out in the dressing room as usual. All Beatrice would have to do was step into the undergarments and dress. It was orderly and she didn't have to leave the privacy of these rooms. Beatrice liked some order to her life, though Augustus sometimes upended things.

Finally, everything in place she nodded to her maid and walked out of the room back into the bed chamber, only to find Augustus was not in bed. Cad, he was probably himself bathing or dressing. The man never knew how to relax for very long. Neither of them did.

She entered the dining room and found him seated at the table, a huge plate full of coddled eggs, sausages, ham, and bacon. To the side he had a plate of toast buttered with jam on one piece. He was reading a newspaper and didn't put it down, pretending she hadn't entered the room.

"Good morning. How did you..."

"What? Get ready so quickly?" He smirked wickedly. "While you were in the bath splashing around, I was in and out of a bath and dressed before you even thought of finishing."

She ignored him. "What have you planned for this morning? Correspondence to catch up on?"

"Nothing that can't await my attention. No, I thought I would come along with you."

"But I have appointments," she sputtered as a footman placed a plate in front of her.

"Quite so and I intend to be there." He raised his hand to keep her from protesting too loudly. "I promise I'll remain at my desk while you're in your meetings."

"But why? I really don't think I need your help."

"It'll allow me to listen and judge each man myself. Also, if I'm there they may be more truthful."

She sighed. "I suppose you're right."

"I'm glad we agree on the matter," he said, setting his paper aside and picking up his fork. He speared a piece of ham.

"You may stay, but only if you promise not to interfere."

"I promise," came his reply. He took his free hand and reached across the table and took her hand. "Last night was incredible."

"Aren't they all?" she replied coyly.

"That they are."

She eyed him warily. Augustus would have to show great restraint. His desk was in her office. Her idea or rather their mutual idea. He had to let her do this on her own, but he wasn't going to leave her to be talked down to by a couple of men who thought they were better qualified.

26

By lunch, Beatrice had already interviewed three possible candidates. While none of them held her interest, she was put out with how they spoke down to her. Her husband had for the most part pretended to be absorbed in his own paperwork while all along listening to his wife's meeting. If he liked or disliked a candidate, or didn't like the way they viewed the way his wife ran her business interests, he would subtly shake his head.

She cast a glance at Augustus after the last of the three left the room. "This is harder than I imagined. Did you hear how they talked to me?"

"Aye. You have time, why don't we have lunch before your meeting with Mr. Collins?"

"It's started to rain, and I don't feel up to going out in it."

"You don't have to. I took the liberty to arrange it with Mrs. Hughes," he said. "Besides it'll give us an opportunity to discuss each candidate."

She nodded as Mrs. Hughes walked into the office behind her was a footman bearing a large tray of food.

"Not much to talk about. I wouldn't let them run my stables let alone my businesses."

Augustus bit back a laugh as he joined his wife at a small table. That was Bea, always blunt and to the point. "You're being rather harsh, don't you think?"

"Not in the least," she said stabbing an innocent piece of chicken. She put it on her plate before looking across the table. "Did you hear what two of them said about my department store? That I should accept my losses and move on? That I can't compete with the others?"

"Yes, I heard."

She tore apart a piece of bread, not realizing the force she was using. "None of them will do. If they can't look past the fact that they'd be working for a woman who's more forward thinking than others, then I don't need them."

"You're unique, Bea. And yes, they probably thought you'd be a business owner who was silent, and not involved."

"This is just so exhausting."

"What is?"

"Everything. Trying to hire someone fit to do the job. Someone who must see that I'm fit to make diffi-cult decisions. And don't get me started on my sister."

He picked up a slice of apple and bit into it. "I thought we agreed. Let Sebastian take care of Theo. And as far as finding someone, how about you meet with this fellow your brother recommends, then sit back and re-evaluate all of them."

"You are right, of course."

"Of course I am." The corners of his mouth edged upward in a smile.

She reached across the table and lay her hand over his. "Thank you. I don't know what I'd do without you."

"Always glad to help my beautiful bride."

She arched a brow. "Flattery will get you everywhere, milord, but I must prepare myself for the final interview. After that I'd like to walk over and see how things are progressing on the store. That is if it stops raining."

"Of course, though I wouldn't count on the rain letting up any time soon. I think it's set in for the day."

"Then we don't have to walk. We'll take the carriage."

He popped the rest of the apple slice in his mouth as he observed her. She had picked at her food, barely eating a thing. A habit he noticed she had whenever she had matters on her mind or was worried about something. He'd be glad when this was behind them and could leave for Scotland to truly begin their life together. There were too many distractions in London.

Rising from his chair he walked around and helped her. The delicate scent she wore caught him off guard, wanting her. The need to be close like they had the night before filled his thoughts.

She walked around her office before settling in the chair behind the desk. Fingers drumming the thick oak top, she sat reading a paper. He recognized it immediately as a list of questions she'd written up. On a separate paper she had scribbled what he imagined were her thoughts on each man she'd interviewed.

"We'll go over each man's answers after I speak with Mr. Collins," she said, her eyes never leaving the paper she was reading.

"Of course."

"I value your input, Augustus. You are the only one who understands what a painfully hard decision this is for me to relinquish some control."

"And you're doing it with grace and dignity."

Her eyes shifted to a clock she kept on the edge of

her desk. "Mr. Collins is due shortly. I shall go refresh myself before he arrives."

He nodded. "Good idea."

She turned at the door to her private room. "Thank you for listening."

"No need to thank me. That's what I'm here for, my dove."

Mr. Timothy Collins arrived ten minutes ahead of his appointment with Beatrice. A tall man with broad shoulders, piercing gray eyes and ginger hair which had been shorn in the shorter style men seemed to favor these days. He was exactly as Sebastian described him. The third son of a successful importer, Collins was Oxford educated, well-traveled and had a keen sense of what the business climate was on any given day. His previous employment had been with Sebastian's solicitor. He'd left, deciding it was time he branch out on his own.

He entered the room without airs and firmly shook both Augustus's and Beatrice's hands before settling into the leather chair Bea pointed him to.

"Mr. Collins, thank you for coming on such short notice," Beatrice said, starting the interview.

"My pleasure. Your brother wrote me and said you were hoping to find someone before leaving for Scotland. Am I correct?"

"Yes, my husband and I intend to reside there for the summer."

"How can I help you?" he asked. His voice deeper than most gentlemen she'd met. A deep, rich baritone distinct from any other man.

She went into depth about the nature of her businesses, what she was looking for and what she expected from the chosen candidate. Collins sat, listening attentively and not interrupting her as the previous men had done. Not once did he dismiss her or speak down to her, rather he praised her on her knowledge of her own companies.

"The biggest project is the department store," Beatrice said.

"I can only imagine. What are your plans for rebuilding?"

"We won't be able to open this autumn like I'd hoped. Clean-up is still ongoing, but once that's completed, we'll be able to restart construction."

He nodded. "Had you begun ordering merchandise?"

"Yes, and a great deal is housed in one of my warehouses. What's on order has been halted for the time being." She told him what had been done with the clothing, which seemed to leave a good impression on him.

"What of your weaving mill in Scotland?"

"No changes have been made as I've only recently purchased it. Since we're going to Scotland, I thought my husband and I might visit for ourselves before making any decisions."

"The mill is well established, I understand."

Beatrice nodded, smiling. "I must say I'm quite impressed with how much effort you've put into learning about my holdings. To answer your question, yes, it is a well-established mill. They manufacture some of the finest tweeds."

"I believe in doing my research."

At the end of the hour, Beatrice rose from her chair. She'd given him more of her time that anyone else. Not one to make a hasty decision she thanked him for his time, telling him she would be in touch in the next few days.

She stood at the window and watched as he climbed into a carriage. The rain she noted had given way to breaks in the clouds. "I like him," she said, turning back to face her husband. "I assume you're in agreement?"

"Yes, and from what I understand his previous employer wishes they had been able to convince him to stay."

"None of the others were anywhere near as knowledgeable. He seems to be very detail oriented and has a keen sense of figures along with transportation and warehousing. Plus, he did his research into my companies before arriving."

"He did. I thought it quite impressive myself. So, what are you going to do?"

"I'm going to invite him back to negotiate salary before someone else grabs him up." She plopped down in a large chair near the fire grate and sighed. "That is over and I'm exhausted."

"Why not take the afternoon off? You haven't ever done that for yourself."

"Much as I would love to, I need to stay here. Everything must be in order before I turn over the day-to-day operations to another."

He crossed his arms and arched a brow. "I know you. Everything is in perfect order."

She flashed him a smile. "Yes, it is. I promise I won't be long."

"Then I'll leave you. I have some things to do before we leave for Scotland."

"Very well. I'll hurry. I promise I'll finish in two hours."

"We know what that means," he chuckled. "I'll leave the carriage for you."

They both knew she would forget all concept of time until Mrs. Hughes reminded her how late it was getting and that it wasn't safe for a woman to stay so late after dark.

BEATRICE STOOD at a table she used for projects. Renderings and blueprints of the department store lay spread out before her. She was determined to see it built and opened. This time, because of the fire the construction would take longer and would be more involved. The building had to be completely torn down, an unexpected expense, but the heat of the fire made any remaining outside walls unsound. The last of the rubble was being removed, and when finished, construction would begin.

Mrs. Hughes voice made her turn and look away as she watched Theodora determinedly march through the door to her office, ignoring the older woman completely.

"It's all right, Mrs. Hughes." Turning, she faced her sister. She was angry, very angry, and Beatrice knew at that moment the reason her sister's visit.

"How could you!" Theo said. Her voice was trembling, and Beatrice could tell her sister was trying to keep her temper under control.

"How could I what? What are you talking about?"

"You know exactly why I'm here."

Beatrice sighed. "If I did, would I be asking?"

"Sebastian – he has forbidden me from seeing Sutton. He has no right to tell me who I can or cannot see."

"Come, sit down," she said. Taking her sister's arm she led her to a dark gold brocade chair. "I'm sure he had good reason."

"He has no right. I'm of age." Theo smoothed her lilac-colored cotton dress with her hands.

"I'm sure it's for the best. It is rumored Sutton is searching for a lady with a large dowry." Beatrice didn't want to tell her sister they suspected the other reason Sutton had chosen her was to get back at Augustus. Marriage into his wife's family would certainly do it.

"That is a lie. Sutton has no need of money. He's quite rich, you know."

"All men want money, Theo. It's in their nature."

Theo shook her head vehemently. "You're just jealous."

Beatrice sighed. Nothing she said would change Theo's mind. "Why would I be jealous? Augustus and I are happily married."

"Who had little money when you married, which was why he married you. But you were too blind to see that," she spat.

"I will not sit here and argue with you, Theo. Our brother has made his decision and you must live with that."

"I won't. I refuse to."

"I don't see how since we both know Sebastian is not one to easily change his mind once he's made his decision."

Theo arched a brow and sat ramrod straight. "He's going to regret ever making such a decision."

"Theo...don't do anything you'll regret."

"Our brother may be a duke, and think he's above everyone else, but he's not and I intend to show him that he's not master of my life."

She watched as Theo rose from her chair. If she had come to her for sisterly advice and sympathy, she hadn't gotten it. Not the way Theo would want it, and it was apparent, she was not going to sit and listen to Beatrice.

"Won't you stay for tea?" she asked.

"Thank you, no. I don't need to keep you from your work. I have a fitting with the modiste anyway."

"Very well. Is your maid accompanying you?"

Theo arched a brow as though she'd been asked the silliest question in the world. "Of course she is. She awaits downstairs."

"You walked?"

"I certainly wasn't about to ask Sebastian for use of a carriage. Besides it's not a far walk."

"You're more than welcome to use my carriage. I'm going to be here a while."

She walked with her sister to the door. "I appreciate the offer, but I'd rather walk."

"Very well."

"Are you and Augustus attending Lady Primdale's soiree this evening?"

She shook her head. "No, I'm afraid we made plans before we received her invitation."

"Well, I must go. Much to do before I prepare for this evening's affair."

"Don't do anything stupid, Theo."

"Really, Beatrice. You need to lighten up. You sound worse than some of the harpies."

"I only want what's best for you."

Theo made a dramatic gesture with her hands and started down the stairs. She watched her sister disappear out the door. As soon as Theo was out of sight, Beatrice found her way to her desk and sat down. She must let Sebastian know of Theo's visit. Their sister was headstrong and she knew Theo would need constant supervision.

She penned a note, and reread it before slipping it into an envelope. Ringing for Mrs. Hughes she waited little time before the woman appeared. Beatrice handed her the envelope. "This needs to be delivered to my brother immediately. It's imperative he get this."

"Yes, milady. I'll see to it right now. Is there anything else?"

Beatrice sighed and shook her head. "No. I believe I've done all I can for today, and my sister's visit has made me lose sight of my own work."

"You mustn't let her upset you."

"I am only afraid she's going to do something she'll regret for the rest of her life."

Mrs. Hughes lifted the letter. "I'll see this gets to His Grace immediately."

"Thank you, Mrs. Hughes."

"Might I say something..." the older woman said.

"But of course, Mrs. Hughes. You know I value your opinions."

"I know you love your sister very much and want only the best for her, but let your brother deal with Lady Theodora. You're newly married. Go to Scotland with your husband and begin your new life. Your sister will be fine."

Beatrice nodded. "I don't know what I'd do without you, Mrs. Hughes. You're right of course. Thank you for reminding me, and don't worry about your position. I may hire a man to run the business from here, but you're an integral part of this company."

"Thank you, milady."

"Besides, I will need eyes and ears here, just in case."

"You can depend on me. Now I'll leave you to your work."

She turned her attention back to the plans laid out on the table, but after a few minutes realized her heart wasn't in it. Her mind kept floating back to Theo. She knew her sister better than most since Sebastian had charged her to help him with Theo and Matilda. Theo had always been quiet, but she was determined. When she wanted something, she went after it and got it, regardless of the consequences. And that scared the hell out of her. She would speak with her brother before she left for Scotland. Once she left Theodora would be left for Sebastian and Cora to manage.

Walking back over to her desk, she arranged her papers. Unable to concentrate she decided to go home. Everything could wait until tomorrow.

27

"You're home earlier than I expected," Augustus said as he walked toward her. "I only just returned myself."

"And where may I ask have you been?"

"Finalizing a few business issues before we leave."

She kissed him on the cheek and walked toward the drawing room. "I couldn't concentrate. The only thing I got done of any consequence was to write Mr. Collins to request another meeting with him. I asked him to send a reply here."

"Any reason why you couldn't concentrate?"

"Theodora. Though after talking with Mrs. Hughes I decided she was right. She reminded me that Sebastian is her guardian and it's up to him to make decisions regarding her future. Not me. Not that I won't worry about her."

She sat on a dark gold brocade couch and smoothed her skirts. Augustus sat down next to her.

"I wouldn't expect you not to worry, though I'm glad to see you're taking Mrs. Hughes advice, though I believe I've given the same advice," he said, waggling his eyebrows.

"Stop that. Yes, I'm aware you have," she replied. "Is everything ready for our departure?"

"Almost."

"Good, I'm ready."

"If Collins accepts your offer, you'll need at least a few days with him?"

"Yes. I'm not sure when he can start, but I'm hoping it'll be immediately."

"As soon as you have all the details, I shall finalize our plans."

That moment the door opened, and a footman brought a tray filled with scones, marmalade and seed cake, sandwiches and of course tea. Beatrice slapped her husband's hand as he stole a piece of cake off the plate and ate it in two bites.

"I ran into Sebastian at White's. I went there for a late afternoon drink, and he was doing the same. Though I think he had escaped his houseful of women for some peace and quiet."

She giggled as she passed him a cup of tea. "I can imagine. He was much the same when all three of us were under the same roof with him. I guess we never realized how boisterous we were."

"He said Theodora refused to accept his decision that she is not to see Sutton again after she snuck off to meet him. So, he's confining her to her chamber."

"I'm sure she doesn't like that one bit."

"No, but he said it's the only way he knows to stop it."

"She is headstrong."

"Like her sister," he smirked.

"What about Sutton? Has Sebastian been able to speak with him? Again?"

"Yes. Sebastian said he thought this time he got his

point across to Sutton, but he still doesn't trust either of them."

"He'll send her to the country if she doesn't behave."

"He mentioned that. Any correspondence could easily be intercepted."

"Yes, he would. I wish him luck because he's going to need it," she replied. "Would you like to sit in on a meeting I have planned with the contractor about the store before we leave? I thought if Lord Collins accepts my offer, he could join us as well."

"Yes, I would," he said reaching for another piece of seed cake. She marveled at how he could eat. He was always hungry and always eating. "Anything planned for this evening?"

"No, and I'm glad," she replied. "I'm happy to spend a nice quiet evening at home with you."

"Part of the reason I enjoy being home in Scotland."

"I'm looking forward to it."

Taking their leave to Scotland could not happen soon enough.

BEATRICE REREAD the note from Collins which had arrived shortly before dinner for a second time. Lord Collins had agreed to meet at her offices and looked forward to it.

"Did he accept a meeting with you?" Augustus asked as he stood by the fire.

"Yes, and he looks forward to it."

"I would say he'll accept your offer."

"Yes, seems so," she said as she folded the paper and placed it back into the envelope.

"If there's anyone else you might have in mind, you need to arrange to meet with them."

She sighed. "No, as I've mentioned before, there is no one else. Collins will be the perfect match for the position."

"Because he doesn't balk at the prospect of working for a woman?"

"Yes, something like that. But more, he's perfectly qualified for the job. His knowledge of business matters is among the best I've encountered."

"Yes, and you won't worry quite as much."

"That is my hope."

She was so thankful to have found someone to marry like Augustus. They may have had their differences in the beginning, but she couldn't imagine herself married to anyone else. While he was very much a man's man, he wasn't one to dismiss women, and knew they deserved more credit that what was given.

How had she been so lucky?

"Where are you? What are you thinking?" Augustus asked.

She shook her head. "Nowhere. I was simply enjoying being here with you."

"Liar," he quipped. "I'll let you have that though I don't believe you."

"Would you rather tell you I was deep in thought with how wickedly handsome I found some man I saw in passing?"

He arched a brow. "No, not at all."

"I thought not," she laughed lightly. "Just because I'm quiet doesn't necessarily mean I'm thinking about business."

At that precise time, the butler entered the room to inform them dinner was ready. Rather than eat in the large, cavernous dining room, Beatrice found the breakfast room more suitable for just the two of them.

Dinner was also a simple affair when they were alone. Five course meals weren't necessary. The thriftiness in her dictated there was no reason for Cook to spend hours cooking a large, multi-course meal. She felt it a crime to waste food when they could suffice on a simple meal of roast chicken or beef roast.

Dinner this evening was roast duck with a variety of potatoes and vegetables. Duck was a favorite of Augustus's she tried to have Cook include it from time to time. It was too fatty for Beatrice's pallet which was one of the reasons it wasn't a regular on the menu.

"Your father appears to be warming up to you," she said as a footman set a bowl of turtle soup in front of her.

"Yes, he does. You might have something to do with that you know."

"How's that? He thinks you've matured because you've married?"

He nodded. "Something like that. I believe it's impressed him how I seem to have found a purpose in life."

"And that's because of me?"

He nodded taking a spoonful of soup. "Yes."

"Well, we do make a formidable team."

His lips twitched as he set down his spoon. "He's also mentioned grandchildren. Insuring an heir, the family line, that sort of thing."

"I'm sure he has. Procuring one's heir was a chief reason for marriage in his day."

"It still is."

"For the aristocracy, but not the common man," she said. "Not to say having male offspring isn't as important to a baker or banker as it is a duke or a duke's son."

This time he grinned. "I'm glad you realize that my dove."

"I don't suppose you'd like to give me a lesson on how that's all done after dinner, would you?"

He wiped his lips to cover his amusement. "I could be persuaded."

"Good."

"You've gotten quite bossy, my dove."

"You knew when we married, I was no meek, cowering maiden." She grinned.

"No one would dare make that mistake."

"Good."

"Now that we have all that straight, would you like to enjoy a brandy in the privacy of our chamber, or would you rather wait?"

She rose from her chair and circled the table to where Augustus sat, lifted her skirts, and straddled him. Her hot breath inches from his skin. "Or we could have our brandy brought here and lock the doors."

"You minx," he groaned as her lips found his. Moments later he broke the kiss, gasping. "Let me see to it that our brandy is brought here and we're not disturbed."

"Have the table cleared. That way there is no reason for us to be disturbed."

"I'll still lock the door," he said breathlessly as he helped her to her feet.

He returned minutes later. The table had been emptied of any sign of the meal they had just enjoyed. A footman followed carrying a tray with a decanter of brandy and two snifters. The young man placed it on the table and turned and left.

"I thought it better than having to go in search of a second glass," he said with a grin.

"How very thoughtful of you, milord." Before she could say another word, he was beside her, his mouth capturing hers in a hot, searing kiss. His lips demanding, taking everything she had to give. His hands found her backside and he pressed her against his arousal.

She wanted him with more desperation than she'd ever felt; her desire getting, stronger and stronger.

"My God you're so perfect," his voice low and seductive. Beatrice threw her head back as his hands slowly roamed her body. Finally, he gripped her thighs and lifted her as he sat in one of the dining room chairs.

Her skirts hitched up to her waist, his hands quickly found she was wearing no undergarments. He groaned. Quickly he felt her raise herself from him to allow him room to unfasten his trousers. Her hand followed as her hands enveloped his hard cock and guided it to her wet passage.

"I don't wish to wait. Fuck me now, Augustus," she pleaded.

"Such a mouth for such an exquisite marchioness." He sucked in a breath as he felt her slide down onto his shaft. She was hot and wet and seated to the hilt. He pulled back, thrusting in once again to be sure they were flesh to flesh.

His hands found their way to her waist as he helped her establish a rhythm, lifting her up, so he could push her down, thrusting deep inside her. She was made for him; they were made for each other.

"Augustus," she whispered.

"Hmmm?"

"I...I can't."

"Yes, you can," he growled, knowing she was at the edge. He pressed his thumb against her bundle of nerves and rubbed as she called out for him as she fell into her pleasure.

His hands grasped her hips and held on to her as he pumped into her. A few moments later he joined her as he thrust one final time. He flooded her with his release. It seemed to go on and on as he continued to empty into her. He held her that way, determined they would stay as one.

When he opened his eyes, he saw tendrils of her hair falling over her face. Her eyes were closed, her breathing still hard. One of her hands stroked his hair while the other held on to the back of the chair. He groaned and held her as he pushed into her. His cock still hard, he began to rock into her.

"See what you do to me," he said raggedly.

Her mouth found his and kissed him with such passion he himself thought he might come inside her without another stroke. She made him mad. Madly in lust and in love. He made love to her a second time. Quickly. This time after they regained their strength, she pulled herself off the chair.

"I don't know about you, but I think we've earned a brandy," she said with an amused smile on her face.

"Yes, I believe we have." He rose from the chair, tucked his errant cock back into his trousers and walked over to the decanter where he poured them both a healthy splash of brandy. She neared and he passed her a snifter.

"Thank you," she whispered.

His lips twitched. "For what? The brandy?"

"Both."

Life certainly wasn't boring for either of them

which made them luckier than a lot of their peers. For some, love would never come.

28

Hearing Mr. Collins' voice outside her office, Beatrice gathered the correspondence she'd been going over and set it aside. To her left were papers she'd had drawn up by her solicitors--a contract and non-disclosure for whoever she chose for this position.

The door opened and Mrs. Hughes appeared, a smile on her face. "Mr. Collins is here to see you, milady."

"Send him in, Mrs. Hughes."

Standing, Beatrice rose from her desk and watched as he walked towards her. She held out her hand and shook his larger one in a firm grip. Sitting, she motioned for him to take a seat as well. He was a large man and pleasant looking.

"Thank you for seeing me, Lady Talisker," he said as he set a case on the floor next to his chair.

"It was I who should be thanking you. I'm hoping you've had time to think about the position I have offered."

"I have, and would like to hear the details from you," he replied.

Beatrice nodded and began to tell him details of

each of her businesses. She gave him quick descriptions of what each of her businesses manufactured or what its source of income was. Most importantly, she told him what she expected of whomever she hired for the job. He was the only man she liked enough to offer the position to. He was well-mannered, well-known, and respected. Most importantly, he did not appear to have a problem with a woman such as herself owning and running a business.

Next, she told him the salary she was willing to pay. More than most, but with her living in Scotland it was going to be enough of a challenge. She needed someone to make decisions, the right decisions, if they had to be made immediately. She wasn't against him making decisions on his own if something came up, but she wanted to be informed and she wanted to make sure he kept her businesses on track.

"Do you have questions?" she asked.

He replied with a couple, which impressed with the time he'd obviously spent researching her business interests. Finally, she picked up the contract she'd had her solicitors draw up for her.

"I would like to offer you the position, Mr. Collins." She pushed the contract toward him. "I think you'll find the salary competitive, and I've also included some innovative ways a bonus can be earned."

He nodded and picked up one of the copies and began to read through it without speaking a word.

"Why don't I give you a few minutes to go through the contract. I'll see to having some tea brought in."

He grunted, his head bent, fully engaged in reading her offer.

Beatrice rose and walked out of her office, leaving Mr. Collins. She found Mrs. Hughes and asked for a pot of tea. She had the feeling once Mr. Collins finished, there would be questions. If he accepted, she wanted to arrange for the two of them to visit all her holdings. That way he would know the job wasn't to just sit behind a desk in the office.

When she returned a few moments later he was still reading--was he rereading? The contract wasn't that complicated nor long. She believed in being straightforward.

"Any questions you might have that I could answer for you, Mr. Collins?" she asked.

He glanced up with deep brown eyes and studied her for a moment. "No, this is quite generous, and you seem to have thought of everything."

"Thank you. Does that mean you're interested in the position?"

"Yes, I am most interested."

She nodded as Mrs. Hughes entered and set a tray on a nearby table before turning to leave. "Would you care for a cup of tea, Mr. Collins?"

"Please," he said. "Plain."

She poured a cup for each of them and carefully placed his tea on the edge of her desk. She returned to the leather chair behind her desk and sat down.

"I thought if you decide this is for you that we could spend a day visiting all the locations, and I can introduce you, before my husband and I head for Scotland."

"I would like that." He set the contract back on the desk and picked up the teacup. "If you can spare the time, of course."

"I already planned to do this."

They spoke for some time; he asked questions, and Beatrice answered them as best she could because until the contract was signed there were things she would not reveal. Though she thought him an honest man, she was keenly aware there was nothing stopping him from telling others about how she ran her businesses. And that simply wouldn't do.

"Would you like time to think on it?" She finally asked.

He shook his head of wavy dark brown hair. It matched his eyes perfectly and suited him. "My decision was made when I walked in here. I would very much like to accept the position, Lady Talisker."

"Please, call me Lady Beatrice. If we're going to be working together there is no need for such formality." She wasn't quite ready to allow him to call her simply by her given name. That privilege had to be earned.

"Collins. Call me Collins."

Beatrice nodded, deciding his given name must be one of those horrid ancestral names parents gave their sons upon birth. "Very well, Collins it is."

"I know you're a busy woman, so I'll sign the contract and leave you for your day," he said. "When would you like to visit your businesses and when would you like me to start?"

"Would tomorrow be too soon? We can take my carriage and visit every local location tomorrow. The day after I can show you what is going on with each business. You know, the joy of paperwork."

He bit back a grin, but Beatrice could see he was trying too hard not to smile. "Yes. There's always paperwork, isn't there?"

"Yes, but I'll tell you a secret. Mrs. Hughes is a wonder with keeping everything in order."

"That's good to know."

Beatrice watched as he signed all copies of the contract. She slid a copy across the desk. "This is your copy. I'll send word about visiting the sites. Would tomorrow work for you?"

"Yes, or day after tomorrow if you have the time."

"Very well. I'll send word to you later this afternoon."

He nodded, rose from his chair and picked up the papers. "I look forward to working with you Lady Beatrice."

"And I you," she said as she stood up.

She watched as he left her office and disappeared. Going to the window she noticed him climb into a waiting carriage. As the carriage pulled away, she felt herself breathe a sigh of relief. Now she could relax knowing her small empire would be well attended to. It was time to call it a day and go home to her husband.

BEATRICE DIDN'T HAVE to look far since Augustus was a creature of habit when at home. He was standing in front of the hearth in a small parlor, staring into the flames, deep in thought. He preferred the intimacy the room alluded to than of one of the two larger drawing rooms.

Next to him stood a gentleman she recognized as someone from the Metropolitan Police who had spent time at the site of the fire.

Hearing her enter he turned to face her as she glided across the carpets to him. He stood, took her hand and guided her to the dark blue damask sofa. "This is Chief Inspector Donald Lindsay of the Metropolitan police. He's come bearing news," he said.

"Ma'am. It is nice to finally meet you."

"Thank you."

"Would you care for a glass of sherry? I can send for tea if that suits you better," Augustus asked.

"A glass of sherry, please," she said hoping it would help calm her nerves.

She gazed at him as he walked to the far side of the room to a sideboard where there were several decanters. He really was a striking man, sinfully handsome. He used to have an aloofness, but now he didn't. He was freshly shaven, and a lock of errant hair curled down his forehead. He handed her a glass filled with sherry. As he did, their fingers touched, sending an electric rush through her. She dared not look at him, afraid he might have felt it too. He handed a whiskey to the inspector and motioned to a seat across from the one Beatrice was seated in while Augustus sat in another.

"You say you have news about the fire?" Beatrice asked.

"Yes. Good news too," Inspector Lindsay said. "I was put in charge of the case. Though my bosses were sure the fire was an accident, My investigation dug up information to the contrary. The fire was indeed the work of an arsonist, and I'm happy to say we have the man in custody."

"May I ask who?" Beatrice asked glancing quickly at Augustus.

"A man named MacRae? I believe you know of him?" Lindsay said.

"Of course we know MacRae. We'd already suspected him," she said.

"I spoke with the man about hiring him as my representative for my whiskey in the Edinburgh area. He seemed to want more. He wanted the London market," Augustus mentioned.

"He has quite a colorful past. He's not to be believed as he is not the real MacRae. We have no idea who he is, but the real MacRae from Edinburgh disappeared several years ago. He was one of the most knowledgeable men of the history of Scotch whiskey."

"Is he cooperating?" Augustus asked.

"No, but I'm not worried about that. Evidence has been found in regards to the fire at your store. He won't get off this time."

"What did you discover?" Beatrice asked.

Lindsay shook his head. "I'm really not at liberty to say. At least not now."

"Well at least you have him in custody," Beatrice said. She took a sip of her sherry before placing the glass on a table next to her.

"He won't be going anywhere."

"You sound awfully sure of yourself," Augustus said.

"We can link him to two other fires, possibly more. It's part of our ongoing investigation."

"Goodness, I'm glad you didn't hire him," she said glancing at Augustus.

"As am I."

Lindsay shifted his weight and leaned forward. "He seems to have a pattern. If a business deal doesn't go as he wanted or someone embarrasses him his solution is arson."

"But why burn my store down?" Beatrice asked.

"Your store was a way to get back at the marquess for not hiring him."

"Please, keep us informed as to what happens to him next," Beatrice said.

"I shall." Lindsay glanced at his pocket watch. "I'll be in touch."

They all stood, said their good-byes and then he was gone.

"That's certainly good news," Augustus said, putting his arm around Beatrice's waist.

"Yes, but I'll not rest easy until I know he's been convicted. MacRae or whoever he is, is as slippery as an eel."

"He is that."

~

AUGUSTUS SAT BACK in the tall leather chair at White's the next day and crossed his legs. He accepted a glass of whiskey from the footman attending them and took a sip. Across from him sat Sutton. He probably had no business meeting with the man. The problem of him wanting to court his sister-in-law was not his affair, but Sebastian had voiced concerns about his discussion of the matter with Sutton. Sebastian was sure the man had no intention of staying away from Theodora. Augustus thought perhaps since they had been friends at one time, he might be able to convince Sutton it would be best for all involved if he ended things with Theodora.

"I never told you how much I appreciated your brother-in-law settling your debts," he smirked.

Augustus found his temper surge and had to remind himself the man was merely trying to get a rise out of him. He took another sip of whiskey before responding. "I'm sure you are. That's really none of your concern. You were paid. That's the end of it."

"Is it?"

"I know the duke was quite thorough in his dealing with you, so if you're attempting to claim you're owed more, I can assure you that your scheme won't work."

"That's old news, Augustus. I've moved on," he said, a smile pulling at the corners of his mouth. "His sister has a very generous dowry."

"Of which you will never lay claim to."

"I wouldn't be so sure of that." Sutton drained his glass and motioned to a nearby footman for another.

"The duke is her guardian. He's made it quite clear you will not court his sister, yet I understand you won't quit."

"No, I won't. I sent Lady Theodora flowers. What's the harm in that?"

"You're playing with fire," Augustus muttered. "I beg you; stop now."

Sutton shook his head. "I have no intention of doing any such thing. I don't care who her brother is."

"She's locked in her chambers and isn't allowed to leave until the duke is satisfied this infatuation has ended."

"There's always ways around that," he said with a smile. "I intend to marry Lady Theodora, and no one will be able to stop me."

Augustus arched a brow. "Hard to do that don't you think, when she can't leave her rooms?"

"Nothing is impossible."

"What are you going to do? Wait as a bird of prey would until she's allowed to leave her chambers, then ruin her, giving the duke no choice but to allow a marriage?"

"You are wiser than anyone has ever given you credit for. Yes, that's exactly what I plan on doing, though I may not have to wait long. Hightower will tire of it. You'll see."

"Then you don't know my brother-in-law very well," he said.

"You'd be surprised. He can't play jailer forever."

Frustrated, Augustus leaned forward in his chair. "What would it take for you to walk away?"

Sutton laughed, a deep diabolical sound that gave

Augustus chills. Why had he never seen this side of his former friend? Had he always been so uncaring? "Unlike you, I can't be bought."

Augustus chose to ignore the slight. He was getting nowhere. It was best to leave things be. Sebastian would just have to stay on top of the situation, which he knew the duke would do. "Fine. I came here today hoping I could persuade you to do the right thing. Obviously, I can't."

Sutton sat there, not moving, a smile still on his face.

He unfolded his frame from the chair and stood above Sutton, who hadn't bothered to move. "If you'll excuse me, the stench in here is more than I can stand, and I have to be somewhere." He turned and headed to the door. He needed to distance himself from Sutton before he said or did something he'd regret. He didn't need to embarrass himself or his family by acting rash. He had a new life, a second chance, a wonderful marriage to a delightful woman he loved with all his heart, and he wasn't going to allow some rogue ruin any of it.

Sebastian could deal with the repercussions of any actions Theodora and Sutton might do. Unless of course Theo came to her senses during the time she was locked in her rooms and cast him aside.

He and his brother-in-law were in talks along with his father about keeping the two distilleries under one marketing umbrella. It would be a smart move to help get word out about his new brand, especially since he'd decided not to hire a man. He and Beatrice would be making regular journeys to London. Her for her businesses, and he for the distillery. There was no reason he couldn't tend to sales then. Besides, his smart wife had a few ideas of her own he was wanting to try.

Outside White's he looked up and down the street and decided to walk home. The day was still cool, but the sun was out and as in Scotland that was a day to savor the good weather by being outdoors and not cooped up inside.

As he began walking, he wondered how Beatrice's meeting with the Collins had gone Hopefully better than his. He decided he would tell her about his meeting with Sutton only if she brought up Theodora. Beatrice was strongly opinionated and might object to the idea he'd taken it upon himself to meet with the scoundrel. Might? Oh yes, she'd object quite vehemently to his meeting with Sutton, but that was one of the many things he loved about her.

Two days later Beatrice and Augustus were on their way to their home in Scotland. Both glad to get away from London and enjoy some time alone with each other. The day was dark and gray, the clouds so low and heavy one expected the rain to begin at any time. Augustus had chosen an early northbound train so they would still arrive home before dark and wouldn't have to stay in Edinburgh.

Beatrice had spent an entire day with Mr. Collins taking him to warehouses, buildings she owned, and finally the department store. He asked questions and didn't fill the silence in the carriage with unneeded conversation. She decided with her earlier assessment. Collins would be a huge asset to her and had no qualms that her businesses wouldn't continue to thrive under his leadership. At last she would have her much needed break.

She needed to make their residence a shining example of a well-run household. Not that she for a moment doubted it wasn't already. Beatrice was simply anxious to make this their home.

They'd been on the train for about two hours when she put down the book she was reading.

"You won't mind if I make changes, will you?" she asked.

"Of course not. You're the mistress. You can do whatever you please."

"I just want it to be ours."

He arched a brow realizing what she meant. "I've never had the opportunity or desire to do that. I'm perfectly content with the way it is."

"Typical man," she snorted.

"I haven't exactly been able to make such changes. If it weren't for the fact the estate's entailed, I might have lost it as well."

"That part of your life is behind you."

"I know and our future is much more palatable, I can assure you."

Augustus rose from his seat across from her and sat next to her. He took her hand and lifted her gloved hand to his lips. "I love you, Bea. You're the best thing to ever happen to me. Even if we did get off to a rocky start."

"You're referring to the incident at the countess's pond?" she asked with a sly smile.

He smirked. "I am."

"I wouldn't change a thing about that night."

"Were you afraid I'd compromise you?" he said with a laugh. "Some thought I had."

"Nosy gossips. Yes, the thought occurred to me, but I knew I had an advantage if I pushed you in the pond."

"Look how far we've come."

"We have."

"Any regrets? Because I have none."

She smiled and lay her head against his shoulder. "I have no regrets. You are the most precious thing to come into my life."

He kissed the top of her head. "You say that now, but I'm sure that compliment will pass on to our first born."

"Yes, I don't doubt it, but children grow up and leave home. You'll always have a special piece of my heart."

"Speaking of children..." he said. Augustus waited for her to say something witty and getting no reply he sat in silence looking out the window at the passing every-changing landscape. A moment later, he realized by the soft snore in his ear that she'd fallen asleep. He leaned down to kiss her. A conversation for another time.

He was glad to see her relax. It was well deserved, and he intended the first month in their home in Scotland would be about them. Getting to know each other's little idiosyncrasies without anyone to interrupt them. Nothing pleased him more and come next spring he would take her on a wedding trip to the continent or wherever she desired to go. He would do anything for this woman, his wife. The world was their oyster and together they would discover what wonders it had to offer.

The End

ALSO BY JR SALISBURY

ABOUT THE AUTHOR

J. R. Salisbury is the historical romance alter-ego of contemporary romance author Jamie Salisbury. Writing romance stories with passion and sass, Jamie Salisbury has seen several of her books soar to #1 on Amazon. Her novella, Tudor Rubato was a finalist in the 2012 RONE awards. The cover won for Best Contemporary Cover. In 2014, her novel, Life and Lies was nominated for a RONE in the Erotica category.

Music, traveling and history are among her passions when not writing. Her previous career in public relations in and around the entertainment field has afforded her with a treasure trove of endless story ideas.

Follow Jamie:
Book + Main
Website